THE HONEY ANT

DUNCAN KYLE

The Honey Ant

COLLINS
8 Grafton Street, London W1
1988

William Collins Sons & Co. Ltd
London · Glasgow · Sydney · Auckland
Toronto · Johannesburg

My thanks are due to many generous and informed West Australians, among them Pauline Gillett and Dorothy Parkman, to Tim
and Ann Lee-Steere, to Bill and Judy Bamford and Bill and Juliet
Inwood – jewels, all of them.

First published 1988
Copyright © Duncan Kyle 1988

BRITISH LIBRARY CATALOGUING IN PUBLICATION DATA

Kyle, Duncan
The honey ant.
I. Title
823'. 914 [F]

ISBN 0-00-223382-7

Photoset in Linotron Trump Mediaeval by
Rowland Phototypesetting Ltd,
Bury St Edmunds, Suffolk

Made and printed in Great Britain by
Robert Hartnoll (1985) Ltd, Bodmin, Cornwall

I

They do a great PR job on Perth. Beautiful setting, they say. (True.) Unspoilt, they insist. (Not quite true). Happily laid-back lifestyle, they'll tell you. (True of some). Everything blessed—by Nature and by God. Among those so blessed are the red-back spider, the great white shark, the brown, the death-adder, the tiger, dugite and other deadly snakes. Plus the mosquito. The Ozzie-Mozzie that is, and may he never bite you.

So there Perth sits, at the far end of nowhere, a million-plus prosperous people in a single city, commanding a state the size of Europe, and surrounded by killers: animal, vegetable, mineral, airborne, marine—yes, and human, some of them.

Still, heigh-ho for the outdoor life in the sunshine. Because the sun certainly shines. Oh boy, does it *shine*! TV ads are an endless round of cars, swimsuits, barbecues, beefsteak, beer, and oh yes, endless warnings about skin cancer. There are zappers and squirters, lamps and liquids that will protect you (some of the time, anyway) against the great Ozzie-Mozzie, which bites like Shere Khan and begins its sweet songs daily at dusk. Still, Paradise always did have the odd flaw, did it not? Many people will tell you Perth *is* Paradise, and bits of it come near, but it didn't feel like Paradise as I walked up the steep incline of Barrack Street the day all this began. The temperature was 36°C (multiply by 2 and add 30, that's the rough and ready way, and it gives you 102°F). The pavements and walls and buildings and earth had been soaking the heat up for hours upon days and were presently releasing it. My guess is that it was 110—115°F in Barrack

Street, and my shirt was stuck to my back and my trousers to my legs and inside my shoes my feet squelched in my sweat. I'd been to lunch and foolishly had a couple of stubbies (beers) and all the liquid was fighting its way out through my pores. I felt, and no doubt looked, like an old slipper well chewed by an enthusiastic puppy.

Anyway I toiled to the top, turned into St George's Terrace and walked along the flat towards my office. There were bits of shade from high buildings, maybe even a trace of breeze. A couple of Abos strolled towards me, black and comfortable, protected by pigment and the evolutionary processes of forty thousand years. No sweat, this heat, to them. Not that I felt envious. The way Abos get treated isn't one of the brightest chapters in Australia's glory-story, and I have absolutely no ambition to be the wrong colour under the Southern Cross.

Funnily enough, another Abo was sitting outside our building when I got there, and as I approached the swinging glass door, he suddenly stood in front of me. A second before, he'd been squatting on the pavement three or four yards away, but they can do these things.

He held out an envelope. Just inside the glass door and visible, and within the air-conditioning, was a sign that said, 'Inquiries. Please ring'. I pointed. He pushed the envelope at me. I shrugged and took it. He vanished. What I mean by that is that I looked at the address on the envelope which was:

> J.R.J. MacDonald, Esq.,
> MacDonald & Slaughter, Solicitors,
> St George's Terrace,
> Perth, W. Australia,

and then looked up and he wasn't there. I stood with the envelope in my hand, looking around. He wasn't this side of the street, or the other. He wasn't dodging down the side street, or into the tea shop. He'd just gone, in the time it takes to read an address. But, as I say, they can do remarkable things, especially the full-blood tribal Abo. He can walk a hundred miles in the heat between one drink of water and the next, for example, and if that isn't remarkable, I don't know what is.

But back to that address. J.R.J. MacDonald, founder of the firm, was near enough contemporary with Alfred the Great, or it may have been Richard III or George Washington— at any rate, he's already spent several decades nestling in Abraham's bosom, and his partner Henry Silas Slaughter has been mouldering in *his* grave for a goodish number of years also. The firm was now MacDonald, Slaughter, Nicholas, Trumble and Paminski. None of them was still extant and none was me. My name is John Close, just to get the matter straight, and on that day I was thirty, six feet exactly, and about four pounds overweight. I was bottom man on the partnership totem pole, with nine above me, none of them named MacDonald or Slaughter or N.T. and P. The boss (technically Senior Partner) was a one-time barefoot boy, born a bastard in Bunbury, a town a hundred or so miles south, and he was given the town's name for his own. So he was Miller Bunbury, bastard at birth, bastard to this day, and husband of the only daughter of the deceased Trumble.

I stopped at the enquiries window and when Sharleene (I suspect that's how it's spelled) opened it and smiled with her big white teeth, and showed me about an acre of tanned skin and her great big vacant blue eyes, I said, 'This came for Mr MacDonald, Sharleene. Make sure he gets it, please.'

'Well, right,' she said, with a great big smile.

I went up in the lift, wondering idly how long it would be before whatever it was reached my desk. It would go first, when Sharleene had stared at it for a while, to Miller Bunbury, whom it would not reach. His secretary would look at the yellowing paper and the Abo fingermarks with *profound* distaste and would use sterilized tongs to place it in the out-tray, unopened. And so it would go on. This was a firm which dealt in the elegant letterheads and pricey and devious works of the millionaires and mining companies.

Deckle-edged parchment might just possibly be opened by Bunbury's secretary. If she recognized it. Otherwise not.

It would take about ten days, I thought, for the pass-the-partner game to run its course. During those days, the envelope and its contents would pass through the hands of, among others, an Olympic Gold medallist swimmer now run to fat, and a breeder of Arab horses—Oh, we're a varied lot at MacDonald and Slaughter!—and the exquisite Marye N. Bright, number eight in the Top Ten, social mountaineer extraordinary. She, of course, would wear her little snow-white gloves to handle it. Girl with nerve, that one. In my time I've seen her patronize Miller Bunbury himself. Ten days to Close's desk.

It was there in an hour. I'd forgotten the one-day cricket at the WACA, two o'clock start, New Zealand vs West Indies, and everybody, including me, invited there to sip champagne with Manning Mining. Pity, still . . .

The envelope was still unopened, and was more than yellowish—the paper was turning brown, and it had been folded in its time, and crushed into people's pockets. I took a tentative sniff at it and BO was what it had. I slit it open like a surgeon, with a single bold stroke of the chrome-plated kris my last secretary brought me back as a souvenir from Kuala Lumpur.

Folded in four inside was a familiar sight: one of those will forms you buy in Post Offices and Woollies and stationers if you want to dispose of your worldly goods without the expensive advice of firms like MacDonald, Slaughter.

This paper wasn't yellow; it was a fairly nasty shade of pale green. On the front were the words: 'The Will of', plus dotted line for a name and another for the date, both blank. On the back was a specimen of how a will should be made. I unfolded the sheet.

This is the last will and testament
of me . . . Mary Ellen Emmett
of Stringer Station
Western Australia

made this 8th day of October
in the year of our Lord
nineteen hundred and forty one.

Mary Ellen Emmett hereby revoked 'all wills made by me at any time' and appointed 'my sister, Jane Emmett and the Yorkshire Penny Bank' to be her executors. She gave and bequeathed 'All to my beloved sister, Jane Emmett and her children, if any'.

There were two witnesses. One in a bold, firm, even a stylish hand. But simple. His name was H. Naismith, S.J. The other, barely legible, said Billy One-Hat.

I read the thing through twice, wondering what it told me that was not immediately obvious from the brief form. I expect I was pulling at my lip: I usually do when I'm thinking.

Well, for a start, that word 'Station' came zinging out at me with neon aglow and bells ringing. Not that I'd heard of Stringer Station. But any 'Station' in Australia is liable to be a fair stretch of real estate, and Mary Ellen's sister Jane, if still living, was likely to inherit something worth inheriting. The second thing was the Yorkshire Penny Bank, of which I'd never heard, either. But I'd heard of Yorkshire right enough. Cricketers: Hutton, Sutcliffe, Boycott, Bowes, Verity, Trueman, Hirst, Rhodes. Great names. There was an Emmett among them too. Tom Emmett.

So Mary Ellen Emmett was a Pom. Certain? Well no but I'd be willing to place a small bet of say, everything I had.

What else? Billy One-Hat would be an Abo stockman— another guess I'd back with dollars. And H. Naismith of the Society of Jesus, he of the fine, plain hand, would not be the kind of bloke you meet leaning on every paddock fence.

Next question.

It was: why were the names of Messrs MacDonald, Slaughter on the envelope?

Answer: at some point there had been a transaction carried out by/for/on behalf of one or other of the founding partners.

Off to the Registry. Deed boxes and filing cabinets. Dust on the old files, untouched for years. A dull modern gleam to others.

E for Emmett . . .

Stone me, but they did their filing *properly* in those days. Papers just about jumped out into my waiting paw.

Emmett, Mary Ellen, spinster, Fremantle. She'd bought a house, MacDonald, Slaughter taking their cut, in Chalmers Street, Freo. Number 14. Funny thing was, I knew Chalmers Street; had even been there within the last few weeks, to visit an old school mate, so I knew those houses, too. Victorian they are—a dunny out the back, probably with the traditional red-back spider under the toilet seat.

She'd paid a hundred and twenty-five pounds, forwarded by a cheque drawn upon the Yorkshire Penny Bank. That was in 1921. When she was . . . was her age anywhere? Date of birth was 25th December 1899 so she'd been an old lady when she died, and a young one when she bought into Freo's wild colonial charms.

It wasn't a thick file, but there *was* something else: I read the papers and learned she'd sold the Fremantle house less than a year after buying it (MacDonald, Slaughter profiting once again) for £120. M & S had charged £15, the thieves, so she'd made a loss of ten quid on her venture into property ownership, and gone away, presumably; there was no reference to further purchases. Indeed, there was no further mention at all of Mary Ellen Emmett. Not until today, sixty-odd years later.

The obvious thing to do was go and hunt in the Land Registry—or send one of our pupil–students to hunt. But times have changed, even since I was young. The young don't like that kind of thing now. Makes their cuffs dirty, gets dust in the hair-do. Anyway, what they do is dodge. They go there and don't look and then come back and say there's nothing. And *I*, for that matter, didn't much want to walk out again into Perth's flaming afternoon.

*

I let my fingers do the walking, and rang the *West Australian*, a newspaper, old-fashioned in all the best ways. It is local and it makes a real attempt to cover its local area—even though the task is impossible because the local area is roughly fifteen hundred miles long and a thousand miles wide. That's no exaggeration, not even a little one. The local area stretches from monsoons and crocodiles in the north, to the Southern Ocean and the Roaring Forties in the south. There are deserts and diamonds; there are cliffs made of bauxite, and beaches of titanium sand, and wheat and gold. It's big.

And so is the library at the *West Australian*. For long years, devoted people with scissors have taken cuttings and squirrelled them away in files and indexed and cross-indexed them.

I telephoned, brimful of confidence. Stringer Station must, at some time, have figured in a report in the *West Australian*.

'Hold on. Sorry. No reference to Stringer Station.'

Then I thought of the Society of Jesus, that tough, intellectual, spare brotherhood of boundless faith and energy, openers-up of continents, wrestlers with the Devil, keepers of records. And listed, with luck, in the reference books.

No worries! Spin the dial and there you are. I gave my name. 'I'm a solicitor with a Perth firm, and I have a reference here to a member of your order whose name occurs as a witness to a will.'

'You need to know he exists?'

'Probably exist*ed*. It's dated 1941. His name was Naismith.'

A pause. 'You don't know of him, Mr Close?'

'Should I?'

Dead silence—which said clearly that I should. Then he said, 'Father Naismith died only a few weeks ago. You were correct in your suspicions of age. He was ninety-three.'

A great clanging bell of recognition was now tolling in my mind.

'We are talking, are we, about the Saint of Bungle-Bungle?' I asked.

'The newspapers liked to call him that. Your signature's bound to be genuine, Mr Close. Nobody north of Hobart would have *dared* forge it!'

Two minutes later I called him again.

'You wouldn't happen to know,' I asked, 'if Father Naismith was ever at Stringer Station?'

He was amused. 'Father Naismith wandered the outback for seventy years, Mr Close, on foot, on horseback, on camels. He must have visited every remote station in Australia at least twice and possibly more.'

'Did he keep a diary?'

'He kept nothing,' said the gently humorous voice. 'He was devoted to poverty.'

'Oh,' I said.

'Surely it's a matter for the Land Registry?' he asked.

I didn't bother any more that night. Other matters required my attention, including a chunk of work on a new shopping mall. Another shark was ashore and this one was gobbling up land. All I did was enter my actions on the daily log— that means there's a keyboard on my desk, into which, each day, one punches the records of one's actions. In each and every case. I won't deny it's useful in its way: some such system is vital in a law office, otherwise chaos comes Friday. The disadvantage to it, as to most things, is Miller Bunbury, the killer spider in his funnel web on the top floor. He just presses a couple of buttons and he's looking malignantly over your shoulder.

It happened next morning. *Brrrp* on the intercom.

'Yes?'

'What's this about Stringer Station?' Bunbury never begins by saying, 'Bunbury here, G'day.' (Bunbury comes on snarling. If he ever wrote a text book it would be Bunbury's guide on *Advanced Bullying, Creeping, Crawling and Unlovely Behaviour.* He looks it too. Nostrils point skyward and personally I believe his spinal column ends in a curly tail.)

'There in the log,' I said.

'Bloody nonsense. All there, my arse. What's this crap about "delivered by hand by unknown Aboriginal"?'

I told him. There is, or was then, because now they're pouring in, a shortage of lawyers in Perth; and though I'm neither F. E. Smith nor Clarence Darrow, I have two permanent standing offers of jobs. Thing is, Western Australia has lots of litigation, and MacDonald, Slaughter gets some of the juiciest; that's why I stayed, for the quality of the work. But talk ever so briefly to Bunbury and you also get to reflect upon the quality of life.

'Should've grabbed the bloody boong by the bloody nuts,' he growled. 'Got his bloody name.'

'Know anything about Stringer Station?' I asked.

'Heard the name.'

'It'd help if you told me.'

'Idle young bastard—bloody well find out!'

Click.

And G'day to you, too, Miller Bunbury, I thought. Up above, the sky was blue, the sun shining. Nine o'clock, temperature 25 or so. But between me and the sunlight Bunbury lurked. One day the partners would get together and toss him out. One day. After that Bunbury would hunt them down one by one. Tear them apart with his bare hands. Not just a bastard in every sense of the word, but a very big, very strong bastard. (Gossip says, indeed, that the father he never knew was a buffalo bull from Arnhem Land. They're impossibly big, strong and malevolent, too.)

Right then. I'd give it a bit more of my valuable time: have to, if I was going to get anywhere. My Qantas flight to London, booked for the next Monday (connection two days later to Cortina d'Ampezzo), was not to be missed, not in any circumstances. For one thing, I'd paid for it.

Okay, Land Registry it would have to be.

I buzzed Sharleene. 'Call me a taxi, will you, please?'

'Yes, Mr Close.' She giggled briefly and hung up.

It wasn't a long ride, but worth every cent of the fare. The heat was building and Sharleene knows this outfit with air-conditioned cabs. And it helps. Visitors to Perth tell me one of the things that startles them, at first, is the sight of bank cashiers in shorts and long socks and short sleeved shirts and ties. It suits the climate; it suits all sorts of places from the Stock Exchange to the Merlin Hotel. But it doesn't suit Bunbury.

'Suits and bloody ties in this bloody firm and don't bloody forget it,' he cries.

Quick work at the Land Titles Office. Western Australia's nearly a million square miles, but the population, all told, is only one and a half million so they can keep track pretty well.

'Stringer Station, PO Box 19448 Kununurra,' said the clerk at once, facts off the top of her head—and correct. 'Registered in the name of Mary Ellen Green—'

'It says Emmett here,' I said, 'Mary Ellen Emmett.'

'Mary Ellen Green née Emmett,' she said. 'Boy, I bet it's hot in Kununurra today!'

'As The Hinges,' I said.

'What hinges?'

'The ones on the gates of Hell.'

'Oh, *those* hinges. Be hotter than that.'

'And Stringer Station?'

'Small one. Eighty-two square miles.' She had a map, for what it was worth.

'Can I have a copy of that?'

'You can for a fee.'

'We're all worth our fees,' I said.

'Wish I believed you.'

I returned to my office and the question of dependants. It seemed unlikely any existed here in Australia. The will left all to the sister in England. But there are phones and radio-phones and all sorts of high-tech wonders in WA. I called everybody from the radio-phone operators to the Flying Doctor Service. There was a radio-phone at Stringer Station, but it hadn't been used for weeks. Not, said the radio-phone lady, since Mrs Green died.

I said as the thought struck me, 'Who told you she'd died?'

'Hold a minute, I'll check.'

I held and she came back pretty soon.

'Father Naismith called in himself, to report it. He'd been there when she died. Issued the burial certificate.'

'Could a priest do that?'

She said, 'He was a doctor before he became a priest, surely you knew that.'

'Must have slipped my mind.'

'So he buried her there and moved on.'

I said, 'Then he died too.'

'Yeh, shame. What a man! Buried her himself, it says here. Even dug the grave himself. Imagine that—a man in his nineties, up there at Kununurra!'

'Probably that's what killed him.'

She said, 'Some bastard in a car killed him. Nobody knows who because the bastard didn't stop! The Father was crossing the road just south of Katherine. My Christ, there's one blacktop road in a thousand miles and he's killed crossing it!'

I thanked her and hung up. Strange that I'd missed Father Naismith's death; it must have been widely reported because he was pretty well-known. When I checked my diary I understood the reason. I'd been off bush-walking for ten days right about the time he'd died, and one of the joys of the bush is there isn't a newspaper under every eucalypt and there's no TV at all. Yes, I'd had a two-way radio in my Range Rover, but I'd left it parked and just listened mornings on the emergency frequency.

But I wasn't in the bush now. This was dog's breakfast country and I was near enough lost in it. Plain enough that Stringer Station would be badly run-down; just one very old woman and a handful of boongs to run it, that's all; and when she died, nobody, except the wandering priest—all things to all men, the Priest—diagnostician, gravedigger, even coroner in his fashion. Then off he goes to his own meeting with his Maker. Funny, just as the radio-phone lady said, that he'd died crossing the only good road in a thousand miles. Though maybe it wasn't so strange at that—I've driven south from Darwin, too, and there's plenty of death on that road, from broken-backed snakes, and flattened rabbits and 'roos to cattle hit six-in-a-bunch by a road train going fast and not slowing. Even saw a dead camel once, four legs in the air, and wondered what it could be till I came level.

So—what next? The big question was whether the papers had been recovered. If Father Naismith had gone to Kununurra first, no worries—he'd have dealt with things there. But if he'd gone off travelling eastward, and been hit by a truck, the paperwork could be in shreds and blown all over the Big Red Centre. I crossed my fingers.

Crossed them to some purpose, too. Everything was neat and tidy. Coroner in Kununurra had accepted 'without reservation', so he said, 'the finding of Father Naismith that Mrs Green was dying of old age and general infirmity when he arrived at Stringer Station'. He'd sat and prayed with her, the old priest had, and given her the Last Rites. He'd given her pencillin first, of course, but it was clear Mary Ellen Green née Emmett had been too far gone in pneumonia to respond. Then the burial, then off to Kununurra with the paperwork, and put it in the right hands before the slammer came down on him too. Efficient, the Jesuits!

Except . . .

And it was a sizeable 'except', this one.

Except—why, when everything else was according to Cocker, had the will been delivered into my hand, on MacDonald, Slaughter's doorstep, by a full-blood tribal Abo without a word to say for himself? Death certificates, Coroner's verdicts, all proper, yes. Will, no.

Somewhere in the far north there were now eighty-odd square miles, unoccupied, probably not being worked or managed. Owned by *somebody*. But who?

Okay, I thought. Look at it rationally. Father Naismith turns up, finds the old lady dying, does his best. She dies. He buries her etc., etc. He also takes a look around, and finds there's nobody there except a few Abo stockmen and their wives and kids. He also finds the will—either that or Mrs Green told him about it.

Right so far?

Possibly. What's he do next? Well, the will is a valuable document. It passes on eighty square miles, probably of grazing land, to somebody. It's addressed to MacDonald, Slaughter. If the good Father's off to Kununurra with the rest of the papers, why not take it with him and make sure it reached the right hands?

Answer: nothing wrong at all. Absolutely correct behaviour. Just what he ought to have done.

So why didn't he do it? The rest of the papers *did* reach Kununurra, and were dealt with by proper procedures. But not the will. No—the will goes into a black hand and a workman's pocket and is handed over without a word by a tribal Abo who promptly vanishes.

Eighty square miles.

Land, lotsa land. Money, money, money.

Money which Father Naismith was protecting.

I pulled out the left lower drawer of my desk, which one of my predecessors had made into a properly-padded footrest; I stuck my heels on it, and thought some more.

The old man was her priest and confessor. Maybe, when he got to Stringer Station, she was still conscious, and capable of giving him instructions, or making requests, or whatever you do with priests. Could she (Mrs Green) have said, *not Kununurra*?

Yes she could. But if she had, why? Could she have been afraid the will would fall into the wrong hands? Again, yes she could.

There could only be one reason for that—a belief the wrong hands would tear it up, burn it, anyway destroy it. And they'd do it, those hands, because otherwise the eighty square miles would go to Jane Emmett, her heirs and successors.

Simple. If true.

I didn't believe a word of it. But it had to be followed through, that particular train of thought. And it ran on in a simple straight line too: if Jane Emmett and her family were *not* to inherit; and if it were thought (and ruled in court) that Mary Ellen Green (née Emmett) had died intestate, to whom would the estate go?

Profitable questions for lawyers? In Miller Bunbury's set-up, the charges to clients go like this. Every hour is broken into twelve five-minute periods, and the client is charged per five minutes or part thereof for time devoted to his affairs. In my case the charge is $A50 per five. That's $A600 an hour. Some people, though, come expensive. Bunbury himself charges like a wounded buffalo.

Where now? There'd be papers somewhere, concerning ownership, and they'd have to be found. The probate process had to be started, but before that, I'd have to track down the heirs. Starting with the Yorkshire Penny Bank, if it still existed.

I telexed the London solicitors who handle things for us. They have an Australian partner name of Greg Tucker, and use another firm in Yorkshire. Well, it's all work for lawyers; and I'd get a reply in due course.

I did, and it didn't take long at all, but the form it took— well that *was* a bit startling!

·

2

I don't know if you've ever done one of those twenty-four-hour flights. Remarkable, say the old timers who used to go by P & O liner and take six weeks. True, they are remarkable. What they aren't is funny. Perth, Monday—London, Tuesday leaves the feeling you've been gutted. You're stuffed with booze and grub, you dozed twice, each time for six minutes, and you've watched horrible movies three times. You are emphatically not at your best, as you stumble out of the Jumbo into the metal corridor and start following the Heathrow arrows that take you six times round the terminal on the way to Immigration. I hadn't got five yards before a Qantas girl asked if I were Mr Close.

'Mm,' I said suspiciously. This couldn't be good news. Called back urgently? Alitalia regret no seats to Milan?

She handed me a note. Mr Tucker was waiting to meet me. Exactly what I needed, a good strong dose of Greg Tucker, in my condition. He's a good enough bloke in his way. Comes from Albany, way down south, like me. Difference is, I say it the Aussie way. 'Al' rhymes with 'pal'. Greg says Awl-bany. We were mates at the University of Western Australia, where he was known as Super-Pom. One of those, and there are still a few about, who wish they'd been born Brits and do what they can to join.

Struggle, struggle, suitcases, etc. Then I was through and he was saying, 'Hello, old chap,' and, 'Let me give you a hand with all that.' He wore his February look: bowler hat, black fitted overcoat with velvet collar, gleaming black shoes, needle-slender umbrella. Wears it all in July, I bet.

'How did you know?' I said.

'Rang your firm. They gave me the flight number.' Looked me square in the eye, he did, and said, 'Jolly efficient they are, I must say.'

Honest, it goes up my nose, and as I said before, I wasn't at my best. I had only vaguely realized there was a girl around, but the dinkum Aussie had risen in his wrath inside me, and I said, 'Who's the sheila, you Pommie bastard?'

Greg draws himself up at this and a small superior smile plays about his raised nose. 'May I introduce Mr Close from Australia? John, this is Jane Strutt.'

'G'day, Jane,' says I, turning with outstretched hand, 'are you his?'

I found myself getting a very flat look. Steady level eyes. Amused, but not much.

Greg was saying, 'Frightfully sorry. Not always like this. These colonials!' But even he must have noticed I was only half-alive. He soon made the sensible suggestion that we all meet a bit later at the Kensington Hilton—I was staying there for a couple of nights to shop for new ski kit—so I checked in there, had a shower to waken myself, and went to join the two of them in what passes for a lounge, by now feeling more attached to the world.

Jane Strutt had been wearing a raincoat at the airport. Now she was in a dark green uniform with pips on the shoulders. Beside her on the bench seat lay the coat and a cap with a shiny badge on it. I approached and Greg rose.

'Captain Jane Strutt, WRAC,' he said.

'And I'm not his.'

'No,' I said, 'I'm sorry. It's no excuse, but Greg and I . . .'

'I've met Australians before, Mr Close. It doesn't matter.'

'So, we can all begin again,' says Greg. 'Coffee?'

'What actually happened,' Greg said, 'was that the old Yorkshire Penny Bank had become part of the new Yorkshire Bank. I spoke to them. Their records are amazingly good. In a twinkling they were back with four generations of account holders.'

'Jane Emmett?' I said.

'Was the second generation. The first was her father,

Henry Emmett; the third was her daughter, and the fourth . . .'

'Fourth and last,' said Captain Strutt, 'is me.'

'Granddaughter of Jane Emmett,' Greg said.

I asked her, 'Why last?'

She laughed. 'Yorkshire's a long way from Aldershot.'

'That's not what you meant, though?'

'Some other time, Mr Close.'

'Do you suppose,' Greg put in, 'that I might leave you two to it, since I'm not actually involved further?'

'Suits me,' I said.

'And me.'

He gathered his bits and went, making me promise to call him on my way home.

Watching his departing back, she said, 'He's pretty mysterious about things, Mr Close. You'd tell me something to my advantage, he said, but it must be at Heathrow!'

I said, 'The English approach always puzzles me. Tell me what I call you—sir, madam, Ms, Miss, Mrs?'

She grinned. 'Excellency, will do.'

'Captain, I'll call you Captain. And the position, Captain, is this: I'm handling the estate—Greg must have told you this?'

'Yes. My great-aunt. Granny's sister.'

'You ever meet her?'

'No, I think she came over once, just after the war. I wasn't around at the time.'

'Your grandmother's dead?'

'Yes.'

'When?'

'Nineteen seventy-one or two.'

'She had how many children?'

'One—my mother.'

'Is your mother alive?'

She shook her head. 'Died last year.'

'Brothers or sisters?'

'My brother found a wartime mortar bomb on a beach when he was ten and blew himself to bits. There's just me.'

I said, 'All of this will have to be checked, of course.'
She laughed.
'What's funny?'
'Mr Tucker said "carefully verified".'
'Mr Tucker would. Now, Captain—'
'Call me Jane.'
'Thanks. I don't want to give you any false hopes, but if you turn out to be the only relative, you inherit the farm and contents. If it turns out there's a long-lost son of Mary Ellen Emmett somewhere . . .' I shrugged.
'Better prospect than a prod in the eye with a sharp stick,' she said. 'What on earth would I do with a farm?'
'Enjoy it. Plenty of people do. I haven't, by the way, any indication at all of other relatives, and the will left everything to your grandmother.'
'What's that mean? Farm and contents—animals?'
'Everything.'
She frowned. 'I know nothing about animals.'
'Perhaps you will want to sell up.'
'Oh, I don't know. Is it big, this farm?'
'Depends by what standards,' I said. 'There are lots of 'em bigger. 'Bout eighty square miles.'
'Did you say miles?'
'It's way up north. Plenty of space up there.'
She was sitting pretty still, blinking a little. What she was doing was coming to terms, slowly, with that fact that, in all probability, she was rich. Fairly rich, anyway. She murmured something. Now I blinked.
'Did you say primogeniture?'
'Yes.'
'Why?'
'Down the female line—that's how it's come to me. Great-aunt to Granny, Granny to Mum, Mum to me.'
'Well, I suppose it's primogeniture.'
'Of course it is. When will I know? And how many acres in eighty square miles?'
'Six hundred and forty acres to the square mile,' I said. 'My calculator's upstairs.'

'But that's fifty-two thousand acres! Fifty-two, four—eight—oh. Heavens, it's enormous!'

'Nice little Aussie farm,' I said.

She looked at me. I looked back. Her eyebrows lifted.

'Something you want to know?' I asked.

'Only if you tell me. I wouldn't dare ask.'

'There are always two questions too delicate to ask in inheritance matters. The first is, what's it worth? And the second is, is there any loose cash lying about?'

'Go on.'

'I can't tell you.'

'Whyever not?'

'Valuation first—that's a valuation of Stringer Station—before anyone has any idea.'

'But—'

I said, 'There'll be a dollar or two.'

'Am I being mercenary? No, certainly I'm not. Honestly, I thought Granny's sister must have died years ago. I never expected—'

'As to ready cash,' I said. 'Maybe there's some at the Station, but I wouldn't bet on it. There ought to be a bank account somewhere, but that's still to be checked.'

'So what now?'

'I've done my duty in informing next of kin. Next comes the legal mumbo-jumbo—may take weeks, may take months.'

'Oh.' She looked disappointed.

'But it shouldn't be too long,' I said, 'before your position as sole legatee is established, and after that, the banks will shower you with gold if you want it. You have expectations. Are you the kind who celebrates—cars and fur coats?'

'Don't talk about cars. Mine was crunched two nights ago.'

'Crunched?'

'By a scout car. Idiot of a corporal ran into it and then over it.'

'Wrecked?'

'Write-off. I'll make that corporal jump before I've done. Men!'

'Some men are all right!' I said.

'Damn few. Certainly not him.' Her eyes gleamed. 'I'm making arrangements for that corporal.'

'Be kind to him—in celebration.'

'Kind? I could kill him.'

'What was it—the car?'

'Daimler V8 two-fifty Sports, 1969.'

'Hey, that's a real classic! Maintain it yourself?'

'Yes, always. I half-rebuilt it. Took me two years. That's why it hurts.'

I said soothingly, 'You can buy two to replace it.'

'But where does one find 'em?' she said wistfully.

We had lunch and by the end of it I was so far gone in jet-lag that I thought it was supper. I had the porter get her a taxi and off she went. By the time I got back from Cortina, I had told her, there might be news. One of the pupil students was ringing round the banks, looking for accounts.

I hurled myself into bed and tried to sleep, but couldn't for a while—too tired, no doubt. My mind meandered. Feminist, I thought. Tough, competent, accustomed to command. Mechanical engineer by profession. God help the Abo stockmen when *she* got to Stringer Station—she'd have 'em jumping as high as the corporal.

My days in Italy passed enjoyably. The best weather in the world comes in two patterns—there's the Alpine sun-and-snow, and the great Aussie sun-and-sea. In the Dolomites, the air was clean and crisp and cold and the skiing was magnificent, and I got tanned and fit and drank too much, once or twice. In retrospect, I think I was being readied for something. Good thing I didn't know what.

I called Greg's office as soon as I was on the ground in London, and said cheerily, 'What's on your barbie, sport?' (local patois—what's cooking).

'When's your flight out, John?'

I told him.

'You might just have time.'

'What's the problem?'

'Jane Strutt. She's in hospital.'

'What happened?'

'Hit-and-run.'

'Serious?'

'Bruises and a broken ankle. She's in the army hospital in Aldershot.'

I said, 'Hold on. Why do I have to visit her? Is this one of your posh Pommie legal customs? My client is in hospital, therefore I must visit. What's your fee per visit, eh?'

'She'd like to talk to you.'

'What about?'

'That's the other thing. I'd a telex from Perth. They've found two bank accounts. Hundred and twenty thousand dollars in one and eighty thou' in the other. She wants to discuss it.'

'Does she know our fees per minute, plus out of town charges, plus delayed flight charges, plus—'

'Do the girl a favour!'

'Try saying that to Miller Bunbury,' I said. 'Okay, I'll talk to Qantas. Delay myself a day or so. Where do I stay?'

He suggested one of the Heathrow hotels. I ignored him, rented a car, stuck my gear in the boot (no skis, I'd rented those in Cortina) and set off for Aldershot, which turned out to be a town in which the dominant colour is khaki-green. Cars, trucks, uniforms, signposts. But the sheets in the hospital were white.

'Kind of you to come all this way,' she said. She looked all right in a blue-and-white spotted silk dressing gown. No visible marks apart from the half-ton of plaster encasing her foot. She winced as she stretched out her hand.

'Hurts?'

'Less each day, so they say. I feel I've been processed in a Magimix!'

'Hit-and-run, Greg said.'

She nodded. 'It was in town. Been to the movies, came

out and went to cross the road and found myself staring at the headlights. If I hadn't jumped damn quick—'

I was thinking, of course, that this was her second involvement with accidents recently. And it does me no credit that the thought passing through my mind was 'woman driver, woman pedestrian'.

She saw me thinking it, and said, 'Not my fault in either case.'

'You'd say that.'

She looked at me grimly. 'I'd sue if I could find him. And if I knew of a half-way decent lawyer!'

I said emolliently, 'Too much traffic on the roads over here.'

'Too many men!' says she.

'On a happier note, Greg told you about the money, did he?'

'Said there was a piece of good news, but you'd tell me.'

'There are two-hundred thousand pieces of good news,' I said. 'That's Australian good news. In English good news it'll be eighty-odd thousand.'

'My God, I'm rich—I really am!' She raised both arms in an emphatic gesture of joy, winced and lowered them gingerly.

'I said you would be.'

She whistled. It struck me as odd. Women don't whistle, do they? No reason why they shouldn't, but they don't. It suited her.

'What I wanted to ask—' she hesitated.

'Fire away.'

'Well, is it *mine*? I've been lying here thinking I'd like to go and see the farm and the Station. I've a month's leave—I can take that, and—'

'Probate,' I said, 'is formal proof of a will, okay? If the will is unquestioned, it is proved in what's known as "common form". Otherwise, Probate court.'

'Is there any question?'

'Not that I know about.'

She was appealingly childlike, all of a sudden. 'I'd *love* to go. I got out an atlas and found this place Kununurra and it looks incredibly remote. How long before everything's settled?'

'I'll get busy as soon as I get back. See what I can do.'

'Thanks.'

'Kununurra,' I said, 'is warm.'

'You mean hot.'

'Certainly do. No place for fair-skinned Pommie ladies in early March.'

'I can stand it,' she said with a certain how-dare-you?

'The lizards go off to hide when it's warm up there. Do you no harm to wait a bit. Anyway, the ankle will need it.'

She scowled down at it. 'They say three weeks to a month.'

'Fine, you can use the leave for convalescence.'

The scowl died. She was a surprising young woman, this one. Made slim but strong: whippy-looking, smooth-skinned with health. Qualified engineer, impatient, prejudiced.

I said conversationally, 'What have you got against the male of the species?'

She looked up. 'What makes you think there's anything?'

'Just the way you say "men" disparagingly at the end of every sentence.'

'You're surprised? One crunches my car. The other knocks me down and runs!'

'And you—you're able to get along without them?'

Jane Strutt laughed. 'I saw your nasty little mind click into gear as soon as you saw my uniform. Absolutely without justification. I just expect to compete on equal terms.'

'But men won't allow it?'

'Usually they won't.'

'But when they do, you win?'

'As a rule.'

I took out my little notebook and a pen. 'While we're still on speaking terms—your family history, please. Male and female.'

For two pins she'd have challenged me to single combat. Her eyes sparkled.

I said, 'Mary Ellen and Jane Emmett were sisters, yes? No other sisters—no brothers?'

'There was a brother, but he died in the First War.'

'Can it be proved?'

'It was seventy years ago, does it have to be?'

'Don't get savage. I'm trying to speed things up, remember.'

'I've got his medals somewhere. He got the MM posthumously. The Somme, that was. And his name's in the Book of Remembrance in the library. Will that be satisfactory?'

'Expect so. He was single, was he—no kids?'

'He wasn't nineteen when he died, so I don't think kids are likely. He certainly wasn't married, and if he had time to father any bastards we never heard of them.'

'Carry on about the sisters.'

'They were nurses, both of them. Mary Ellen was a year older than Grannie—than Jane, that is. They trained at Leeds Infirmary, and nursed in France at the end of the war, then they went off to Australia after it all ended.'

'Go on.'

'They were in a place called Free-something.'

'Fremantle?'

'That's right. Then Perth. They got jobs together there. I think there was a house.'

'There was. Mary Ellen bought it.'

'Mum told me they were going to buy it together. But guess what came along?'

'Adam,' I said, 'the old Adam in person. Men, as *you'd* say.'

She shrugged. 'Grannie said he drank. He was brought into the hospital one night, horribly drunk. Injured himself, I forget what it was, doesn't matter anyway. Mum couldn't stand him. Mary Ellen could. Thought the sun shone out of him. Devoted sisters up to that time, but he split them up. Grannie came home. He married Mary Ellen. Man called—hold on, I'll remember—'

'Green,' I said.

She shook her head. 'Stringer, of course it was. That's why it's Stringer Station, I imagine.'

'Solves that. Go on.'

'He was a betting man, this fellow Stringer. Horrible and

rough, Mum always said, and he drank and gambled. He was—' She looked at me. 'There's a word, an Australian word.'

I grinned. 'Solicitor?' I said. 'Or do you mean Ocker?'

'Ocker, that's it. Anyway he gambled.'

'On what?'

'Anything, Mum said. Two flies on a window and which flies off first.'

'That's wet-weather betting, Captain.'

She wasn't listening; her mind was on that villain of long ago. 'Grannie said gambling would be the ruin of him.'

'Was it?'

She had the grace to smile. 'Sadly, no. Within a year he'd actually won a farm!'

'Gambling?'

'I forget what game. Something to do with tossing coins.'

'It's called two-up,' I said, 'and it's Australia's national sport. When you say he won a farm, did he win—?'

'Stringer Station, do you mean? Eighty-two square miles! Maybe he did. Gosh! I bet the man who lost was cross.'

'Drunk more likely. Anything more?'

'I don't think he lasted very long, the drunk, I mean—this fellow Stringer. Died after a year or two, far as I remember.'

'So who was Green? She was Mary Ellen Green—Mrs Green—when she died.'

'Not sure, Grannie never really said. She—Mary Ellen—didn't write much, a few times in fifty years, that's all. I think this Green just came to the farm one day—'

'The Station.'

'Yes, the Station. I'd better get used to it. To me a station is Waterloo or Paddington. Well, he arrived and never left. I think that was how it was. And eventually they must have just got married.'

I don't know how she pictured it. Farms English-style, I imagine, with thatched houses and five-bar gates, and casual strangers knocking at the door. She didn't appreciate, or understand, the kind of country they were in, the scale of it. From the sound of things, and just for a start, Stringer Station wasn't far from the fringes of the Great Sandy Desert, and anybody moving around too casually there is likely to perish fast of thirst and heatstroke. In my mind, I saw something different: the lonely widowed woman on the big remote Station; a few blacks for company, no one else for miles; then a man comes from somewhere—a jackaroo maybe, on the move, fired by one station, looking for work or whatever. A white man probably—there's never been much intermarriage—and she offers him a job and he stays. That seemed the way of it. Then the jackaroo married the Station and bought a brewery. It had the marks of probability.

I told her, 'Come and see me when you get to Perth. I'll point you in the right direction, and see what I can do to make some arrangements.'

'You see this rotten plaster-cast, Mr Close? I hate it!'

'Maybe it was put on by a bloke.'

'I'm not sure I don't hate you too.'

I said, 'Can I ask you a question?'

'A question? It's *the* question. Everyone asks it. Why did I join the Army? Is that the one?'

'Along those lines.'

'Have you any idea what a good career it is for women?'

'Okay, fine. But isn't it a bit, er—'

'Butch? Could be if you let it. But it's a lot of fun.'

'Right, ma'am,' I said. 'See you in Perth in a month or so, when you come to claim your inheritance.'

But I saw her well before. The hotel at Heathrow, the one recommended by Greg, was the most neutral place you ever saw: machinery clicking, smiles also mechanical, vacuum cleaners going all night like the restaurants. Twenty-four hour activity, much of it noisy. I woke at two feeling a bit sick and wondering about some prawns I'd eaten. An hour later I woke again, vomiting and with a low-belly pain. Two hours after that I was on the operating table having my appendix whipped out.

Greg came to see me next day, carrying a neat pack containing six glass-size bottles of champagne.

'More suitable, in your case, than long-stemmed roses.'

He then pulled out a telex. The message, from Bunbury, said there had been a satisfactory offer for Stringer Station and it was my job to persuade my client to accept immediately.

'Immediately's a good word,' I said. 'He doesn't waste them. Sprays expletives around, but leaves out necessary information. Offer *from* whom, satisfactory *to* whom, and of *what*? I mean, you'd think—'

'I would,' Greg agreed. 'Will she sell?'

'She's angry she can't fly out today to start ploughing at dawn. No, she won't sell. Any rate, I'd be amazed if she did. Would you, in her place? Eighty square miles of cattle station, think of it!'

He said judiciously, 'She's young.'

'Thirty. So am I.'

'She's well qualified and very presentable. Likes her career. She's English. I'd have thought she'd prefer the civilized pleasures available here to wrestling with, for instance, crocodiles and other local fauna. Gently nurtured young lady, or so she seemed to me.'

'There are times, Greg, when you sound like a very bad pastiche of Noel Coward. She's as tough as pemmican, used to doing things for herself, self-confident and bursting for adventure.'

'Mr Bunbury will be thrilled to hear it,' Greg said.

'Even Bunbury must sometimes face reality.'

'You intend to tell him that? I'd like to see it.'

'What does Bunbury matter to me! There are jobs all over.'

'He may be right, have you thought of that?'

'I've thought of it. If she wants to sell in a year or two, okay, she can sell. Her choice, though.'

'I suppose so.'

'Not Bunbury's!'

'Indeed not. Oh, there's something else.'

'Go on.'

'For when you're up and about.'

'Tell me.'

Part of Greg's pleasure in his effete-Pom act, is riling people like me. It works too.

'What is it, Greg?'

'I mean, not until you're fully recovered. Mustn't risk anything.'

'I *beg* you.'

He smiled. 'The Skeffingham royalties.'

'What about them?' The Skeffingham family, in England, owned an enormous deposit, in Western Australia, of bauxite, the ore from which aluminium comes.

'Price is drifting down,' Greg said.

'Renegotiate, you mean?' The Skeffinghams aren't the only people with bauxite ore. There's lots of it about—more than the world needs just now.

He pointed at the floor.

I said, 'Downward, naturally. Down how far?'

He pointed to the floor again. 'About that far.'

'Or?'

'Mining stops.'

'That's true?'

'Near enough, I gather. Have to be cut by more than half, or mining does stop. The rest is negotiable.'

'Why not you?'

'You know the family, don't you? They'll accept things from strong-jawed, clear-eyed Australians where black beetles like me are not believed. Still, it's for later.'

Appendicitis nowadays is not what it was. I was on my feet later that day and tossed out with my belly in sticking plaster the one after, once they'd found I had somewhere (my hotel) to go to. I loafed in my room watching TV for three more days and then, bored out of my mind, went off to screw down the Skeffinghams. If they'd been little, white-haired old ladies eking out tiny incomes, I might have been gentler, but they aren't—they're arrogant as only the English can be. Booming men who think Australia's still a penal colony; and nose-in-the-air, icy women so strangled they can barely talk, even if they wished to. And rich—on Australia's back. Millions out and nothing back, and too mean and too stupid to hire good negotiators for themselves. The whole drawn-out business was a pleasure. An innate cruelty surfaces in me.

32

At intervals there had been the odd telex from Bunbury, who was exhibiting his habitual patience in the matter of Stringer Station, but I ignored them. Bunbury was on the board of the company mining Skeffingham ore and that simple fact determined both his priorities and mine. No sooner had I closed the revised deal with the Skeffinghams than I was being ordered to re-open negotiations with Jane Strutt.

She was out of hospital, I learned, and back at base. I phoned and said, 'Why aren't you on convalescent leave?'

'Two reasons. There's plenty of work to be done, and secondly, I'm saving all my leave. Are you ringing me up from Perth?'

'Harrogate,' I said. 'It's almost a local call. I'll be in London tonight. Look, when you say you're saving your leave—'

'For Australia of course,' she said. 'I've been waiting to hear from you.'

I thought: there'd have been activity of some kind on the Probate front in my extended absence, and the fact that Bunbury was requiring Jane Strutt to sell must indicate that her right to the estate wasn't much in doubt.

'Can you walk?'

'Doesn't worry me too much. Aches a bit if I overdo things.'

'You want to be sure of that ankle before you take it up North. Listen, I'll be in London tomorrow. Could you hobble up for lunch?'

'Yes.'

'Don't soldiers have to salute and ask for permission?'

'I have automatic permission and I was going anyway. What's more it's Friday today, Saturday tomorrow. Don't know what it is in Harrogate. Where are you staying in London?'

'Place called the Selfridge.'

'Right by the store. Good. I want to buy some shoes.'

'It's bush boots you'll need up there in the Top End.'

'I'll get boots in Australia. Bush boots wouldn't go with my new blue dress.'

3

Over lunch I told Jane about the offer to buy Stringer Station.

She shook her head, as I had known she would. 'Not on your life, cobber.'

I explained that cobber was not a word much in use in Australia: merely a part of the legend, like the hat with the corks.

'Then no.'

Next she asked, as she was bound to: 'All the same, how much *is* the offer?'

'I don't know.'

She raised her eyes from the pepperoni. 'Funny sort of offer.'

'I imagine there'll be a figure somewhere, I'm just to tell you the offer exists.'

'Good guide to the value, though,' Jane said.

'It might be.'

'Why only might?'

I thought of Miller Bunbury, who'd be a bit displeased by what I was going to say. 'Some smart operator offering low in the hope that the far-off English lady will say, "Hello money"—and grab it.'

'But wouldn't *you* protect me?'

'Me, personally, or lawyers in general?'

'I see what you mean.'

'But don't go dreaming dreams about running cattle stations up there,' I said warningly. 'It may sound like romantic pioneering—but the reality is damned hard work in a climate that's hard for Europeans, even third-generation

Australian Europeans. If you keep the station on, you'd have to find a damn good man to run it for you.'

'Why a man?'

I shrugged. 'Slip of the tongue. You're free to run it as a feminist collective if you want to. Just don't be too surprised when you go bust!'

'You think I'm a feminist, do you?' She was smiling.

'You give a passable imitation.'

'I've been tangling with people like you—'

I interrupted. 'You mean *men* like me.'

'That's right. Not engineering, dear, you'll break your fingernails. Not the army, dear, not for a girl. Listen to yourself doing the same thing! Not the North, dear, not for a woman. I'm *not* a feminist, especially. But if I'm able and efficient, why shouldn't I tackle worthwhile things?'

Argue that one? Not me, mate. But you have to have the last word don't you? I said, 'I'll make this prediction—you won't like Australia.'

'Why not?'

'Because if there's a party, you sometimes find all the men at one end of the room with their mates, and all the women at the other.'

She shook her head, amused. 'They can't all be as bad as you.'

'You'll find,' I said, 'that I'm among the enlightened.'

I flew back next day.

She came in three weeks later on a British Airways jumbo via Hong Kong, carrying those little parcels that always contain silk blouses. Perth Airport at noon. As I waited to cross the road from the car park to the terminal building, the shadow I threw was about two inches wider than my feet. The sun was overhead. Crowds thronged the arrival area: Australians, especially New Australians, are meet-and-greet champions of the world. When young Gino flies back from Milano, he's met by everybody from grandmama to the latest bambino. Jumbos carry about four hundred, every passenger met by an average of, say, four. So there were sixteen hundred or so sweltering in the terminal, and I joined them reluctantly, my mind still adjusting to Miller Bunbury's instructions.

'*Make* her sell,' he'd ordered, brusquely.

'She won't do it. Told me so. In fact she has an idea she could run it herself.'

'She can't. She's not wanted.'

'Who by?'

'By bloody Australia, you damn fool. Days of the Pom are over.'

'Who made the offer, anyway?'

'Came in from Cadge & Co in Adelaide.'

'How much?'

Bunbury came as near as he ever comes to smiling. His teeth showed briefly; no humour in it, though.

'What it takes.'

'Why the game-playing?'

He shrugged. 'She's not wanted. That's it. You got it?'

'Clear enough, even for me.'

'Make her unwelcome, make her uncomfortable.'

'But make her sell,' I said. 'Is it the graziers?'

Australia's graziers, those people smart enough, or quick enough, to grab themselves great tracts of grassland a century ago, are a native aristocracy, and to be reckoned with. That much land and money, acting together and with strong common interests, is powerful. Some of the feudal barons are in the North of WA.

'Shit, it's everybody. Get her out and get her selling, even if it takes a scorpion in her boots!'

Damned if I would. And damned too, if I knew why he was so keen. He was always ferociously anti-Pom, of course, but then he was anti-everybody. Bunbury got notions wedged in his head that couldn't be shifted with blasting powder, and this must be one of them.

I waited. They're not quick in Customs and Immigration at Perth and even they were having an off day. It was two and a half hours after touchdown before Jane Strutt appeared, looking happy and giving me her engineer's handshake.

'Good trip?'

'Just like every other jet I ever flew in. Grub's not bad, though. Gosh, look at this sunshine!'

I pushed her baggage trolley to the car, loaded her case, started the engine and switched on the air-conditioning too soon. The car stalled, as they do, but after two or three times, I had everything working and off we went.

'Business first,' I said. 'You've got common form Probate. I'm acting as administrator and it was granted on my oath. Okay so far?'

'What's it mean?'

'Means the will's proved. Valuation's still under way. How are you fixed for money?'

'I'm okay. Granny left me her house when she died and I sold it then.'

'You may have to wait a bit here.'

'Don't worry.'

'You get two days to look around. Then we're off adventuring. That suit you?'

'We?'

'Well, you can't go alone.'

'Sounds lovely.' She looked happily around her. 'Looks lovely, too.'

'Remarkable place,' I said. 'Remotest city on earth—on the edge of a million square miles of nothing—but try parking your car.'

'Don't you like Perth?'

'Love it,' I said. 'But I don't like what's happened to it. Small number of very rich men have got the whole state, let alone the city, by the throat. Perth's changing the way they want it to change.'

I didn't convince her, but then I wasn't trying very hard and she was already bedazzled by the skyline and the shimmer off the Swan River.

She was serene and happy by the time I drove past the giant jarrah tree and found a shady place to leave my car while we walked over to the back of the King's Park restaurant. It's one of those places that soothes the soul, and

I'm enough of a good West Australian to want to show off my state. So we sat out in the sunshine among the big trees, under vine leaf shade, and looked out across the city and the river. Yachts were scudding about, and boat crews rowed, and ferries went smoothly across the Swan. We ate local: from avocado pears, pineapples and bananas to sea food and steak; all was local produce. Likewise the Margaret River fine wine. Below us the water sparkled, around us the grass was green and well-watered. The air was absolutely untainted. The high buildings a mile away showed clean and clear. If you plan an idyll, that's the scene for it.

'Where,' said Jane, at one point, as she sipped the crisp Chablis from the Swan Valley, 'is all the red dust you hear about?'

'Monday,' I said, 'you'll see enough red dust to last you a lifetime.'

So, Monday we boarded an Ansett WA flight bound ultimately for Darwin in the Northern Territory, but making intermediate stops at the old pearling port of Broome, at Derby, and at Kununurra, where we got off. You may wonder why it was 'we'. There were a couple of reasons: first, that Bunbury had told me on the phone, 'Show that Pommie Australia's not for bloody Poms,' and he insisted that experienced solicitors accompanying clients new to the country was 'bloody correct, understand!' The second was that, North being North, there might be legal matters connected with the estate to be dealt with. Mary Ellen Green might have had a solicitor in Kununurra or Wyndham. Quite likely there were outstanding accounts to be settled for supplies to Stringer Station.

The earth below grew redder as we flew north, and in an hour we looked down on red ochre landscape stretching endlessly beneath us. But there's usually something to soften airport arrivals. At Broome, it's the Indian Ocean and the old harbour. At Derby there's King Sound—more water; then as you come to Kununurra there's Lake K itself and the vast expanse of man-made Lake Argyle in the distance. All looks pretty and inviting.

But, boy, oh boy!—the *heat*!

It hit her like a club. Couple of minutes before, the airline captain's reassuring voice had been murmuring 34°, and bright sunshine and clear skies at Kununurra, which sounds nice. Apply the formula though: double the number and add thirty, you wind up with 98°F and a pitiless sun. I watched Jane step out of the air-conditioning on to the tarmac, and move in an instant from comfort to astonishment.

'Come on,' I said, 'there'll be cool air in the building.'

There was more than cool air: there was a small grizzled man in his forties, who picked us out effortlessly from the dozen or so other arrivals, and came over, hand outstretched.

'John Close? G'day, I'm Bluie Stainsby.'

I introduced Jane and hands were shaken. This was our pilot, pre-booked by the airline.

Jane said, 'Warm here, Mr Stainsby.'

He grinned amiably. He had a number of teeth, but it was not a very large number. 'You a Pom, lady? So am I. We don't spend a hell of a lot on coal fires in Kununurra. I'll tell you that.'

'I'll bet.'

'Drink a lot, that's the trick. Water, Coke, beer. And stay covered. Don't let that old golden bastard up there get at your skin.' He turned to me. 'Wanna go now?'

Jane said, 'Yes, we might as well. There's nothing to keep us.'

Stainsby gave her an uncertain glance, then looked to me for confirmation.

'Yes,' I said. 'This, by the way, is the new owner of Stringer.'

He nodded a couple of times, then said, 'You're a right smart-looking lady, Miz Strutt. Reckon you'll have some changes to make out there.'

'You know Stringer Station?'

He shook his head. 'Where it is, that's all. Never landed there. She never left the place, old Miz Green.'

'Never?'

'Not that I heard of, and I been here twenty-three years,

ever since Kununurra was a joey.' He showed us his teeth again. 'The town's new, only founded in the sixties.'

'Supplies?' I asked. 'Do you know how she got—'

'Everybody knows everything here, mate. There's a boong —an Abo—think he's stock foreman, been there years. He drives over now 'n' again in a big four-wheel-drive Land-Cruiser. Kind of old.'

'The man or the truck?' Jane asked.

'Man'd be maybe fifty. Truck seven or eight. I've some tucker loaded in the plane for you: tins of things, few veggies, water. You're there for what, five days?'

'That's right.'

'Keep you going that long. Got some venin in there too, not that you'll need it.'

'What's that?' Jane asked.

'Snake-bite, but you won't see one,' Stainsby said. 'You people okay now?'

He had a little six-seater Piper. Single-engined, which never seems a very good idea to me when there's a lot of hostile land or water to cross; but these blokes have to have faith in internal combustion engines, especially petrol ones. When I have to have engines, I'm a diesel man, but they don't put diesels in the sky. Still, he got us there.

Stringer Station is a tiny, a very tiny part of the enormous sweep of grassland which runs right across the top of Australia from the Great Sandy Desert in the west, to New South Wales in the east. Not all of it is year-round grass. You've got some genuine tropical savannah but a lot is temperate grassland, and a lot is seasonal, and it's a very good place indeed to graze the kind of cattle that can stand heat. Only trouble, nowadays, is finding markets for the beef.

We'd been an hour and a bit in the air, when Stainsby, the chart on his knee, pointed out to the left side and called out, 'There—say g'day to Stringer Station.'

Jane and I looked down as Stainsby put the plane into a wide circle designed to show off Jane's fiefdom, the first thing I saw was a ragged mob of cattle put to a run by the racket of the air engine. Then, as the turn continued, a tin-roofed house—the tin dark with age—came into sight, with a scatter of buildings round it. There was a wind-pump, too, and it was turning, which was a good sign. Not much else—but what else *would* there be on a cattle station except cattle and living-quarters and water?

One thing I saw no signs of was a landing strip. 'Where do you put her down?' I called to Stainsby. He turned his head to grin at me and yelled back. 'No worries, mate,' and a minute or two later brought us in on hard, bare earth and taxied to a stop not more than a hundred metres or so from the house. He switched off, beamed at us, and said, 'Stringer Station, ladies and gents.'

He helped us to get the baggage out, not that there was much: we'd a suitcase apiece plus the food he'd brought for us. We carried the cases, and Stainsby the food, over to the house, and when we got there, sweating, I said, 'The water, where's that?'

'Ten-gallon drum for you,' said Stainsby. 'In the plane. Mind, they'll have a good supply here. See the windmill?'

'Agreed,' I said, 'But . . .'

'Oh, yes, *but*,' Stainsby said. Then he said, 'See you in five days.' After that he flew away, leaving us to look.

That first look was informative. Stringer Station, to put it kindly, was run-down. Neglected would be a mild word.

'Not a lot of maintenance lately.'

'Or anything else.' She turned to me and gave a little resigned smile. 'Don't know that I expected fresh paint exactly—'

I said, 'Look at it this way. It must have been well-built to start with.'

'Or it would have fallen down long ago?' she said.

'Let me,' I said, and turned the handle and pushed open the unlocked door, and stamped my feet a couple of times, hard, in case anything had crawled or crept or slithered inside.

'Why do you do that?'

'There's only one good thing to be said about Australian snakes,' I told her. 'They're nervous. They get out of the way if they can. You have to give 'em the chance.'

'All of them do that?'

'Maybe not the King Brown. He's nasty.'

'Is he here?'

I nodded. 'Wouldn't be too surprised if he's somewhere on the Station. Hope he's not indoors here.'

I listened, but heard no sinister small sounds from inside, so, leaving her at the door, in I went.

Chaos. It was a single big room, kitchen-cum-sitting, the windows were shuttered, so the only light came from the doorway, itself in shadow. But there was light in plenty to see that every pot and pan had been tossed on the floor and that many were broken; so were the straight-back chairs, and all the drawers had been emptied either on the table or the floor. The door of the old, cast-iron cooking range stood open and the trays and racks from it were strewn about. The ruins of two picture frames lay among it all. The radio, too, had been tipped over and smashed. Then I was looking in through the doorway of what was clearly the main bedroom, and at a slashed mattress spilling stuffing like Niagara Falls. I heard a tap, then, and Jane's gasp behind me.

Swinging round I saw her in the middle of the main room and behind her, in the doorway, in silhouette, what had wrung the gasp from her.

A man with a rifle; and it was pointed at her.

4

As I turned the barrel moved to cover me. I stared across the twenty-odd feet that separated us, trying to make out something of him. He was big, that much I could see at once, and the bulk was crowned by a wide-brim hat.

He said, 'You—out!', gesturing with the rifle, and backing as he spoke.

'Go on, Jane!'

She strode towards the door, stopped there and said, 'I'm the owner of this station!' Then she stepped outside. By the time I reached the door the whole scene was changed. The man was a big Abo, and now he stood with his hat in his hands, saying, 'Aw, sorry, missus,' over and over. The rifle lay on the ground at his feet—an old, bolt-action .303 Lee-Enfield of World War Two manufacture.

'Who the hell are *you*?' Jane was rasping in her best barrack-square style. 'What are you doing on my land?'

'Billy,' he mumbled.

'Say that again! Clearly this time.'

'Billy One-Hat, missus,' he said, clear as you like.

'And why are you here?'

'Missus, I live here.'

She turned to me and nodded. Stainsby mentioned an Abo.

'You're the stock foreman, then?' Jane Strutt asked crisply.

'Yes, missus.'

She took a step forward, hand outstretched. 'You looked after Mrs Green, I hear. Hope you'll look after me.'

It was like one of those *Sanders of the River*-type movies: proud white girl and hulking native chief. Evidently the magic remained potent.

'G'day, missus,' said Billy One-Hat, 'glad you come to Stringer.'

'I'm a stranger,' she said, 'and I know nothing about all this.'

He blinked at her. 'You welcome, missus. You hubban' too.'

I laughed and she smiled. I said, 'Not my wife, Billy.'

He nodded, blinking, and I said, 'I'm law—like police.'

'What happened in the house?' Jane asked him.

'Not here,' I said. 'Let's go indoors and brew some tea. Get out of the sun.'

The kettle was dented but not destroyed, and the cooking-gas bottle stood in a little brick housing where it had not been disturbed. While water boiled, Jane asked him if he had a family, when he'd been paid last, putting him at ease. I hunted up cups and found only old enamel mugs, chipped and stained but survivors of the assault that had wrecked the pottery.

When he held a steaming mug in his great paw, I said, 'Who did it and when?'

He'd been shy, as his people have always been. But the questions put him on fresh ground; he was angry, and the words came rushing. 'Four come in plane—' he pointed '—from that way. Into everywhere. Break door—' he gestured at the rear entry '—go through Missus Green's things, break everything.'

The unworthy thought had just crept into my head that maybe Billy and his Abo mates had been looking for grog one recent Saturday night and had turned nasty when there wasn't any. They have a reputation for liking the bottle. The thought didn't last long.

Billy One-Hat said, 'Hit me, my wife, two boys.'

'Hit you—why?' Jane asked.

'Try stop them. They say no. Knock me down, beat me.'

'When?'

'Three week.'

'Who were they?' Jane asked.

He shrugged.

'You mean you've no idea at all?'

They were strangers, he said. He was a quiet man and he spoke the English necessary to his life, but no more. In Australia these days you have Abos in Government and the media and all sport, but it's recent. You also have the full-bloods who haven't fully opted into the white world, and don't want to, because their traditions pull too hard. In any case, too often they're not accepted.

I asked lawyer-type questions: descriptions of men, colour of aircraft, that kind of thing.

Jane asked why they'd come to Stringer.

He didn't know, couldn't imagine. 'Maybe drunk?' I asked.

He shook his head. 'Not drunk.'

Had they been before? No. Nor since. We were getting nowhere—there were things to be done before night.

'Generator, Billy?'

He showed me where the machine was—in one of the outbuildings. It was an ancient American diesel that must have been left to run down because its tank was dry. But there was fuel aplenty in store, and with a few gallons in the tank, she started as soon as I touched the light switch. I was glad about that—hand-cranking old diesels in baking temperatures isn't humorous work. The wind-pump, wheel turning away easily on top of the thirty-foot mast-pylon, provided a big tankful of water.

Everything domestic, it seemed, was in working order. I went and told the owner so.

She frowned and said, 'It's weird.' She was busy trying to bring a bit of order to things indoors.

'Weird?'

'Don't you think so?'

I said, 'Do you mean the place, or the country, the house being vandalized—what?'

She glanced at me. 'Everything in order—except the house. You tell me that the generator works, that there's water. But in here everything's smashed.'

'There's something weirder than that,' I said.

'Is there?'

'Come outside,' I told her. And when we were out in the sun, 'Look round you.' She did so. 'What do you see?'

'You know what I see. Old, run-down buildings, broken fences, cattle running wild.'

'They always run wild up here. That's the system.'

'Okay,' she said, arms akimbo, 'what's your problem?'

'The place has produced pots of money,' I said. 'Two hundred thousand in loose cash!'

'Perhaps the money has been there a long time. Earned when the place was in better order.'

'Maybe. We'd better check that later.'

There were no answers for us; that particular conversation ended there. I went and hunted through the outbuildings until I found the Land-Cruiser in an old red-painted tin barn, hotter inside than a baker's oven. Glow-plug going, the old Toyota gave a grunt and chattered cheerfully.

I switched off and continued wandering. There was a feed store, with not much in it except some maize. Presumably Mary Ellen Green had kept a few chickens at some point and indeed I did find a chicken run with what had been fine mesh wire, but it was more holes than wire now. No protection, no chickens. No eggs either.

Four or five hundred yards away stood a trailer. That, I thought, must be Billy One-Hat's home. Eight or nine people stood and sat near it, grouped in the shade of a boab tree: plainly his family. They'd be discussing us, I thought. New mistress who looked a bit on the bossy side, and her tame man. I'd have liked to go over there, pump Billy for more information, but I didn't. It was too hot to stroll over and too hot in the tin shed to encourage getting the Land-Cruiser out. Morning would do. Early morning.

Then I opened the door. No, that makes it sound easy, and it wasn't. It was a barn door for a start, and askew on its hinges, so I had to lift and pull and tug and sweat to shift it. Inside was a chapel—an old tin tabernacle complete with two rough pews and an altar; and a Bible on a lectern and paintings of Christ and Mary. It was dusty in there, but somehow serene, the way empty churches are. In my mind's eye I saw an old lady and an ancient priest, and the simple service they must have held on his occasional visits.

It was somehow touching, and when I went outside again, and round the far end of the building, there was something there that touched me more.

'Found the graves,' I said to Jane when I saw her. She'd meanwhile discovered a ladder and put it against the house side, and was halfway up it with a pair of binoculars having a good look round. By now the heat was beginning to ebb, but not much.

'Show me.'

There were three of them, behind the chapel and in the shadow of a big rock that reared ten or twelve feet close behind them.

'Mary Ellen Emmett,' Jane said softly. She was standing at the foot of the grave on the right. It wasn't much of a grave: this was rock hard ground, probably only two or three inches of dusty earth over the rock, so there could be no six-foot digging. The grave consisted of a narrow hump of reddish earth, set with flat stones. At the head was a wooden cross with her name chipped into it, and the date of her death. There was also a little piece of white pottery to serve as a vase, and a couple of thin burned stalks that must once have been flowers.

I moved along. The next one had a headstone: black marble, lettering carved by a stonemason. Here lay:

BILL STRINGER

loved husband of Mary Ellen
died November 2nd, 1923
in the 40th year of his life.

It was a handsome chunk of marble and would take centuries to erode, that being the general idea. This was the man who'd won Stringer Station—not the wreck of a place we saw now, but the Station as it had been more than sixty years before, when the good building work had been recent.

This was the man who had won it in a game of two-up.

I moved to the next one. Another headstone, this time one of those black and grey things, stone chips ground up and then mixed: modern and looking as though they've been moulded rather than carved, as possibly they have. The inscription here was carved impressively deep and gold inlaid: *Sacred to the memory of John Joseph Green, beloved husband of Mary Ellen Green, died Sept 1971, aged 76.* There were two more long black stones of the same composition-material, one either side of the little earth-ridge. Churchyard stuff, looking odd out here.

The sun drops quickly out of sight in those latitudes, and soon after six we were indoors with the shutters tight and Ray-ban squirted in all the corners against mosquitoes, making some dinner out of the considerable assortment of tins Stainsby had provided.

'What kind of food would Mary Ellen cook?' Jane asked me.

'Bully-beef stew and damper, or her own beef.'

'What's damper?'

'Kind of bread you make in a billy.'

She knew what a billy was, and she had a lot of other questions about life in the remote stations. Some I answered, some I couldn't. I'm a city boy myself, and even if I do go bush-walking, the notion of handling a longhorn steer was as remote from my life as it was from hers.

After we'd eaten, Jane wanted to draw diagrams of family trees, and we sat at the rickety table on equally rickety chairs to do it.

'Imagine, sixty years in this place!' she said.

'Devil's Island might be more fun.'

'Oh! How can you!'

I said defensively, 'At least there'd be a spot of company. Mates to talk to.'

'She had a mate, as you put it. Here. For a lot of years.'

'Yair,' I said. 'Just the two of 'em, and every now and again you say G'day to the boongs for a change.'

48

'You don't think they were happy?' Her voice was wistful; she *wanted* past happiness for the people under the earth behind the chapel.

'Imagine they must have adapted. People do.'

'You think it was dull, don't you? Sixty dull years. God, think of it!'

'She had two-hundred thousand dollars, Jane. Plus this station. All hers. If she'd thought she'd like it better in Perth —or in Paris for that matter, she could have gone there, no worries. She chose here. QED.'

'But there was *him*,' Jane said. 'You and your QED. Maybe *he* didn't want to live in Perth.'

I got the cracked teapot and poured a strong cup for her. 'Drink it,' I ordered. She drank half. 'Did you ever meet her?'

Shake of head.

'Then don't get all romantic about her. She's as remote from you as Captain Cook.'

'All the same—'

'And we're pretty remote ourselves, without the radio,' I said.

It brought her back from her private dreamtime. She looked at me soberly for a moment then said in a bright voice, 'Have to get another teapot, if this one can't be repaired. And Mr Stainsby'll be here in five days.'

'It's not Stainsby I'm thinking about. What do we do if the others come back.'

'Why should they?'

I shrugged. 'Why did they come in the first place?'

'Probably to see if there was anything worth stealing. If there was and they took it, we'll never know. Why should they come back?'

I laughed. 'You're an unusual woman.'

'Why?'

'There's a very well-known and common reaction to intruders. People get the shudders, women especially. Invasion of our private space, intruders in the nest. Offends against man's need for security.'

'Man's?'

'Mankind's, then. Including womankind. Doesn't it give you a touch of the shudders?'

'It wasn't my house, not then.'

'Oh, but it was.'

'But not my *home*. Maybe that's the distinction.'

'Maybe.'

She asked, 'You think they'll be back?'

'Either that or they're plain sadistic.'

'What do you mean?'

I said, 'Look, you know where we are—we're way out the back of Bourke, as the saying goes. There's all sorts of services up here. Flying Doctors, police. You've heard of them. They come out at a run if somebody's seriously crook. But we can't get in touch. There's no way!'

'So if they do come back here?'

I said, 'Well it may be eighty-odd square miles, but it's like being stuck in a cell. Nobody coming near for days.'

'I still can't see why they would come back. There's nothing here!'

'Wrong,' I said, as the thought struck me. 'There's us!'

5

In the second bedroom, no mattress, ripped or otherwise. The room was small and plain and furnished with an iron bedstead, army narrow, and with criss-cross wire springing, plus a rug of that ancient type made by threading strips of cloth through canvas, and a picture of the Virgin Mary. This would be where Father Naismith slept when he visited. The rug lay on the bedsprings and was presumably all the mattress the old priest had needed, accustomed as he certainly was to a blanket under the stars.

The ripped mattress we simply tossed outside to be burned next day, and Jane, following Father Naismith's example, put a rug on the mattress.

Rudimentary. But I slept well and when I asked her, Jane said she had too. It was six in the morning and the temperature at a guess—the barometer/thermometer was a part of the smashed furniture—was about twenty-three. While Jane boiled water I went to fetch the Land-Cruiser. A cup of tea and we would be away on our first tour of the Station. The big diesel again started easily, after I'd done a checklist of oil and tools. We weren't going that far: but in those parts you're careful. Always. I filled the water tank and drove round to pick up Jane at the house, where she handed me a dented tin-mug of tea and a biscuit. Two minutes to ingest, then we left. Jane at the wheel.

'We could pick up Billy One-Hat to give us the full guided tour,' I suggested.

'Let Billy sleep on,' she said. 'I just want to see the place. The detail can be filled in later.'

The Toyota's sturdy old engine rasped and clattered as Jane drove cautiously over the hard earth. But the first notable thing on the voyage of discovery was not agricultural but aeronautical—a plane, which flew fairly high, more or less across us, the morning sun reflected in flashes off its silver body. The sky was enamel blue and cloudless and even though the plane must have been about nine thousand feet up, clear air brought it almost close.

Beside me, Jane said, 'Where in hell—!'

'What's the matter?'

'Plane up there. Know what it is?'

I looked at it. 'No.'

She said, 'Distinctive—it's very unusual.'

'What is it?'

'Old P38 Lightning.'

'So?'

'Well, it's World War Two. American. Twin engines. Twin booms, see 'em?'

I saw them. 'How do you know?'

Jane laughed. 'It's one of the famous silhouettes. Anyway, I'm interested in aeroplanes.'

I watched it idly. 'Wartime?' Forty-plus years. Hard to get parts.

'What's it doing in these—?' She broke off as it lifted an elegant wing and began to turn. 'In this region?'

'Watch the road, Captain,' I said. 'I'll watch the plane.'

And I did, until its wide turn took it out of sight behind us. But then, not many seconds later, it came roaring over us from behind in a ferocious blast of sound that had us ducking involuntarily for cover. The whole thing was over in a second. It just flew, waggling its wings, and then climbing; in a couple of minutes it had vanished.

'Funny thing,' Jane said.

'What's funny?'

'Did you see any markings?'

'Tell you the truth, I wasn't looking.'

'Plain silver aluminium,' Jane said. 'No registration letters, no roundels, no nowt.'

'What's a nowt?'

'Where I come from,' Jane said, fixing me briefly with a hard eye, 'it's a nothing.'

'Discuss,' I said.

She laughed. 'Thank goodness all my exams are over.'

They were just beginning, had we known.

This was strange ground we began to cover: flat-looking, it seemed at first, but in fact seamed and wrinkled. The best parallel I can think of is the skin of an old woman's face, smooth from a distance, but deeply lined close to. I don't suppose there was any part of it more than fifty feet higher than the next, but you could have hidden an army there, comfortably. Half the time the Toyota was in second gear on sudden, sharp little slopes, up or down, and dozens of small gulleys intersected each other like the grid of a crossword puzzle. Down in the bottom were the dry tracks of wet season streams, but no sparkle.

'Where's the water?' Jane demanded.

'In the grass, I expect. There's plenty of grass. Not your English meadow exactly. The grass at this time of year is always brown and dried and fairly thin, but the hot-land cattle up here thrive on dry grass.'

'Nothing thriving about that beast,' she said.

A cow had turned away nervously at our approach and scrambled off up a slope and then out of sight.

'It's nimble.'

'Shouldn't it be fat?'

She knew nothing about livestock, and nor did I, but she'd hit the nail on the head. Cattle at Stringer Station *were* thin and nimble: swift of foot, sensitive of nostril and ready to run. They saw us coming and off they went. There was no contented cud-chewing, no watching the world go by.

Jane said, 'Do Australian cattle get branded, or is that just in the Wild West?'

I remembered the beer ads in Perth: six sweating men branding one calf and then opening six cold stubbies. 'They get branded.'

'Not here, they don't.' Jane clearly had an eye like a circling hawk. 'Haven't seen a brand yet.'

I hadn't been looking—a herd manager I'm not. But I began to look now, and she was right. 'No brand—they're called cleanskins,' I told her.

'Shouldn't they all be branded?'

'As I understand it—and you realize it's a lawyer you're asking—branding's a once-a-year job. Round up your calves and brand 'em before your neighbour gets in first. That's a local sport called poddy-busting, and it's provided work for people like me over the years.'

'Don't you have fences?'

'Australia, lady, has fences of all descriptions. Some are rabbit-proof, some are dingo-proof; some are fifteen hundred miles long and some are only a thousand.'

'And some,' she said, staring ahead, 'aren't too good.'

Right again. Travelling west we'd come to a boundary fence and there was barely enough left of it to mark the ground. Rusty wire and insect-eaten poles, canted over. 'Been a bit neglected,' I said.

'For years and years. Not a bit—a lot!'

'Surprised there's any livestock left,' I said. 'Must be honest people hereabouts.'

She turned the Land-Cruiser away and drove on, silently for a while. Then: 'Where would I learn?'

'Farming you mean?'

She nodded.

'Well, there's a good agricultural college, but hold on! You've taken one short look and you're chucking your career in and going back to school. Let's not be too impulsive!'

'Two things,' she said. 'One, it *has* to be done. Two, I own the place and it's my responsibility. Known as *force majeure*.'

'The facts of life—' I began.

'I'm thirty. I know 'em, thanks.'

'Of Australian agriculture,' I went on, 'are that we are very efficient. We produce everything from bananas to buffalo. Problem is finding somebody to sell it all to, now that the Poms are in the Common Market. We sell to Arabs and our new friends in Japan, but they don't buy enough. Result, please?'

She shrugged. 'Stockpiles.'

'Lakes of wine and mountains of grain in Europe,' I said. 'Here it's bankruptcy. We have farmers walking off their land because they can't pay their way. And it'll cost a fortune to put right—this station of yours.'

She said, 'I have a fortune. The station made it. Time to put some back perhaps.'

'Tell you what'll happen,' I said. 'Listen to the old fortune-teller. You'll put your money into fences and improved stock, and it'll be sucked in like sand swallowing water, and it won't be enough. Then you'll have to borrow heavily from Mr Cheeryble the Benevolent Banker, and he'll only charge you twenty per cent and you'll work yourself to a standstill and worry yourself half to death, and as you collapse the bank will foreclose and take the place. Goodbye inheritance.'

'What's brought this on?' Jane demanded. 'You weren't so bright and happy yesterday!'

'It's a feeling,' I said. 'It's happening a lot now. In wheat, in grazing, in sheep.'

'What it is,' she said calmly, 'is that boss of yours. He says I ought to sell, and you're trying to persuade me.'

I thought of Miller Bunbury's unreasoning determination that she sell, and became unreasoning myself. Every word I'd said was true, if you allowed for a bit of over-emphasis here and a touch of hyperbole there. Able and experienced men *were* going to the wall all over the state: men who knew the land and the climate. Jane Strutt, impressive as she was, knew nothing about life and work up here. She wasn't mentally equipped or educated for the job—not *this* job—and she wasn't physically equipped for the climate, and for the unrelentingly hard life she'd have here.

'Funny thing is,' I said, 'Miller Bunbury—though it's the very last thing he'd intend—might be doing you a favour.'

'Let us,' she said, 'halt this vehicle, and I will race you to yonder ridge. And back.'

'There's nothing to prove,' I protested.

'I think there is. Out.'

Air-conditioning in the Toyota: Nature's air outside. Hot. Perhaps a mile to go. Lunacy! She was pounding off. Let her, I thought and strolled along behind, feeling sweat break out all over me. No place even to be strolling! Suddenly I heard her shout and then she'd turned and was running towards me, and a few yards behind her trotted a cow, wide of horn and eye, calf at foot. Having chased Jane off, it halted, watching her and making sure. Jane, meanwhile, had now slowed to a walk and was mopping her brow and looking frequently over her shoulder.

'It's not even a bull!' she said indignantly.

'More deadly than the male.'

'Cows are?'

'The female of the species,' I said. 'Kipling.'

She scowled at me—it was a good tempered scowl—and got in the truck again. The cow looked at us menacingly as we ground past, and gave way not a millimetre. As we left it I glanced back and saw the tail twitch.

'There's no mistaking the message,' I said. 'Those animals are independent.'

She gave me a big grin. 'So am I. Question is, do I want to be, isn't that right? Sell up, pocket the money, and back to the service of Her Majesty. That's option one. Or—as you paint it—go bust in the service of the banks.'

'Does one seem just a bit more attractive than the other?' I asked.

'Hey, look at *that*!' Jane said.

'That' was water: a roundish pool, roughly a hundred metres across. Not much water in it at that moment, but lines on the banks showed how high it filled in the wet season. The sun gleamed at us from the surface.

'Must be worth a few dollars,' I said, 'a thing like that.'

'It's beautiful!'

'Dollars you won't have to spend, Cap'n Strutt!'

'That's beautiful, too. Is it natural, d'you think?'

We investigated. It wasn't natural, and it wasn't new, but

whoever had built it had built well. Looking carefully, you could begin to see that a substantial area drained to this spot. The high-water mark, plainly visible, was about twenty feet above the present level, and the dam, when we got to it, looked impressively solid: an earthen wall about fifty yards long and thirty feet high, baked hard now; and although there were millions of tiny cracks in the wall's surface, they weren't important. What was important was that there were no significant cracks, and no leaks at all.

Jane said, 'That looks to me like a valuable asset.'

'And to me. But—'

'But indeed. How on earth did they build it?'

'I was going to ask you the technical stuff.'

She ran her engineer's eye along the earth face. 'In England in the 1840s and 50s they had enormous gangs of Irish labourers building railway embankments. A bit like that.'

'Convicts did it in Australia.'

'Convicts didn't do *this* job!'

I said, 'You're absolutely right.'

'Then who did?' Jane asked innocently. 'Was it the Aborigines?'

'You could say that was doubtful.'

She looked at me. 'Sure?'

'Positive,' I said.

She walked forward and began to prod and poke at the wall. 'We're daft even speculating,' she said after a few moments. 'This was done by machine.'

'Bulldozer, you mean?'

'Muck-movers of some kind.'

'Jane,' I said, 'listen to me. This place, right here, this patch where we stand, is about as close to the backside of absolutely nowhere as you'll find on this entire earth.'

'Even so—'

But I bored on. 'It's the aeroplane,' I said. 'On it in one place and off in another, coffee and cold beer as you go. Blinds people to reality.'

'John, look—'

Didn't stop me. 'Perth,' I said, 'is the world's remotest

city. Next nearest city's Adelaide and that's twelve hundred miles off. So now we're a thousand miles north of Perth, and a damned long way from Kununurra, even. And you're talking about bulldozers!'

'Has to be,' she said. 'Bet you.'

'Well, by normal Australian standards,' I said, 'I'm not exactly a betting man. But—'

'Can you afford to lose a hundred dollars?' she asked sweetly.

'Make it five,' I said. 'You can afford to lose it and I'll enjoy spending it.' I could feel the heat increasing: the sun leaning on my shoulders. 'I'll buy cold beer—maybe give you one.'

She stuck out a hand for shaking. 'Five dollars, was that?'

'Five hundred,' I said. 'Bulldozers!' And I laughed.

We shook on that. The nearest bulldozer, I was pretty sure, would not be less than a hundred miles away. Ord River, somewhere, or Kununurra. To bring one out here, cross-country would cost a fortune. But that water was valuable. 'I'm not sure of this,' I said, 'but the water probably prevented your cattle scattering. They like a nice cool drink lying handy—just like the rest of us!'

She grinned with pleasure, and some imp of mischief made me wipe the grin away when she said, 'Do you suppose other animals drink there—kangaroos and things?'

'Everything,' I assured her. 'Including the snakes. The edges of the dam will be alive with them.'

'I was thinking about swimming.'

'Some of them swim, too.'

So off we went. It was high morning, and the nocturnals weren't about and she was a bit disappointed not to see her first 'roo. For a couple of hours or so we just drove, not talking too much, just getting the hang of the place.

When we got back to the station house, she raked on the handbrake and stilled the chattering engine, and said, 'What do you think?'

'I think you'd better knock off the air-conditioning, or your battery'll die in about thirty seconds. Remember always to do it.'

When she'd done it—'What do you think?' she asked again.

'I don't know enough to have an opinion.'

'Don't be a spoilsport!'

'Well,' I said, 'I have a kind of impression that once upon a time—possibly a long time back—Stringer Station was a bonzer place.'

'That means good?'

'Very good.'

Jane said, no little determination in her tone: 'I have a feeling it will be again.'

For lunch we opened tins and made a salad and drank Swan Export and then I set about shifting wreckage from inside to outside, and Jane kept saying, 'No, not this, and no, not that.' Chiefly it was the personal things. When I told her that hoarding junk was bad housekeeping, she agreed, but then said, 'It's the only chance I have of getting to know Mary Ellen. If I pitch it out, nothing's left of her.'

So a number of ratty bits of embroidery were put back either into roughly-repaired frames, or stuffed into her sewing box. Mary Ellen had been a neat worker; no great artist or designer, but neat and precise; and she'd certainly kept busy. Obviously she had sewn a lot for pleasure—what else was there to do at Stringer on twenty thousand long evenings?—and usually she'd worked on things from her memory.

'Look at this!' Jane said, holding up one piece.

'What is it?'

'Pub in Thornton, where we come from. Still looks like that and she can't have seen it since she was twenty!'

'Nostaglia's powerful stuff.'

'Mmm.' Then Jane said, 'That's funny!'

'What is?'

'The name. I'd have sworn that pub was called the Green Man. Still, perhaps it wasn't in her day and it's been changed since. She seems to have liked embroidering lettering, doesn't she?'

All this was going on while I walked in and out with wrecked chairs and general matchwood. Some of it could be repaired, but whoever had searched Stringer Station had been ruthless and persistent, and I wasn't taking too much notice as Jane talked, suspecting that she was, in any case, talking chiefly to herself. Junk dealers in Perth would have glued the matchwood together and charged high prices for it as Victoriana or Edwardiana or whatever it was.

Then, when the big living room was, if not straight, at least straighter, a thought struck me. Where, I wondered, was Billy One-Hat, foreman of this place?

'Your employees are giving you a wide berth,' I said.

'Must have seen us drive off this morning,' said Jane reasonably.

'Also seen us come back an hour and a half ago.'

'I wonder what Billy One-Hat does?'

'Not too much, I suspect.'

She said, 'I suppose Mary Ellen just gave up, towards the end.'

'Probably.'

'And he looked after her.'

'Maybe.'

'He seemed okay to me,' Jane said. 'Admittedly I don't know much about Aboriginals, but—'

'Yair. He seemed okay to me, too. But I don't know too much about 'em either. I keep telling you—I'm a lawyer.'

'A lawyer who's wondering about Billy One-Hat. Why's that?'

'There's a weevil of some sort in my mind. It keeps muttering Billy One-Hat as it weevils away.'

'Let's go see him.' She bundled the pieces of embroidery together and put them away, then headed for the door.

'Hat,' I said.

Jane picked it up. It's what we call in Australia an okubra hat: flat crown, wide brim. She put it on and looked at herself in the mirror. 'I look like John Wayne.'

I shook my head, 'Like Jack Palance,' I said, and dodged as her boot swung at my behind. She was laughing and so was I, and that's a dangerous state of affairs for bachelors of thirty.

It was the last laugh for a while.

6

The Toyota stood in shade, but getting in would still be like entering an oven. I opened the door, reached inside and turned the key. With the engine running, I switched on the air-conditioning. Jane said was this elaborate procedure really necessary, and I said that depended whether you enjoyed sitting on a hot barbecue and I liked my behind raw not rare. I was looking across towards Billy One-Hat's little camp: at the trailer and tents for his family. It seemed like meagre accommodation for the foreman, but making hasty judgements about Abos and housing is foolish, because many of them don't want to live indoors and won't, even if you try to make them. Plenty have tried to enforce it, over the years. Here's your little wooden house, the missionaries have said, and here's the stove and this is the bathroom. And your full-blood, tribal Abo, who's a member of the oldest race on this planet, with forty thousand years of sleeping under the stars behind him, and the knowledge, instincts and pigmentation to cope with Australia's size and climate, says only, 'Thanks for the wood and water,' and chops it up and enjoys dancing in the firelight. For that he's called names. Ungrateful, for one. He's impossible to civilize, say the wiseacres. He drinks too much, according to a lot of people with beer bellies. My view, for what it's worth, is that the Abo's simply wary of the white man— and with damn good reason, considering the way the white man's treated him.

As Jane drove closer, she gave a cheerful toot or two on the horn to announce herself. I expected heads to bob up, but nothing happened. When we halted she tooted once more—longer and a bit more peremptory, now—Captain Strutt ordering atten-shun.

But nothing happened. So she switched everything off and out we got. The camp was deserted, the caravan empty. No fire burned.

I said, 'You've frightened them off.'

She looked at me seriously. 'Where have they gone?'

'Dunno.'

'You don't seem surprised.'

'I'm not. I don't pretend to understand, that's all.'

'Is there much to understand?'

I gave her the standard introductory lecture, all about the Dreamtime, which is the essence of an unbelievably ancient culture; about the deep mysticism of the Abo's attachment to the land itself; about the curious lopsided inventiveness that produced boomerang and throwing stick when nobody else did, but not the wheel when everybody else did; about the millennia of their endless migrant life.

'You think,' she said when I'd done, 'that they've all gone —what's the word?—walkabout?'

'Not necessarily. New things are happening. You for one. Maybe they just want to consider things for a bit.'

'Where will they be?'

I shrugged. 'It's a big country, and those blokes know it like nobody else.'

'No point in looking, you mean?'

'They'll be back.'

'Sometime—is that it? But we've only a day or two.'

'Relax. There's nothing you can do—'

'But—' She didn't believe it, and was ready to argue, but at that moment both of us heard the approaching drone of an aircraft engine, turned our heads to look, and then followed the Piper with our eyes as it swung round and dropped to a landing close to the house, on the same spot Stainsby had chosen.

Through the windscreen, as we drove back, we saw two men get out and stand waiting. Jane ran the Land-Cruiser directly into its parking spot in the shade, and switched off, and we went to meet them.

The smaller and older of the two men wiped his hand on the seat of his pants as Jane approached and gave her a grin. 'You must be Miss Strutt. I'm Jim Procter, kind of a neighbour. G'day.'

'G'day,' said Jane.

'And this is my cousin Harry.'

Hands were shaken all round as Procter said, 'Heard you'd got here, thought I'd drop in and introduce myself.'

'Glad you did,' Jane said. 'How near a neighbour are you?'

'We're all neighbours up here, you can have neighbours a couple of hundred miles away, and I'm one. You're from the Old Country, I hear?'

That phrase, as much as his appearance, placed Procter at fifty-plus. The Old Country's not a phrase or a concept much in use among the young of Australia. But he seemed amiable enough. His cousin, a lean, quiet man, said barely a word beyond the muttered G'day of greeting. We took them indoors and I got cold lager from the fridge while Jane apologized for the state of the place.

'Had a bunch of boongs in, while it was empty, eh?' Procter asked, looking round.

'That's who it would be?' I asked.

He nodded. 'Like as not. Drink the drink and break things after. Pointless, but if you turn your back it happens. You from a farm family?' Procter asked, and corrected himself. 'But of course you are—old Mrs Green was your aunt, that right?'

'Great-aunt,' Jane said, 'and I'm no farmer. But we've been having a look round and even I can see there's a lot to do.'

He nodded sympathetically. 'Let it go, after her husband died. You can't blame her—she'd have been seventy, then, herself. Before that Stringer was a smart station.'

'And will be again,' said Jane.

He laughed. 'Good on you, Miss Strutt. But you're going to find it costs a lot of dollars in fences and fertilizer.'

'Just have to do my best.'

Procter gave that little sideways twitch of the head which signifies approval. 'Don't say you're the first woman to take on a thing like that, but you're the first for a while. Wish you luck.'

'Thanks.'

'Just one thing, miss—don't kill yourself doing it. It's not worth that. You are miss, that's right? No husband?'

'No.'

Procter said, 'Better introduce Harry again. He's single.'

Jane smiled. 'There's a chap at home, I'm afraid.'

'Bad luck, Harry,' Procter said. He'd been jovial from the moment he landed. Now he became serious. 'Let me say it plainly, Miss Strutt, I'd like to buy you up. There's a lot of work here for a woman all alone. Man'll have a wife to see to the station house while he works the land and animals. You haven't. But you're strong and healthy and I can see you're determined. Maybe you can handle it all. But if you find you can't—'

'I think I can,' said Jane steadily.

'—or if you find you don't want to go on—just let Jim Procter know.'

'You mean—before anybody else?'

He laughed. 'That's dead right.'

'No promises.' Jane smiled, extended her hand. 'But thanks for dropping in, and thanks for offering.'

They left after that, the little plane vanishing in moments into the clear sky, and I turned to Jane.

'Who's the chap at home?'

'The alternative,' she said, 'was Cousin Harry. What did you think of that pair?'

'Procter seemed all right. I didn't look at Harry much.'

'I felt like something in an agricultural show with those two looking at me. Class for farmer's wife complete with farm: first prize. Pin a rosette to her ear and lead her off to the kitchen!' Genuine anger edged her tone.

'*Men!*' I finished for her.

A couple of hours later, we were in bad trouble. It began

with another aircraft engine in the distance. I remember thinking when it was still a faint drone that if things went on like this we'd be notching up more traffic movements per day than Jandakot. I smiled at the thought and went out to see who was paying a neighbourly call now. As I searched the sky, Jane came and stood by me and in a minute or so we had in sight a six-seat, single-engined workhorse Cessna. I watched idly as it descended.

'No registration letters,' Jane said suddenly. 'I don't like this!'

That now made a pair of us. I said, 'Quick—into the Land-Cruiser.' These could be the people who'd searched and wrecked Stringer Station.

We scampered away as the light plane made its turn. It touched down as Jane switched on the key, and was running towards us as we moved off in the Land-Cruiser.

'Where?' she said.

'Doesn't matter. Somewhere it's hard to follow.'

We tore out of the sheltering shade and made direct for open ground a couple of hundred yards off. Our path and the Cessna's were converging, but its speed had begun to decrease, while we were accelerating. We'd pass twenty or thirty yards clear of it, I guessed, and once that happened we'd be okay whoever our visitors turned out to be—there was no way a light aircraft could follow a four-wheel drive.

They must have been ready; must have had it all worked out. As we raced to pass clear of the Cessna, I saw the window open on the starboard side and a rifle barrel poke out, and a second later Jane was wrestling with the steering, because the nearside front tyre had gone. But she got hold of it, and the sturdy old Toyota began to roll ahead on three. How far we'd go like that on rough ground I never did discover, because a second shot collapsed the rear nearside and we were suddenly broadsiding slowly and out of control.

The Cessna missed us, but not by much. We flung the doors wide and began running for the house, heat or no heat. But we'd still fifty yards and more to go when the flat, authoritative crack of that rifle stopped us, the bullet passing neatly between Jane and me. Another followed it an instant later. Whoever had that rifle could use it, I thought, and those two shots were warnings. The next might bring down either of us. So, reluctantly, I stopped running, Jane did the same, and panting and sweating we turned to face the oncoming plane. It had been taxiing at an angle to us, presumably so the rifleman wouldn't shoot up his own propeller. Now the plane straightened, came near and halted. Nothing of pilot or passengers was visible through the blur of the spinning prop; but then the door opened. A man emerged, jumped down from the wing and walked round it.

And he was a chilling sight! Like the terrorists in news photographs he wore a black fabric helmet with eyeholes cut into it. The rifle in his gloved hand pointed at a spot somewhere between Jane and me, and considering he'd just shot out two tyres on a moving vehicle with two shots fired from another moving vehicle I took no comfort from the fact that it wasn't quite aimed directly at me.

Now the Cessna engine cut, the prop slowed and slapped and stopped and three other men emerged one after the other. All wore the black helmets and the black gloves. All wore jeans and denim jackets. Two of the three carried handguns and the third a short-barrel shotgun. It was like an invasion of malign creatures from Space.

The shotgun gestured to us to move. I looked at Jane and saw how helpless she felt, saw her hesitate.

'We have to,' I said, and she gave a little nod, her face set.

Another gesture of the shotgun moved us towards the Toyota. We kept walking, obediently, and as we came to it, a voice behind said, 'Change the wheels.'

'Who are you, and where are we going?' I demanded.

'Quiet, change the wheels.'

It was horrible work. At four-thirty there was still plenty of heat and neither of us had a hat. Sweat coursed over faces and down arms. Soon our clothes were soaked. And everything we touched was too hot to touch. Try jacking up a Land-Cruiser in high heat sometime, and then unscrewing two lots of wheel nuts and all the rest of it. The only good bit was that all four of them had retired into the shade by the station house, leaving us to it. They were quite safe in doing so, of course: that rifle's reach in still air was a great deal more than a hundred and fifty yards.

Jane, working as hard and possibly harder than I was, suddenly said in a despairing voice, 'We have to *do* something!'

'There's nothing.'

'What if I start the engine.'

'I saw him take the key.'

'Even so. If I lift the bonnet, I can join the ignition circuit.'

'Don't try it, for God's sake!' I said.

But she did. She'd barely begun to work the bonnet catch when the shot rang out and she came scuttling back.

I said, 'They're not going to kill us, or they'd have done it. All we have to do is wait.' I didn't believe it for a moment. These anonymous men, their unmarked plane and masks, and their assorted weapons, had an extra air of menace about them.

Plainly Jane didn't believe it either. 'Don't damn well patronize me!' she snapped. '*Think!* Why are we changing these wheels? Answer, because they need the truck. *Why* do they need it? What are the *answers*?'

I had no answers. What I had was a wheel brace in my hand and a brake-fluid pipe a foot from my nose. 'If I clout this with this,' I said, 'what then?'

'The brakes wouldn't work. I can't see sabotage helps.'

I grunted. I was lifting the front wheel into place, trying to match bolts to holes and it was heavy as hell. But into my sweaty misery a thought came. 'If we disable the plane, they're stuck here.'

Jane looked at me. 'Control surfaces,' she said.

'What?'

'Flaps, rudder—the hinged bits. It's fairly thin aluminium sheeting, I expect. Give the rudder a good thump and they'd have bother.'

I looked at the tools. 'Best method?' I asked humbly. She forced a tyre lever handle into a piece of pipe and told me: 'Jam the blade into the gap just below the lower hinge and lever it loose. That'll fix them.'

When finally we'd finished, I jammed my twenty-inch prise bar into the back of my belt, and we began walking slowly and exhaustedly back to the station house. To get there we'd have to pass within ten yards or so of the Cessna. Perhaps try to narrow that a bit on the way. Then, when we came level, Jane was going to faint. It would be natural enough for a fair-skinned woman, just out from Britain, to pass out in that heat, and it ought to distract their attention long enough for me to jam in my crowbar and heave at that rudder.

Walking, we drifted slowly rightward, nearer the plane. The invaders stood in the shade, watching. It's hard to look from bright outdoor sunlight into deep shade but as we came close, I thought one man had binoculars on us.

Then we were getting near: fifteen yards, no more, from the tailplane. Damage it, I thought, and they're stuck! No way out except a very long ride in the Toyota to Kununurra, where they'd be seen and maybe identified.

Ten yards. 'Now!' I said to Jane, and as she began to crumple I wrenched out the makeshift crowbar and raced for the plane.

The rifleman shot it out of my hand. Clean as a whistle, and instantly—I hadn't gone six feet. Pain shot through my hand and up my arm and as I stood nursing it, a voice yelled, 'Walk forward. No tricks.'

We'd no tricks left. What we had was more work. I was sent out to the truck again to bring in the punctured wheels and then we were set to repairing them. If it had been up to me whether the job was done, it never would have been. I was bone-weary, no good with my hands, one of which, in any case, ached a lot. But Jane was all the things I'm not: she had deft, strong hands and all the knowledge she needed. To see her levering off the tyre casings was an education.

But it still got us nowhere; not at any rate, in the sense

of improving our position, which was bad and worsening.

'Can I have some water?'

'No—and get away from that tap!'

Jane did the job, more or less single-handed, in half an hour or so. Then she, too, asked for water.

It was refused.

'What about a wash? I'm filthy.'

'No.'

Otherwise there was silence. We were thirsty and uncomfortable; they watched us being thirsty and uncomfortable. One of them occasionally glanced at his watch.

Eventually: 'Outside!' I looked at my own watch. Five thirty-five.

'Where are we going?'

No answer. We were made to tie each other's wrists with thin rope, and the result was inspected for proper tautness. Then we were shoved into the cargo space in the back of the Land-Cruiser, and three of our captors got into the seats. In a few minutes we were off, heading south.

'Where are they taking us?' Jane muttered.

'Can't imagine.' The truth was, I could imagine all too many things, none of them reassuring. The only comfort for us was that the air-conditioning in the truck was on. As time went on, even that became chilling.

We drove for endless hours. The night was lit brightly by a moon two days from full, but I learned nothing more than that, squinting upwards as I was from the floor, except that my first guess had been right—we were heading south. And not on a road. If we bounced off the floor and crashed down again once, as the Toyota ground over some bump or other, we bounced a thousand times. With wrists tied behind us, we could neither sit up comfortably, nor protect ourselves against the constant bash, bash, bash from the bumping truck. But after a while the bumping eased and it was plain the wheels were running on a different surface. From time to time I heard the hiss of sand, and gradually more of it, and then the rattle of shale.

The three men in the seats didn't talk, or not much, and neither did we. I heard a bottle being passed round and some beer cans being opened; from time to time there was the scrape of a match, the smell of cigarettes. Beyond that—nothing. I even caught myself yawning. Perhaps, if I'd been less uncomfortable, I'd have fallen asleep. But the discomfort was considerable. For one thing, bound as we were, and jammed into that smallish space, we were privy to endless small, threatening cramps as the night wore on, and to bruises by the dozen. The worst thing by far was the ever-increasing thirst!

Thinking back to the last drink I'd had—that cool beer with the earlier caller, Jim Procter—I calculated that he must now have been without liquid for something like fourteen hours, half of them very hot hours. If you're reading this in some temperate place, that may not seem long; but even in your temperate place you'd be thirsty.

I'd already asked for water several times and been ignored. I asked again.

'Shut up.'

This time I persisted. 'Look, it's fourteen or fifteen hours since we had a drink! For God's sake—'

'No water.'

'Please!'

'Shut up.'

A while after that it began to get light. The Toyota stopped and fuel was poured into the tank from the cans of spare diesel oil on the side racks. Though I knew we couldn't have drunk it, even the sound of running fluid was a torture. But it was a brief stop, and then we went on. By now there was only the soft swish of sand beneath the wheels. And a fearful suspicion in my brain—I was beginning to believe I knew where we now were.

The sun climbed and its warmth began to reach us. Air-conditioning was switched on again. The Land-Cruiser ground on.

Two more hours and we stopped. The back doors were swung wide. The sun blasted in, and already it was hot.

70

'Out!'

We obeyed slowly and with difficulty. At a guess we must have been in there something like fifteen hours: we'd started off six-ish the night before; now it must be about nine. My legs seemed locked in the position they'd had to adopt in the truck. My arms were still tied and had no sensation in them.

Jane's condition was the same. The pair of us, unable to stand properly, staggered and reeled like drunks on legs that didn't support us properly. I tried to ask again for water, but could produce only a croak from a throat that was growing drier almost by the second. And that croak wasn't heard. I saw that two of our captors were busily looking round, one of them using binoculars. I couldn't actually see number three, but soon there was the sound of metal on metal, and then another sound, and suddenly I knew exactly what he was doing! And it was then, as though to confirm that knowledge, that the sound of the aircraft engine floated into my consciousness.

I heard one of the men say, 'Right on time!' The other laughed with pleasure.

I looked at Jane. She was blinking and puzzled, like me, but stood steadier now: circulation was returning to her legs, as it was doing to mine. She said, 'Why's he draining the radiator?'

The sound of water ceased. I heard footsteps approaching in the sand, and behind me my wrists were held and I felt a chill something on my skin, and then they were free. The man, still gloved and helmeted, moved to Jane and cut her wrist binding.

Almost abruptly they were gone. The plane—the same unmarked Cessna in which they'd come to Stringer Station the previous day—had dropped to a landing not far away, and the three who'd been with us, were walking towards it. They reached it, climbed in and the Cessna took off. I'd hoped the sand would have bogged it's wheels, but it must have been sand on rock. The plane lifted easily—no worries! —and turned north.

Which left *us*.

'I think you know where we are,' Jane whispered.

I was trying to find a drop of spit to move round my dry mouth before I answered, but there wasn't one. I said, 'I think so,' and felt the words grate in my throat. 'We're in the Great Sandy Desert.'

'With no food or water,' she said.

At that time of day—my watch said 9.30—the sun still slanted and there was a little shade beside the truck. In two hours there'd be none, except under it.

Jane said, 'Tell me.'

There was a biro in my pocket. No point in speaking words that could be written. Paper? There were fuel receipts in the dash pocket.

I wrote: *Survival without water, two days.*

She looked at me, eyes wide, then took the pen and wrote: *19 hours already.*

I nodded.

Can we walk back?

No hats. No water. Heat stroke.

How far?

I shrugged. Could be anything. We'd been a lot of hours on the move.

That must have been one of those times when knowledge is dangerous. I knew about the Great Sandy Desert. Kids in Western Australia learn the horror stories early and the message: without water, you're a gonner, mate. I don't say I'd already given in, but I wasn't far off. A couple of hundred miles on foot in the desert is beyond all of us without proper equipment. And we had nothing—no water, no map, no compass.

But Captain Strutt hadn't had all the terrible desert tales dinned into her young head at school. She'd had *survival* dinned into her head by the army. While I was mentally looking round for a shady spot to die in, she was busy and purposeful, hunting through the interior of the Toyota like a terrier at a rabbit warren.

First thing she came out with was a pair of beer cans: empty unfortunately, except for about six drops. But the six warm drops were wonderfully welcome. So was the other discovery: an old fertilizer sack, made of heavy-gauge black plastic. She found it under one of the seats and held it up in grinning triumph. I wondered to myself where it had come from—Stringer Station had seen no fertilizer in a long time.

But the Toyota had first to be moved before a solar still could work. Hands up those who've never seen the movie where soldiers hand-crank an army lorry backwards up a sand dune with the starting handle? Well, that was in the good old days when engines were low-compression and there *were* starting handles, and in any case that one wasn't diesel-engined. So the Toyota had no handle, and even if it had, a giant would have been needed to turn it. So I upped the bonnet lid and joined the wires and prayed and she started, thank God, and I leapt in and flung her into reverse, and back she went ten feet or so, and I switched off quick and kept praying that no permanent harm had been done.

Ready!

So here's how a solar still works: you begin by digging a hole, preferably where you know water to be. No worries about that—we knew exactly where the water from the emptied radiator sank into the sand.

Then: having dug a hole, you cover it with a sheet of plastic, first placing a suitable receptable (a beer tin's a bit narrow, but it had to do) beneath it.

Next you make a hollow in the plastic, prodding down with your finger, so that the hollow is just over the receptacle, and any vapour which appears runs down the plastic and drips into the container. If there's water, you get it. And we knew there was water.

All of the above is well-proven technique—it's the application of scientific principles. It works. Water vapour condenses and water is produced.

Eventually.

Drop by drop. One every, say, fifteen minutes.

And the temperature by now was 110°F and rising. The

sky was deep blue enamel, the air shimmering in the baking heat, and we hadn't had anything to drink since lunchtime yesterday, except six drops. Worse, there were two of us.

We stayed in the shade and sweated, losing more fluid through our pores than the solar still seemed to make. We hadn't any food, either, but though an empty tum isn't pleasant, it doesn't get dangerous for quite a while. You can probably live nearly a month without food if you keep still and you have water.

After a couple of hours, I began to get seriously worried. I'd thought the still would save our bacon at least for a while, but now it didn't look like doing so. If we'd been full of water to start with, and could wait for it to work—fine. But we were already half-dehydrated and getting more so. I kept glancing at Jane's face, looking for the signs, the skin tone going, the eyes getting sunken.

I also kept looking at the still: unable to stay away, yet knowing it was a destructive thing to do because the vapour's supposed to condense, not escape when some idiot lifts a corner of the plastic to peer inside.

By four o'clock we'd got about a third of a can. Two good swallows apiece, except that you sip instead of swallowing, and you make sure that every bit of mouth and throat gets moistened. We sipped, and put the can back, and crawled back under the truck and waited for the heat to drop. The idea was to set off towards the north-east at dusk, hoping to find some kind of trail—maybe the old cattle route which ran, once upon a time, right down through the continent southwards from the Kimberleys. If we found it—well, the route had water wells at one-day intervals.

In the late afternoon, the still did better, for some reason. Not much, but we'd half a beer can full when we started getting ourselves ready for departure, and that included another search of the Toyota for anything that might be useful. There was nothing.

'What chance have we?' Jane muttered painfully and for-lornly, just before we left.

I forced a smile and said, 'It's the only chance we've got,

large or small.' Fact is, we hadn't a hope. Not one. Not of any kind. The water we had wouldn't last the night, given the expenditure of energy, and we ourselves wouldn't last far into next morning. There'd be no shade to hide in without the Land-Cruiser.

The way I saw it we needed one of two things. The first, a nice cool cave inhabited by the almost-legendary animal slow enough to be caught and big enough to be eaten. Rabbits and 'roos are no good, but a snake would do. The second was the cattle trail, though even if we found it, the blessing would be debatable because it's been out of use for decades, and there'd be no food, and you must have food for energy if you're to keep moving.

We turned our backs on the Land-Cruiser and off we went. We were breaking every known rule for survival in the desert, and with reason! First law says: stay with the vehicle, because it's the machine the searchers will see first. But we knew that for us there would be no search. Survival codes also say: use the vehicle's water, its shade, any supplies it contains. No water in ours, no supplies. You wait, says the Golden Rule: you wait—and you're patient! But we knew we'd die if we waited. So we walked. There was no other choice, no other chance.

Within five minutes I began to realize we were already weakened by thirst and salt loss. And though the sun was down and the moon up, the heat hadn't gone. This was a desert in northern Australia, and chances were the temperature would be ninety-odd for a good while and drawing moisture out of our bodies. But we had determination, at that stage, if we had nothing else. Foot kept being placed in front of foot; step by step, the ground was covered, though ground isn't the word: we were walking on four or five inches of soft sand lying over rock, and damned hard work it was.

We didn't talk; that was common consent. Talk dries the throat and ours were too dry already. But thinking gave some small relief from the stress of walking, and my mind, at least, was busy.

75

Why were we there? But I had the answer to that, no worries! Why had that brutal group driven us all the way from Stringer Station and deliberately left us to die on one of Australia's—and the world's—most hostile places? Again —no worries, I had the answer. I plodded on, brooding about it all. Jane had moved into Stringer Station as owner. *And* she was a complete tyro! A Pom and a woman, up in the hard country; furthermore, the Australian with her was a city softy. And off they'd gone sightseeing—that's how the story would sound—they'd gone off for a barbie in the bush, a romantic excursion into the open spaces. Not enough water, not enough food. Breakdown and death. It's happened often enough before and would ring very true in Australian ears.

So all that's needed is the finding of the Land-Cruiser, followed by the finding of the bodies and *bingo*!—Stringer Station's on the market!

That's how my mind worked over things as we forced our aching bodies forward, over a brutally harsh landscape silvered into beauty by a shining moon and a pack of bright stars. I looked at them sourly. Those stars had seen a lot of death in the Great Sandy Desert, and were likely to see more next day.

Before noon, too. Though I didn't say so to Jane.

7

Time ground on. We found no cool cave and no slow-moving edible creatures. The Great Sandy's not famous for game; occasional snakes and lizards and scorpions, yes, but we didn't see any. And the ground was flat, so the chance of coming across a cave was nil. But the cool did come, the desert lost yesterday's heat, and the night actually began to be cold, and then colder, and the cold was almost more debilitating than heat, draining the warmth and energy from deep within us, as it did from the sands and stones around us.

We were already in a bad way when, after about two hours, we halted for our sip of water. The beer can was jammed in the breast pocket of my shirt, with paper for a cork where the ring-pull tab had been. With an aching throat I warned Jane not to gulp, and she nodded and sipped a little and then her cheeks moved as she swilled the small mouthful over all the surfaces inside her mouth. With an aching heart, I thought that, there was now one, or perhaps two tiny sips each before all the water was gone. Then we would have to walk forward dry, into death.

I fell before her—a trip, not a collapse, my foot catching a stony bump I hadn't noticed. But there I was, down on my knees and finding it curiously hard to get up again.

'Are you hurt?'

I shook my head.

'The water?' Jane's words were no more than a whisper. There was little strength in her either.

'Christ, the water!'

I grabbed for my pocket and heard the little swish as it moved in the beer can.

'Okay.'

But it wasn't okay. We truly were going down fast. When midnight came we'd have been nearly thirty-six hours without food and with no more than a cupful of water between us. Looking at Jane's face in the clear silvery light, I saw that already her eyes were sinking back into her head, and the skin of that healthy, fine face was slackening. Mine, I knew, would be the same. Or maybe worse—Jane's fitness, when we started, was greater than mine, and women, with that layer of subcutaneous fat, have a greater capacity for endurance than men.

Staggering is the word. Staggering how fast the deterioration happens once it's under way. You're walking, and then you're suddenly weaker and you're staggering and you stagger for a while, with strength going fast, and next you're suddenly floundering, and you know there's only one stage beyond. You're going *down*!

Half an hour after the midnight stop I was down. The water had moistened our lips, no more, and I'd been down once before, but Jane had dragged me to my feet again. Now, ten minutes later, I knew I was down for good. It's like that —you just know; like one of those sudden bouts of flu where all of a sudden you're so weak you can't move and all strength has gone—from your mind as well as your body.

I knelt, while Jane held me up and took the beer can from me, not that it was much use now, with no more than a teaspoonful inside, plus the damp paper stopper to chew. I was muttering, 'Got to rest,' or something like that, and letting my body fall forward gratefully, so that the Earth could take the weight instead of my aching legs and hips.

'Sleep for an hour,' Jane murmured and I slid into sleep instantly, aware that this sleep was the last one, and not caring, not really. Grateful, if anything . . .

Dimly I could feel that somebody was shaking my shoulder. She shook me till I woke. I was shivering and shuddering in the cold night air, and cold, probably, was the only thing that made my exhausted mind work.

Jane was listening, head cocked, and pointing with a finger. There was a sandhill off to the right of us, a few feet high. 'Hear it?' she whispered.

I didn't at first. Then I thought it must be some kind of aural mirage, ear and brain conspiring to create a fantasy.

But it *was* there, and it went on; then it stopped and there was a brief, terrifying pause before it began again. Tinny. Faint. But—

Somebody was playing a tape recorder! A tape of a pop group, which of them it was I don't know, but there was that faint endless, mindless thump of drums and guitar, which in all normal circumstances I avoid.

But not then.

I looked up at Jane and croaked, 'It's real?'

She nodded. She was sitting on the ground and she, too, shuddered with cold.

'Who?'

She shook her head.

I tried to rise, and couldn't.

Tried again.

Jane tried, got to her knees and couldn't move more.

When I tried to call out, my throat could produce only a kind of choking hiss. I looked at Jane, hoping her strength had lasted. But Jane, too, was silenced—by thirst and the accumulated dust of the Great Sandy Desert; by lack of salt and lack of water. Help—some kind of help—*must* be just beyond the sandhill! I couldn't begin to imagine what form it might take, but it was there! And for lack of the strength to rise, to stagger a hundred yards, to climb maybe ten feet —we were going to miss it! You hear it said that desperation lends strength. It didn't to us.

I began to cry, but no tears came because there was no fluid in me to find a way through the tear ducts. Limply but angrily I punched at the sand in despair, and hit the beer can, and over it went and I grabbed at it, knowing its contents, the last three or four drops of precious water were—

A *bell*!

With arms and hands that seemed to be made of used Kleenex I rummaged for and found two or three tiny stones in the sand around my face. Into the tin they went. I pressed my palm against the ring-pull slot and began slowly to shake it. After a second Jane took it from me. She shook harder and more often.

She stopped to listen. Still, distantly, the drums and guitars thumped, but so far away! Oh God, I thought, the bloody music will drown our sound!

Jane kept shaking that can. I rummaged for my handkerchief with two weak fingers, tied a knot in the corner, took the can and jammed the knot in the hole. A bell now? I hit it with my door key, from the other pocket. It didn't toll musically, but the click was now louder. I tapped out Di-di-di-da-di. Once. Then again. Then a third time.

When I stopped to listen, there was silence. No drum, no guitar, no nothing.

I tapped again. Da-di-di-da-da-da-da.

Silence followed.

Silence—and a bright beam of yellow light straight in my eyes. Followed by a voice which demanded:

'Who goes there?'

There was no strength to shout a reply. Jane held the can up in the beam and shook it again.

Luck? My oath, but that *was* luck! You could back the Melbourne Cup winner every year for life and still not be lucky like that! Takes a bit of believing even now: those blokes were *Norwegian*! Of all people to run across in the middle of the Great Sandy at four in the morning, how about Norwegians! There's something else on top, which multiplies the odds a good bit—those blokes had stopped for one hour only. Ten minutes more and they'd have been well on their way; and we'd have been well on *our* way to becoming a few more bleached bones in the desert.

They were Nato troops—commandos on hot-country exercises. They'd been at the Jungle Warfare School in Malaysia, and now it was the long-distance desert trek—a three-hundred-and-fifty-mile march from Eighty Mile Beach to Gordon Downs, more or less nonstop. Rest—five minutes every hour and one hour every eight hours. Through the night; hide from the sun in the daytime: that kind of stuff. The soldier on watch had had a Walkman, though why anybody'd want to carry an ounce of extra weight on a forced march across desert is beyond me. Anyway, that's what we'd heard—the Walkman. The tape was something called Meatloaf, and it saved our lives.

Unbelievably, our luck continued. We were really in with a bunch of pros. Before you could say Nils Nilsen we were topped up with water and salt tablets, chewing on emergency rations and being helped into sweaters and sleeping bags. We put the troops behind schedule, but we were an interesting subject for study. As their corporal pointed out: we'd been in the same danger they were training to avoid.

I said earlier that when thirst and heat drag you down, the process is swift and gets swifter. Happily, the same is true of recovery, unless you're too far gone in heat-stroke. Funny how things happen, really. If the sun had got up again, and we'd been a few more hours in the open, it would have taken weeks to come good, if we'd survived at all.

There was a young Norwegian officer in charge, a skier from his looks, slim and strong, and eventually when our bellies were full and we were drinking more of his hot sweet tea, purely for pleasure, he began to ask questions. He had to decide what to do, because we couldn't set off with his bunch, and he couldn't leave us.

He was Second Lieutenant Andersson and when I croaked that Jane was actually Captain Strutt he looked suitably surprised and came briefly to the salute.

But he wasn't pleased, however polite. He and his men had been preparing for months for the pattern of exercises of which this march was a part, and the probable need to call it off, however temporarily, grated on him.

Where were we from?

I muttered, 'Well, matter of fact the lady's English and I—'

Jane said, 'Stringer Station, two hundred miles, roughly, north.'

Recognizing the takes-one-to-know-one nature of the military minds, I left them to it, listening, but resting my throat and anointing it with tea, and they sorted things out soon enough. Andersson not only had good maps, he was navigating by stars and sextant plus more modern electronic devices, and he knew his position to an inch, more or less.

Which made it simple. He could radio. Something or somebody could come out and get us. This was Captain Jane, composed and confident now.

But come from where? Lieutenant Andersson asked, pointing out that we were a couple of hundred miles from anywhere at all.

So now, having been saved from certain death, we had a little bureaucratic problem of who-does-what, and who pays? Andersson can give us a little food and a little water, can radio his base on the coast, or the Australian army at Gordon Downs. Maybe a helo will be sent, and maybe that will be costly for us. But the thing he can't do is transport us anywhere, or supply enough water for the Toyota, or help us find it.

Finally, and grandly, Captain Strutt says let's get a helo laid on, on the basis of she'll pay. But even that leaves a problem. What about the Toyota? You don't just abandon several thousand bucks' worth of four-wheeled drive in the middle of the Great Sandy Desert. Not when it's the only mechanical form of transport on a remote, broken-down cattle station. What we needed was to get ourselves and the Toyota back to Stringer.

So we were marooned once again—this time in an austere intellectual territory known as logistics, and I've already outlined one or two factors in the problem. Another was the possibility that as things stood at that moment, we might have trouble finding the Toyota; also, that if we abandoned it completely, even for a few days, it might vanish forever. Not that anybody would steal it. But a wind could begin to blow and the desert would simply ingest the machine. But, if we returned to Stringer Toyota-less, it would at once be necessary to obtain another such vehicle—from Kununurra, probably. Cost, cost, cost. Jane had money, of course. For that matter, renting a helicopter for an hour or two wasn't beyond my own rather flimsier resources. The question was: when we'd got it, what the hell did we do with it?

Strictly speaking, logistics concerns the movement and supply of soldiers, not lawyers or cattle station owners; and serving officers are trained and must be proficient to win promotion. So those two wrangled with each other for half an hour or so before coming to a decision.

At that point Lieutenant Andersson got on the radio. A helicopter was chartered, to (1) pick up forty gallons of water; (2) pick up forty gallons of diesel fuel; (3) fly direct to the six-figure map reference of which please make note carefully; (4) on the way, please keep eyes skinned for abandoned Toyota Land-Cruiser several miles south of six-figure map reference quoted; (5) if Toyota found, pick up from six-figure map reference, two passengers to be transported to Toyota along with fuel and water; (6) bring six bottles of champagne (Australian).

We were going to *drive* north!

There's a competence about blokes who work machines in remote places that pretty well takes your breath away. George, the pilot, asks Bill for the tanks and the water, then picks up the fuel cans from Al, and chilled champagne from Bob who runs the store, and he's off the ground licketty-spit. Try the same thing in your cities!

Fact is the helo arrived in not much more than an hour and a half, and it had spotted the Toyota on the way so before the heat started building up, we'd said bubbling goodbyes to our saviours and were topping up the Toyota's radiator and fuel tanks, both of us now with a shade too much liquid inside *us*, which made a nice change from a few hours before.

I asked the pilot to notify Stainsby at Kununurra that we'd be glad to see him as arranged, but that if we failed to turn up at Stringer before he arrived, any search should begin along the old stock route, to which we intended to adhere closely, like treacle to a woollen carpet.

So we lifted off and we drove off. We knew now that the stock route lay north and east of our position, so it was a matter of using the dash-mounted compass to keep the bonnet pointing in the right direction and we were bound to hit it. In the event, even that didn't have to be done because tracks that the Land-Cruiser had made on the way south were still plainly visible, and they'd followed the stock route.

So we followed them. The line ran near enough dead-straight home, becoming less clear, of course, as we began to cross the desert's fringe, making towards the grassland; by the time we reached it, the tyre tracks were gone. But by then we were simply following a line. It was a long line, and certainly it was a tiring line, but when the roofs of Stringer finally came into site on the horizon to the north, just before dusk, Jane happened to be at the wheel.

I said, 'Tired?'

She smiled. 'I'd be happy to drive this beast for the rest of my days. After walking like that, riding's marvellous.'

We ate and we slept.

Next morning Jane was on her feet soon after dawn and so was I, neither of us bothering with morning tea, sacred in Australia—instead drinking hugely of water for the sheer pleasure of feeling it glugging down our throats. After that we had bacon and eggs and beans, and after that, we went looking and found Billy One-Hat had returned.

Where had he been? He didn't say, and neither Jane nor I asked. We needed information now, but not that information. We needed to know who'd tried to murder us.

Why not call in the police? Easier said than achieved with the radio broken and police far away in Kununurra. No, we'd be flying there soon ourselves. Plenty of time to see the police then. But what we needed, when we talked to them, were facts to back our complaints. We had to make complaints that would stick, complaints that would nail the bastards who'd marooned us in the pitiless desert, and would nail the other bastards behind them. It was clear the four who'd flown into Stringer Station were somebody's functionaries—cruel men carrying out murderous instructions.

'Listen, Billy,' Jane said. 'I'll tell you what happened to us.'

Billy One-Hat listened round-eyed. Then, 'Same men beat me.'

'Any idea who they were?'

He shook his head.

Jane said, 'Billy, come to the house. We need a long talk.'

There, tea began to flow. It was needed. Jane was determined to learn the history of Mary Ellen Green and Stringer Station, and there was only Billy One-Hat to tell her. He, though friendly and co-operative, didn't use two syllables where one would do, or one when he could shake his head.

'Billy, where were you born?'

He was born there. The first wave of his arm took in all of Stringer Station. Then he led Jane to the door and pointed to his little camp: born there, where he lived still.

Jane told him that Mary Ellen was the sister of her grandmother. He must have known her well?

Not well, but for many years.

'How old are you, Billy?'

He thought he was fifty-one.

'What was her name then, Billy, when you were a boy?'

Stringer, he said, like the station. But she (he called her The Missus) worked it for years with his father, also a Billy, but Billy Two-Horse, as foreman, and a few stockmen, most of them itinerants. She worked with him after Billy Two-Horse died. Only when she was getting very old, he said, did she stop being—he used the word again and again—strict. She was strict about horses, about branding, about health, about the children, who had to be clean—always, and *strictly*, clean.

We got the story, or a story, in the end. What he knew, mixed in with what Jane knew herself, went like this. Mary Ellen Emmett of Thornton, a village near Bradford in

Yorkshire, having met and married Tom Stringer, who'd won the Station playing two-up, went north with him while her sister, disgruntled and disapproving, repatriated herself.

Tom Stringer died about 1923. 'Little bit snake, little bit grog,' said Billy. You could guess the story. Weak man, weakened further by the bottle, no resistance to anything much, let alone snake-bite.

So he'd died and she soldiered on alone for a dozen years with Billy Two-Horse. And then, sometime in the middle 1930s, a second husband arrived.

Where from?

From the East, Billy One-Hat said. Billy, of course, was only a boy then. Yes, the man was from the East. Where? 'Aw, right over!'

Sydney, then, or Melbourne.

Jane thought Mary Ellen had had her luck, finding a second husband while virtually stranded for life at Stringer Station. By that time she must have been there fifteen or sixteen years.

'Man sick,' Billy said. 'Man Green bad sick when Daddy Billy bring him to Stringer.'

Daddy Billy had found Mr Green during one of his own peregrinations, somewhere in desert country, and had brought him safely to Stringer, where Mary Ellen Emmett was strict with him for a while and Green recovered. In due course, she turned herself into Mrs Green.

Then, together, they worked the Station, content, like Billy, not to stir from it much.

'When they did go, where was it to?'

'Wyndham.' This was before Kununurra was built as a base, when the Ord River was dammed.

Then war.

They were married a long time, the Greens. Around thirty years, anyway. But he died, 'one day sudden fall down', Billy One-Hat said, which made it sound like a heart attack, and which left Mary Ellen alone again.

So, once more she soldiered on alone. By this time she'd been half a century at Stringer.

'She never went away?' Jane asked. 'I thought they came to England once, the two of them. Just after the war.'

He remembered she was 'away long time', but in those days he too had been away. Not in the army—Billy One-Hat's absence had been tribal. Long treks and secret rites, I guessed. Initiation into manhood. Survival. There was a good deal of such matters, then, in the Abo tribes; in the forties the old traditions still had a strong hold. Eventually, Jane let him go when he'd promised to return later to give us the rifle.

That, then, was the history. The plain facts. Plus small and occasional glimpses of character.

In the evening, as we were making a meal of bully beef and spuds, I happened to say, 'Mary Ellen did her share of enduring.'

Jane pursed her lips. 'But I think she was quite impulsive. I've seen pictures of her, you know. Nurse's uniform and very prim and proper, hands held just so. But she certainly jumped to some purpose!'

'The first husband, you mean? Impulsive about him?'

'I mean the pair of them. First time out she grabs a gambler —a very lucky one, incidentally. Second time of asking, a kindred spirit comes wandering in and fails to get out again! She seems to have pinned both of them down efficiently. Funny,' Jane went on, 'but I've got a clear picture in my mind of the first one, Stringer—'

'Long streak of nothing,' I said. 'Got lucky one day.'

She nodded. 'But the other eludes me. What sort of man is it who arrives at a remote place like this, far from any-where—'

'Beyond the Black Stump,' I said. 'Right at the back of Bourke.'

'But what sort of man is it, who comes here and barely leaves again? He was here thirty years, so he must have been reasonably contented, you'd think. That's unusual, if nothing else.'

'People do lock themselves away,' I said. 'Look hard and they're all around you. They don't like the world so they withdraw from it. I could show you a few like that in apartments in Perth. What's interesting about the Greens is that they lived entirely peacefully. Yet no sooner is she dead and gone than violent things begin to happen: the search, the beating-up of Billy, the attempt to kill us.'

'Plain enough to me,' Jane said. 'There's something here that somebody wants. Very badly. Or there was.'

'Nothing's been found.'

'Maybe there are two things. The station itself—and something else.'

'Like what?'

Jane shrugged. 'How do I know?'

'It's the land,' I said confidently. 'She had it for sixty years and intended to die here. Now she's gone, it's available.'

'It's *not* available.'

I laughed.

Jane said, 'But there's this. Somebody's looking for something, and so far, they haven't found it—yes?'

'You mean—so it's still here?'

'We'll look tomorrow.' There was one full day to go before Stainsby's return.

But there was a surprise still to come that day. I was thinking perhaps Billy had forgotten and was about to put out the light in my room when there was a knock on the front door. Billy had remembered after all, I thought, and here was the rifle, as promised.

When I opened the door Billy One-Hat stood there as expected. But he hadn't brought the rifle. On the floor at his feet, its barrel resting in a tripod, lay a machine gun.

8

It was only a light machine gun, but that was a quibble—a machine gun, this certainly was, dull, blue-black and deadly, and a more-than-adequate defence against any small groups who came a-murdering. Billy had three curved magazines with him, and he showed me how it worked.

'Who told *you* how it worked, Billy?'

'Mr Green.'

'Where did Mr Green get it from?'

Billy gave me a look of deep seriousness, and said, 'Tomorrow.'

I went to bed leaving the light machine gun set up under the table in the living room, pointing at the door. Safety-catch on. But it would be off if I heard any stray engines, aero or diesel, or sensed a little touch of horror in the night.

Jane, of course, could actually handle it. Before breakfast next day, when she recovered from the surprise of seeing it, she gave a brisk demonstration of how to strip the gun down and put it together. 'Do lady soldiers get to fire machine guns?' I asked, surprised.

'Not in action. Not yet. But you never know.'

After breakfast Billy arrived, nodded approval at the gun, then went out and started the Toyota. He was grave and somehow formal, more like one of the guides at the Tower of London than an Abo foreman on an Australian cattle station. He was unmistakably in charge for the moment and Jane and I went with him, silently and obediently, not even speculating about that gun. All, it was clear, would be revealed.

About two miles from the house, Billy One-Hat steered

the Toyota off flat ground, down a kind of natural ramp into a gully, along which he drove for perhaps a hundred and fifty metres before halting.

He then got out and waited. He held a flashlight in his hand. When we joined him, we could see, in a kind of vertical fold in the ground behind him, the entrance to a cave. Billy pointed inside, into instant, profound darkness.

'Let's have some light,' I said. Coming out of sunlight into this I could see nothing.

'Here. Look—' he paused '—here.'

If somebody says to me on my dying day, what's the most amazing moment of your entire life?—that's bound to be it! The thing wasn't just unexpected: it was utterly astounding! For the beam of Billy's torch was shining upon the dull-green camouflage paint of a full-blown battle tank. An army tank, that is, not a thing for storing fuel. This one had a damn great turret.

I expressed myself a little rudely, and in one syllable.

Jane, typically, said, 'My God, an M4 Sherman.'

About twenty minutes later, when both of us had managed to winch up our lower jaws to stop them scraping on the floor, we began to ask questions.

As to where it had come from, Billy said only, 'Come in war.' He knew no more except that Old Man Green had used it.

'Used it? What for?'

Still standing in the entrance Billy swung the torch so we could see the front of the tank. Welded to it on two arms was a big blade, making a bulldozer of it.

'Now we know about the dam,' Jane said.

But that was the only answer we got. We kept on asking, but since nobody present knew anything, the questioning ceased. All the same, 'Come in war', wasn't much of an explanation for a stray battle tank on your block.

'Anything else?' I demanded of Billy.

He shook his head.

'Will it go?'

Jane said, 'Probably, with fresh fuel.'

But we didn't try to start the engine. Mainly we just walked round and round it making surprised sounds. There was ammunition high up at the back of the cave, too, for the two machine guns. Jane, having opened one of the two sealed ammunition boxes said she thought it had been well wrapped and insulated and was probably more or less sound.

'More or less?'

'I wouldn't want to be the first to try it.'

We were outside the cave again, half an hour or so later, still with a million unanswered questions ringing in our heads, when I thought of another; one that Billy could answer: 'Did the Missus know about the tank?'

'Must have,' Jane said. 'She couldn't not know a dam was being built.'

'Okay. Billy, did she know where it was kept?'

He nodded.

'Did she ever come here?'

He nodded again. She'd been here many times, how many, he didn't know. The Missus had had a pony, an old one, now dead. Until near the end, she had been able to get about the station with the pony pulling the little cart.

'You think *she's* been hiding things?'

'Jane,' I said, 'there's something. Has to be.'

'Let's find it.'

Jane and I went back into the cave and began looking. It had been workshop as well as garage; a long metal bench ran down one side, with a pair of vices and a lathe. A small petrol engine was hitched to a generator, for power. Didn't work, of course. But there was a paraffin lamp that did, and by its light we hunted.

First find was a fat manual for the tank, cased in some early clear plastic—Perspex, probably. Captain Strutt thought it would be fun as bedtime reading. But after that not much. The usual old tins full of old nails and nuts and bolts and pebbles and drill bits stood on a shelf. A few spanners littered the bench. I blew the sand and dust off to see if it meant anything to me; nothing did. Turning my head, I looked at thirty tons of Sherman tank behind me, solid as Ayers' Rock and almost as big. A safe? It had armour plate and defences. But hard to imagine an old lady clambering into it.

Captain Strutt beat me. While I thought about it, she climbed. The lid of the turret came up after a good heave or two, and Jane was wriggling in, then emerging not long afterwards to say, 'Nothing in there!' And then, 'Don't scowl.'

But I felt like scowling. There was a secret here: on the station, or in the cave—there was a secret somewhere and we had come close to being killed for it. What it was and where it was hidden, and how we'd know it if we saw it— all that was a mystery.

Yet somehow, standing in that dry old cave beside the ancient tank by the light of a paraffin lamp, I felt I was near. In the children's party game, you're hotter or colder as you move about. I felt the warmth of such an indication.

I said, 'You won't be offended if I double-check?', swiped Billy's torch and shinned up to the turret before she could utter.

Getting inside was quite a shock: first, because it wasn't easy even though I'm slim; secondly, because the interior was so very small. I suppose those of us who don't ride in tanks get our notions of them from the cinema, and the tank interiors photographed for movies are spacious mock-ups built in studios. But that tank felt full with just me in it, and Shermans were supposed to have a crew of five!

I shone the torch around me, looking for hiding places and finding none. I fumbled one-handed in tiny spaces under two seats, but nothing there. It didn't affect my feeling that there was something important—

'John.'

'Yes?' I looked up. Jane was looking down—through the turret opening.

'There's a kind of tool-chest built in, according to the manual. Behind you, to the left—yes, there—that's the lid of it. May be something in there.'

I near enough dislocated my shoulder. The lid was hinged,

heavy and reluctant and I couldn't get decent purchase and then Jane said, 'Hop out and I'll do it,' and that gave me the extra strength. The lid creaked up, sounding like a door with Boris Karloff behind it. I turned and shone the torch . . . on a collection of spanners and braces, and a half-hidden contraption I couldn't quite see.

'What's that?' Jane demanded. 'Give it to me.'

She reached down and I reached up and between us we heaved it up, and I began climbing out. I was no longer either hot or cold, in the hunting sense, just neutral and a bit disappointed.

I jumped down. 'Well?'

Jane had the thing on the bench. 'Looks like a machine for model-making,' she said. 'Maybe Old Man Green built toy steam engines.'

'Funny place to work. You couldn't swing a kitten in there, let alone a crankshaft. You're sure?'

'Not a thousand per cent, no, but I'm fairly sure. There's a pulley for the drive belt, and here are the centres and a chuck could go there. It's unusual, of course.'

'Wonder what he used to make?'

'Well, it wasn't spares for General Sherman here, not with this.'

'Must have been for something. Let's take it with us.'

'Why?' she asked reasonably. 'It's just a little lathe. You can get better ones anywhere.'

I gave the sign of the uncertain hand. 'Perhaps I have just a little feeling.'

'Touch of male intuition, eh?' Jane said gaily. 'Okay. Sure you can carry it?'

We tucked it in the back of the Toyota when we left, and Jane speculated most of the way back about what Old Man Green had done with it. She'd seen no sign of any small-scale engineering, and had I?

I hadn't.

'Did you ever see Mr Green working in the cave, Billy?' she asked.

Shake of head. 'Not go in cave.'

'But you went in today.'

'He didn't,' I said. 'Only stood in the entrance.'

'Why?' Jane asked.

Billy shook his head, and I said, 'Probably it's an important place in the Dreamtime. Is it, Billy?'

He nodded, and Jane said, 'In what way?' at which he shook his head again.

I said, 'Don't ask. No business of ours and these are deep matters.'

'I'm sorry.'

'She's an ignorant bloody Pom, Billy,' I said, 'and you'll have to forgive her. She'll learn in time.'

He smiled. We drove in silence for a few moments, and then, after that characteristic display of Billy's quality of self-containment, he began to talk—volubly, for him. 'Mr Green,' he said, 'he work there many times. Many times. He go there all day, then another day, then another day.'

'Doing what—making things?'

Billy shrugged, then smiled. 'Making noise. Smoking pipe, making noise.'

'What kind of noise was it?'

Billy made a sound. It was a kind of a quiet, high-pitched Ee-e-e-e-e, and he kept it going.

'The lathe,' Jane said.

'Do you remember other things about Mr Green?'

He nodded.

'Tell me.'

'Go walkabout,' Billy said.

I have a feeling that I'm portraying Billy One-Hat as some kind of Neanderthal idiot, and if I am, it's quite wrong of me. Nothing wrong with his intelligence or anything else. The things he needed to do, or wanted to do, he did as well as the next man: excellent driver, for instance, and manually deft. But the things he wanted to do didn't include much talking, or perhaps not to whites. For all I know, to his family he'd be Chatter-Box Billy. But it's necessary always to remember that the tribal Abo is the product of a culture already ancient, if fairly simple, when Moses was coming down the mountain. They like it, and haven't wanted to change. We made them change, and it's not to our credit.

'When Mr Green went walkabout—did he go often?'

'After wet season.'

'For long?'

He shrugged. 'Three, four weeks.'

'Every year?' Jane said.

He nodded.

'He stop.' Billy volunteered. 'Old, he stop.'

'Did you go with him?'

'Walkabout alone.'

'Did he walk, or drive?'

'Camel,' Billy said. 'Mule, horse.'

He was packed with surprises.

Jane was in the process of making corned-beef hash for lunch when the engine noise began. Not exactly a favourite sound, to us! I nipped out quick to see who it was before he got his wheels on the ground and thought that anybody without registration letters was in for a surprise. It turned out to be Stainsby, who wasn't due until next day. I carried the LMG through into my bedroom out of sight and told Billy to take it away and hide it after we'd gone. I didn't want Stainsby to see it, for one thing, because if ever I saw an old gossip, he was it. And I certainly didn't want it falling into the hands of unwanted callers.

'Like this, it is,' Stainsby said apologetically. 'Feller wants me to take him to Broome tomorrow, then to Hedland, then to Tom Price, then to Mount Magnet, then to Perth. It's a five-day charter I'd have to turn down, five full days, lot of money, you can imagine, so I thought maybe you'd be amenable. I mean, I want to be fair—you'll get a little rebate from your charter, see?'

'If we leave today?'

'Fair?' He was looking both pleased, and at his watch, having heard more keenness in my tone than I'd intended to put there. I looked at Jane. 'Well?'

'I seem to remember I'm paying the charter,' says she.

Oops! 'Quite right,' I said hastily. 'I'd ask Mrs Strutt, if I were you, Stainsby.'

'Sorry, lady,' Stainsby said. 'But you heard me say my piece, didn't you?'

'You were talking to him,' she said.

'Ah, I thought he was—'

'Well, he isn't!'

'Right.'

'Why should you *assume*—?'

She was quite cross. I was amused but keeping the lid down hard. You can't blame her, really you can't.

But she couldn't browbeat Stainsby. 'Look, my dear,' he wheedled. 'It's worth a pile of money. How'd you like fifty bucks back?'

'Make it a hundred,' Jane said stonily, 'and I'll throw in a plate of hash with a fried egg on top!'

'Seventy-five and two eggs?'

They shook hands on that. I'm not at all sure whether honours were even.

Stainsby made us move now. He was like a walking manual on salesmanship: first close the deal, then shake hands, then get things ordered, then move on to the next customer. He knew we hadn't brought much luggage in when we came, and guessed we wouldn't be taking much out. And if we weren't, we wouldn't require much time. Speaking for myself, I wasn't sorry to be going; not this time, anyway. It wasn't beyond the bounds of possibility that I'd be back, but if and when I did return, a good radio would travel with me, because I'd had quite enough fright already.

Mind, it's fair to say there was another problem. I was going on not long ago about Billy One-Hat and the inaccurate picture I've been painting of him. But it's twice as bad with the Jane I've been describing, because she's a very attractive girl indeed, and several days of her company had given me a fancy for more of it. One could argue that for us to remain at Stringer Station a while longer, with only Billy One-Hat as chaperon, might be just great. But I'm an admitted solicitor and the profession has its rules, and making passes at heiresses while the estate's still warm is the kind of thing the rules are built around.

So it wasn't much more than half an hour before we were away. Stainsby flew like good drivers drive, with easy but complete competence. No formalities: in, taxi, off, climb, level off, trim, fly. At the level-off point, while he was busy adjusting trim, Jane said, raising her voice over the rasp of the engine, 'You ever heard of aeroplanes without markings hereabouts?'

'Aeroplanes, eh?' He turned his head, grinning. 'Only Poms say aeroplanes, nowadays, my dear. Everybody else calls 'em aircraft like the bloody Yanks. Including Australians. You mean, no registration letters?'

'Yes. But no other markings either. None at all.'

'Seen one, have you—where was that?'

'It flew over—P38 Lightning.'

'Aw, yair, there's one of those. Two maybe.'

'Is it legal?'

'No, but it's hard to stop. There's several of the buggers —six or so, I believe. Best known is a Spitfire, but there's two Lightnings like the one you saw, then—oh, let me see, there's another American thing, a Grumman something, never seen it myself. Oh, and a Typhoon. I think that's the lot. There's talk of a Jap Zero, but nobody I know's seen it.'

'Where do they come from?'

His grin widened. 'It's all from the war—Germans, Japanese, that war. You're too young to remember and I can only just.'

'On with it!' Jane said.

'Well the Japs were on Timor, just across the sea from the Top End—the NT.'

'NT?'

'Sorry, that's the Northern Territory. Japs bombed Darwin and Broome, you know, and everybody was sure they'd invade. Didn't, in the finish. But in case they decided to, a lot of war material was shipped north. Big stuff, too. Tanks, aeroplanes in crates all ready to be assembled fast if the need arose. But it never did arise, and by the time they were sure it wouldn't, all the effort was going the other way, up to

New Guinea. Some war material was taken out, but a lot stayed up here.'

Jane said in astonishment, 'You mean the Australian government just *left* it?'

'I did hear they forgot where they put it in the first place,' Stainsby said, grinning. 'But maybe they were just too busy. Anyway, three or four years later, when the war was over, a lot of the stuff had got up and walked away.' He laughed.

'Stolen, you mean, don't you?' Jane said.

'Liberated, that was the word at the time. Most of it was American anyway.'

'My God, how much vanished?'

Stainsby laughed again, happily. 'It was, let's say, adapted. Swords into ploughshares kind of thing. In this case, tanks into bulldozers. Not hard, you see—just a decent welding job. Half the dams on half the stations in the north-west were built by tanks, so the story goes.'

'Didn't the Americans come looking for their lost supplies?'

'Not them. Couldn't wait to get home. You can see why.'

'And these planes are still flying about? Where'd the Spitfire come from?'

'People have wondered that. Wouldn't be American supplied, would it? But it's here right enough. I've seen the Spit myself.'

'Do you know who flies them?' I asked. It could be the Lightning was linked to our kidnappers. If so—

'Nobody knows. Big country, this one, and it's empty.'

'Radar?'

'Oh, there's monster bloody radar, yes. But it's military —ANZUS stuff, and little blokes like me buzzing about all over, and the radar boys don't want to be watching *us* when they're supposed to be watching China and Russia, do they? All you have to do is drop to three hundred feet and they lose you. So—well, someone's stuck a Spit in a barn and runs it as a hobby. Lots of fun for a young lad to take station wing-tip to wing-tip with an airliner and look at the worried faces. Then off and vanish. Jandakot's got tons of reports.'

'Jandakot's the private flying airfield near Perth,' I explained to Jane.

'It's also got the aviation museum. Lots of info, if you're interested.'

Stainsby had things well organized. Before leaving to get us, he'd reserved a pair of seats on the afternoon jet out of Kununurra to Perth. I told him to cancel them. There were things to be done in Kununurra.

''Kay,' he said. 'You want somewhere to stay?'

We accepted his recommendation and found ourselves at the local chain motel, air-conditioned and with a pool. Both were welcome.

It also had a phone and I busied myself calling local banks to ask whether Mrs Green had had accounts, or safe deposits. All said no, except one. She had withdrawal facilities there from an account in Perth that I knew about already. There was a deposit box, too. I got a taxi to the bank, leaving Jane bikini-clad beside the pool, reading. On the way I imagined a salesman, over-nighting at the hotel, and spotting the great little sheila in the swimsuit beside the pool and trying his luck. 'What's that you're reading, darlin'?' And Jane replying, 'It's the engineering manual of a battle tank.'

Bloke at the bank was cautious. I was thoroughly checked and my authorization examined, then he went to a lawyer's office in the bank building to check the Law List. Then he telephoned Perth and gave Sharleene my description.

'Have you long eyelashes?' he asked me drily.

I batted them at him. After that we went into the vault and he opened the box. A small, blue booklet lay inside.

Nothing else.

I signed for the British passport issued in 1947 to Mary Ellen Green. The bank manager put it into an envelope for me, and that was that.

Back at the motel, I put on my bathers and made for the pool. Jane looked up. 'Hi. Any luck?'

I held up the envelope. 'Her passport.'

'What's in it?'

'Gimme a chance to look.'

The passport had been issued, but never renewed, so after the first five-year validity it had expired. There was a photograph, of course, and it showed Mary Ellen Emmett to have had a face which, if far from glamorous, was handsome in middle age: grey-white hair, high cheekbones and clear, steady eyes, the gaze direct. She was approaching fifty at the time, and looked it. Mary Ellen Green née Stringer, née Emmett, had not exactly had a simple life.

I turned the passport so that Jane could look at the picture, and she took it from me, studied the face for a while, then said, 'She looked like that at twenty.'

'White hair and all?'

Jane ignored me and turned the pages. 'Just the one big trip, from the look of things.'

'So it seems.'

She said, 'There's no stamp for departing Australia, or for arriving in England.'

'Mary Ellen was a British citizen.'

'Were Australians British in those days?'

'Not so privileged. Australians were "British (Australian)"!'

'I wonder if she remained British?'

'She did,' I said. 'She had dual nationality anyway. Mary Ellen was a Pommie to the last.'

'Good for her!'

'Good *on* her, if you don't mind. When in Rome—'

'Damn!' Jane said. There had been a rubber band, badly perished, round the spine of the passport, holding in place various health certificates then in use: yellow fever, small-pox, TAB, etc. It snapped in Jane's hands and the papers fell out. Collecting them, she held one up, smiling, and read, 'Cabin 147, *S.S. Asturias.*'

'Did they go to England?'

She turned a page. 'Nope. Nederland. She went to Holland. Port of entry—The Hook.'

'*They* went,' I said. 'Mary Ellen wasn't travelling solo?'

'Odd that it's only *her* passport.'

'You mean Old Man Green's is missing?'

'Well, she went to the trouble of putting her own in a safe deposit. Why not his?'

'True.'

'And where is it?'

I said, 'Lost or thrown out. Why keep it when he's been dead umpteen years?'

Jane added quietly, 'Or stolen.'

'I can't imagine why. The thing expired in 1952 and Green expired in 1971. Not much use now, was it? Possibly she couldn't bear to be reminded of happy times and burned it.'

'Hmmm.'

'You don't sound convinced.'

'I'm not *un*convinced.' She gave a little frown. 'It's just— we know remarkably little about him, don't we? We've no marriage certificate—'

'Obtainable,' I said.

'And no photograph.'

'There's a chance the passport department might still have one.'

'But meanwhile we know he was John Joseph Green and he died in 1971.'

'We know more.'

'Like?'

'Either bachelor or divorced when they married.'

'Maybe he was a bigamist.'

I said, 'Don't look *too* hard for other offspring. Think of the estate!'

'You said it was already mine. Probate granted and things.'

'Won't help you if a legitimate son pops up.'

'Let's hope he doesn't. Why would they go to Holland?'

'I've never been. Tell me.'

She said, 'Tulips, cheese, duty-free booze and fags and perfume on the ferryboat.'

'They'd just got off a damn great liner, remember. Anyway there's no sign either of 'em drank a lot of grog. I didn't see any empties, or any ashtrays.'

'I'm sure *she* didn't drink!'

'Why?'

'Methodists, she and granny. Teetotalism drilled in young and deep so it lasts for life. They signed the pledge together when they were six. Granny used to have it in a little wooden frame.'

'Was it binding, this pledge?'

'Matter of honour. You must have it in Australia?'

'It's fairly rare here, Jane. Fair to say that. Care for a beer while we're on the subject?' We were under shade-netting, but hot even in the late afternoon.

'I don't think I'll ever refuse a drink again.'

When I came back with my pair of stubbies, each in its little, insulated, stubby-holder to protect fingers from the cold, cold bottle, she said, 'From Holland they went to Belgium.'

'Major expedition, eh?'

'Never mind the jokes. I can see why they might have gone to Belgium. She had a brother killed on the Somme.'

I said, 'I thought that was France.'

'It's all Flanders. French Flanders and Belgian. Miles and miles of war cemeteries. I bet that's why they went—to see his grave.'

'Likely you're right.'

Jane said, 'Holland's the funny part. Going to The Hook.'

'Why?'

'It's an awkward journey—if you're in Yorkshire.'

'Maybe they weren't in Yorkshire. Not all the time, anyway. Easy from London, is it?'

'Well, yes.'

'So they'll have gone from London.'

We were worrying at it, but fairly light-hearted. The horrors were behind us, though not so far behind as to be ignored, let alone forgotten. Though neither of us said it, what had happened before could happen again. There was a dangerous mystery attached to the death of Mary Ellen Green—a mystery important enough for murder. Until we had some idea of the nature of the threat, we couldn't *begin* to defend ourselves!

9

We flew down to Perth the next morning. I grumble about the place sometimes but it was good to look out of the window and see the Swan River with the sun on it, and those high, clean buildings lining the Terrace. Then thoughts of Miller Bunbury wiped the smile off my face; I wasn't looking forward to meeting the old brute, but I'd no way of avoiding him. At the office, Sharleene would intercept me with a summons. Then Bunbury would rip into me. Had Jane-the-Pom agreed to sell, and if not, why not?

So I delayed. Took Cap'n Strutt, her luggage, and her tank manual to the King's Ambassador, which is a comfortable, busy hotel in Hay Street, and where she ought to be fairly safe. The lathe I hid in the loft of a friend's house (his wife thought I must be mad, but asked no questions). After that, I went to my office. In the entrance hall, Sharleene smiled her vast vacant smile and moved to intercept me.

'Mr Bunbury wants to see me at once?'

'That's right,' she said. Then added, 'The minute he gets back.'

'Where is he?'

'KL,' Sharleene said dreamily, no doubt recalling that glamorous holiday. There's a lot of Malaysian money in Perth, and some of it finds its way into Bunbury's pocket, I imagine.

'Due back?'

'A few days.'

The mouse was free to play. One way and another, there wasn't much pending on my desk: I'd been away so much lately that other people had handled anything needing quick attention. The rest would come to no harm by being delayed a while longer.

I sat back and picked up the phone, then changed my mind. Keep this private, I thought. So I went home and used the phone there.

First call, to Bob Collis, retired police superintendent, father of a sister-in-law of mine. Bob was a Pom once, way back. Came to WA long ago and is wise in its ways. Grows asparagus and wine, and plays golf off four.

'Sit down,' I said, 'and listen.' Then I told him.

He heard me out in silence, then said, 'Bloody funny! What's the legal position?'

'Simple, but pretty unusual. Jane's inheritance is okay because there was a sound will. But she's the last of the line. No uncles, aunts or cousins—not even second and third cousins.'

'So, if she dies?'

'It passes to the Crown—*bona vacantia*, if you want a bit of Latin. Tell you the truth, though, Bob, I think the State could take it anyway, on grounds of years of neglect.'

'This girl of yours is going to go on neglecting it?'

'She's a Pom, an engineer *and* a woman, Bob. She's no grazier.'

'But will she neglect it?'

'I shouldn't think so.'

Bob Collis laughed. 'So she's in danger only because she's the last of 'em. If she had ten scattered brothers?'

'I suppose they could all be hunted down one by one.'

'Get complicated, though.'

'Yes, it would.'

'So marry her, quick.'

'*Eh?* Who, me?'

'Be saving her life, sport. How many Closes are there scattered about Australia? Seemed like bloody thousands of you at Mary's wedding.'

'That's because you were paying the bill.'

'Champagne drinkers the lot of 'em. Where's the youngest now?'

'Ian? He's in the Antarctic for two years with the Survey.'

'Have a job to knock *him* off, wouldn't they—see what I mean?'

'Bob, the thought never occurred, not to me. Nor to her.'

'Don't you want to save her life?'

'Not by sacrificing mine.'

He laughed again. 'What's she look like?'

'Pretty good.'

'Well, then.'

'Professional ethics,' I said. 'Let's change the subject.'

'To what?'

'Your holiday place.'

'At—'

'That one, yes,' I said.

'Good place for a proposal, I'd say. You want to borrow it?'

'Yair.'

'All yours, mate.'

'Another thing—you could do some work for me, if you wanted to.'

Having briefed Bob, I hung up and the phone rang.

Sharleene. 'Jane Strutt's yours, isn't she, Mr Close?'

'Yair.'

'Just got a packet of stuff for her in the post. From England. What do you—?'

'I'll call in and collect,' I said.

Mine's a Range Rover. It's not that they're more reliable than the old Toyota up at Stringer, but they're more fun, more versatile, and they don't kick your bottom quite so hard. I put a little case with a change of clothes and a toothbrush inside, parked in the multi-storey next to the King's Ambassador, then took the packet to Jane.

She said, 'Oh, good,' and went to work with scissors. It was personal papers because the Customs label on the back said so. Jane elaborated. 'These are the letters granny had from Mary Ellen. I asked for them to be sent.'

'Who had them?'

'Old friend keeps a suitcase for me with all the family stuff in it. Photographs and birth certificates and things. And these—' She pulled off the paper and held up a small bundle of letters in airmail envelopes, the blue paper pale and faded.

About a dozen: not much communication between devoted sisters considering the time they spanned, but a few more than Jane had said when she'd mentioned them before. She sat and read them through while I put on a kettle of water, made some tea, and waited to be invited to read them, too. I wasn't, so eventually I asked. She said, 'Of course, sorry,' and I was reading about the early thirties, with Mary Ellen still alone after Stringer's death, coping with a drought plus desertion by stockmen, when Jane said, 'She's writing about Green!'

'What does she say—and when?'

'It's a Christmas letter, written in December 1942. Listen.'

Heaven knows if this will ever reach you, Jane dear. Perhaps, if it does, you will think ill of me for this piece of news. The plain truth is I am to be married again, and the reason is that, although I haven't complained (why should I complain, when in many ways I am so fortunate?) it is sometimes quite lonely here.

I must tell you all about him, Jane, for he is, let us not forget, to be your brother-in-law. He is John Joseph Green, a man of my own age, and he was born in a place named Picton, which is near to Sydney. If you look at the map, my dear, you can see that is nearly three thousand miles from here, so I have never been there, and such a journey would have no purpose, because he has no family left— like so many, they died of the 1919 flu. He is a very nice man, quiet and fond of being alone, as I am, and we get along together very well; and he is, moreover, a wonderful help with the work of the station. John has travelled a great deal in Australia and really has been a kind of explorer, but he wants to settle in one place now. So, you can see that we are suited to each other and you, therefore, are not to worry. Nor must you think I am foolishly romantic, marrying in my forties, for it is a very sensible match I am making. Yet I will admit (though only to you, dear Jane!) that I saw him first in a way more suitable to a book by Ethel M. Dell. My first sight was of a man riding towards the station on camel-back, John having been engaged on one of his expeditions.

(No mention, I noticed, of Billy's father rescuing him!)

We are to be married quite soon, I hope, when the travelling priest, Father Naismith pays his next visit here. In my imagination, I see your eyebrows rise very high at that, Jane, and hear you say, "Has Mary become a Catholic?" I have not, of course! But Father Naismith is a fine man, a Jesuit (does that make matters worse?) and spends his life in the service of God in remote places. What is more important, he is able to marry us. Were he not, we should have to make a long and inconvenient journey.

I hope to have your Blessing and Good Wishes, Jane, and I am certain Jacka and I will be happy together.'

Jane looked up. 'What's this "Jacka", do you think?'
'Nickname, what else? Like me calling you Oilcan Strutt.'
'Don't you dare! Is Jacka short for John?'
'Expect so. Jack is.'
We read on. I found nothing new, of course, because Jane's eyes had preceded mine. But she did. 'Listen.'
I listened.
'Here's what she writes in 1970. It's just an ordinary letter, really. But there's a P.S. Quote: "Jane, I have never inquired as to your financial state, but since your health is a little less robust now, do not feel you need suffer hardship, for I have more than enough for my own needs. I have made a

deposit at the Yorkshire Penny Bank in Bradford in an account opened in your name. Use the money as you need it. If you don't need it, so be it, but please do not hesitate for the sake of pride, or feel it is not right, because, even though I am not with you, I think a great deal about you!"'

'More money,' I said. 'The estate gets bigger and bigger.'

Jane smiled, almost ruefully. 'I just have to live to enjoy it!'

'I'll tell you what we're going to do.'

'Not until I've read this last letter.'

She read quickly and put it aside. 'Nothing much. What *are* we going to do?'

'We're going to the Land Titles Office, to discover who the neighbours are at Stringer Station. Then we're going to run a check on all of them.'

'What about the police—they might do better?'

I told her about Bob Collis. 'You can call him a kind of informal contact. The police know and they'll be interested in anything else. But at the moment they've nothing to go on.'

Jane walked to the window. It was evening now, with the lights coming reflected across the Swan River, sparkling on the water. She looked at it for a moment. Then she said, 'This *is* a heavenly place!' And after that, 'Will those terrible people know we didn't die?'

'Bound to.'

'How come? They couldn't know about the soldiers.'

'If we'd just travelled straight through Kununurra, perhaps not. But we stayed, made phone calls, all the rest. They'll know we're alive, whoever they are.'

She turned. 'They'll know we're in Perth, then—or guess.'

'That's why we won't be.'

She said, 'Oh, goody, more travel! Where are we going after the Land Registry?'

'I have a friend with a cottage.'

'Does he know you're taking a youngish person of the female kind?'

'Matter of fact, he does.'

'Used to it, is he?'

'He thinks I ought to marry you,' I said, stung.

It set her off, naturally. Heavy sarcasm (How *generous* of him to *think* of conferring a *man* upon *her*!) was followed by indignation (Do you think that if I'd *wanted* to be married I'd still be single *now*!) and then into personal abuse about Perth lawyers so helpless they got themselves kidnapped by persons unknown—unknown at the time, and unknown *still*! She sat glaring at me, nostrils flared, and demanded, 'Why?'

'Because I have about ten thousand uncles and cousins and aunts.'

'Who would all like to get their calloused, greedy, Australian paws on *my* money!'

'You,' I said, 'are like one of the Australian insect varieties.'

'The mozzie, you mean? Thanks.'

'There's an ant,' I said, 'which secretes a honey-sweet fluid. Great delicacy. Front half's ant and back half is honey reservoir. Everybody wants the honey sac; nobody wants head and thorax. You,' I said, 'are the Honey Ant in person and don't you forget it. So my relatives would stand in serried ranks, guaranteeing your safety.' I explained why, and she simmered down. Gradually. But she was touchy the way these determined, modern women are. I reflected that Jane had all the virtues, except tolerance on that one topic. On any other subject she was intelligent, cool, balanced. But at the slightest suspicion she was being patronized, touchy as fulminate. All of this cost us about half an hour and made the Land Registry visit impossible that day, so instead I took her to Mandurah, and then to dinner.

Mandurah is Perth's southern seaside resort. Jane, now reasonable as can be, said, 'Why does Perth have to have a seaside resort miles away when it has other resorts very close?'

She was making the same kind of inquiry a bit more snappily by the time we'd both walked through a cloud of Mandurah mosquitoes in the lamplit entrance to the restaurant and had begun to itch and scratch. In spite of which, we enjoyed ourselves. Mandurah's a place for fish, the Australian varieties were all new to her, and she began quite soon to talk about starting an export business supplying smoked albacore for London's dinner tables. The red wines of Mount Barker triggered further and similar ambitions. It was, as I say, enjoyable, and marriage was not once mentioned.

But Jane's safety was. I told her she'd be fairly safe around Mandurah. Perth was another matter; it's a big place right enough, with more than a million people in it, but though the city's sizeable, its centre isn't. Spend a couple of hours in the middle of Perth—shopping in the big stores, or wandering in Hay Street Mall—and you might as well stand on a ladder and ring a handbell. But all this talk was by way of preparation. My plans for Jane in the next couple of days were centred several miles south. Bob's cottage is actually in a tiny place named Dawesville, on the edge of Peel Inlet. I drove her there after dinner.

There were two advantages to Bob's cottage: first it could be reached either by road or by water. Bob, when he uses it likes to go prawning and crabbing, and keeps a boat there: kind of a general-purpose entertainment boat so he can putter along with a small outboard. Fit the bigger engine and it will stand up to the water skiing his grandchildren use it for. He also keeps an old blue Commodore car there as a runabout. I took Jane inside, carefully closed the door, switched on the lights, and sprayed Ray-ban everywhere in the hope of murdering all the mozzies. The care I'd taken was necessary because of Bob's system of nets. He's got them rigged just about everywhere and I'm pretty sure they're technically illegal. The intruder who forces a window and climbs in finds himself instantly enmeshed in miles of strong nylon net. It just drops down on him from the ceiling. I know—I've been one of Bob's guinea pigs. Once you're caught, you're caught for keeps: struggle and it just gets worse; try to be cool and rational and *find* a way out of it and you fail, because there's too much netting and Bob has several cunning twists worked in each individual net. It's only vulnerable to a sharp knife, should you happen to have one in your hand. If the knife's not in your hand, but in, say, your belt, you'll have wriggled yourself into immobility before you even understand what's got hold of you.

I have said to Bob: What if it's just a boy and he gets caught and starves? Bob takes the hard line: one, the intruder has no business being there, and two, each outside wall has a notice on it which says 'Beware—this property is efficiently protected'. The notice must work because nobody'd died yet.

All this I explained, but did *not* demonstrate! But I did demonstrate that the freezer was working and full and likewise the dry-goods cupboard. There was also the small, concealed cupboard in Bob's room, which contained a police-type revolver and a hunting rifle, for both of which he possessed licences. In wooden houses, concealed cupboards are easy.

She said brightly, 'Well, we should be all right till morning,' and on that note, we went off to our separate rooms.

Next morning, before I left for Perth, I knocked on her door, and called her name, but got no answer. Repeating the process gave the same result. Then I looked through the house. Still there was no Jane, no disturbance, and the nets were in place. Seven or eight acres of bush surrounded the cottage and I yelled for her from the door, not really appreciating, at first, that quite a stiff breeze was blowing. When I did, I put on boots and began quartering the ground. Couldn't find a sign of her towards the road and was beginning to be a bit worried. I've said before that Australian snakes tend to be both venomous and shy. Given the chance, they'll get out of your way. Step on one, though, and you pay the price; so to walk in the bush without boots is pure stupidity. As I hurried towards the water, it seemed likely Jane must have gone the same way—perhaps for a morning swim. But in slippers. Then I heard the sharp, high rasp of a little engine starting. She was inside Bob's boathouse, with the toolkit out and grease on her hands.

'It's Oilcan Strutt again,' I said, 'the Kickstart Kid.'

'Just checking the engines. The little two-stroke wouldn't start. It does now. The big four-stroke runs as smooth as silk and twice as silent. What's wrong with being barefoot?'

I told her that it might be the Tiger snake, or it might be the Dugite, or in those parts it could even be the Death Adder and if I found her barefoot again she could fend for herself in future. She took the point and followed in my footsteps as though I were Wenceslas himself on the way back to the cottage. We saw no snakes.

After breakfast, and with a choice of routes back north, I drove over to Pinjarra—a place which looks like every other small town, but has its own unpleasant niche in the history books because there the last deliberate mass murder of the Aborigines took place. Fifty people or so. We've a young country in WA and a lot to be proud of. Also a good bit to live down. I took the Western Highway due north to Perth, stuck the Land Rover in a car park at the far end of Wellington Street by the Markets. Not only would it not be found there—nobody would even look there.

Taxi to the Land Titles Office. Phone call to Dawesville. Jane said she was reading about tank engines and sounded contented. I went in and began digging. Two hours later I knew the properties that bordered Stringer Station and, within limits, who or what the owners were. With the notes in my pocket, I took another taxi to the home of a retired schoolmaster I know.

Tom Kendrick is in his eighties now, slender as the proverbial reed and about as straight. He has two passions; one physical and one intellectual. The first is daily sea-bathing in the surf at Scarborough Beach (which can flatten you, or freeze the strongest, but doesn't flatten or freeze him) and the second is the history of Western Australia, to which he came as a baby from Glasgow, and has loved deeply all his long life.

'Come in, John Close,' he said. 'What mischief are you considering?'

'No mischief, sir, not at the moment.' He's one of those teachers who invites former pupils to use his first name and they never can. I know nobody who calls him anything but 'sir'!

'Then you're changing.' He serves only tea, and sniffs at it and looks at you through wreathing steam. I told him about my five ownerships and leases and that I needed to know more. He advised the Land Registry first and the top floor of the new library second, and frowned when I said it was quicker to ask him.

'Then ask me.'

I gave him names, one by one, starting with SEVERY.

'Henry Severy?'

I shook my head. 'George.'

'Of course. Henry died, didn't he? Well, they're a very old WA family. Are we speaking of Matilda Station?'

'The bottom right hand corner of it, yes.'

'Good people. Been up there since Heaven knows when. First pioneers they were. You'll have read *Kings in Grass Castles*, Mary Durack's book?'

I had.

'The Severy family's a lot like the Duracks—hard-working and intelligent.'

'Is it possible,' I asked him with such delicacy as I could manage, 'that one of them could be up to no good?'

'A Severy?'

'Yes.'

'You're involved in some malpractice, then?'

'Not me, sir. Somebody else.'

'The somebody else is not a Severy.'

I nodded. 'The second name is Azzi.'

He gave me a look. 'Come now, even you must know about Azzi.'

Azzi came as an Italian immigrant to WA just after the war. He made millions in the building business and spread it about and the millions made more millions.

'Is he straight?' I asked.

'Nobody who makes a million is straight. But there are degrees in these things.'

'And?'

'He does considerable good by stealth. I gather he bought the cattle station for one of his daughters.'

'The showgirl or the vet?' Signor Azzi's two beautiful daughters appear often in the Perth papers.

'Guess.'

'The vet.'

Kendrick shook his head. 'The showgirl. He's building a hotel for the vet.'

'Is he—where?'

'Queensland. The awful Gold Coast.' To Tom Kendrick, Queensland, and all of Eastern Australia, were far-off, Godless places.

'You think he's all right, then?'

'There's Azzi, his wife, and two unmarried daughters. Unless it's a building development matter I should cross him off your list of suspects. Who's next?'

'Somebody called Nixon.'

He gave his short, barking laugh. 'Nixon,' he said. 'Would that be "x" or "c-k-s"? Not that it matters with the scoundrels.'

It's rare these days to hear people speak the word scoundrel: even someone like Tom Kendrick who relishes a good, old-fashioned turn of phrase.

'With the "x",' I said. 'The Nixon Land and Grazing Corporation.'

'Of which the chairman will be Bad Billy Nixon?'

'Well, it's William. Don't know about Bad Billy.'

'Before your time.' Tom Kendrick was looking pensive. Fragrant steam from his cup wreathed round his longish nose. He inhaled, drinking a little, sorting through his files in his mind. 'The Nixons come originally from the Scottish borders. They were Border reivers—cattle thieves and cut throats, the lot of them, and always the same. You'll recall there was one of them became President of the United States. You remember that, John Close?'

'I remember.'

'And what became of him? Bad Billy was a professional man, an accountant in the beginning. After that he was anything for a shilling. Moneylending was his principal line. Evicted a lot of widows, starved orphans. Made farmers bankrupt.'

'Why haven't I heard of him before?'

'I can't imagine. Yes I can—the thirties was his time. And the war. But he may be retired—he's even older than I am.'

I looked at my notes. 'The chairman is a William and there's another William on the board.'

'Chip off the old block *he'll* be!'

'They're crooks. You're sure?'

'Not a word I'd use. Where's the company registered?'

'Sydney.'

'Went there in the war, Bad Billy Nixon did. Where the money was. No, not crooks. Too clever to be convicted of anything at all. They work by using the law to the limit. Grasping, greedy people. Not a scruple among a thousand of them.'

'Northrop?—That's the next name.'

He shook his head. 'Means nothing. Is it a big holding?'

'The maximum.'

'Company ownership?'

'Private company. Subsidiary of another. All well-hidden.'

Tom Kendrick blinked again and said irritably, 'It's age, you know. One forgets all the names. Could this be an American? There are numbers of Americans, these days. Into everything. Cattle, wheat, iron.'

'You disapprove? Tom Price was American.' Tom Price found a mountain made, literally, of iron ore.

'And a public benefactor, of course. It's the culture I dislike, the guitars and the terrible English they use. Like mixing the lyrics of mawkish songs with the deliberate obfuscations of Finance Acts. Your man could perhaps be American.'

'One final outfit. Exotic name. They're called Horn & Hoof Pastoral Grazing.'

Tom Kendrick smiled. 'I wasn't certain of Northrop, but Horn & Hoof I do know. Meat for hamburgers for American teenagers.' (It's worth a few dollars just to hear Tom Kendrick enunciate the word teenagers!) 'Suppliers to the corrupters of public taste. Not that there's anything to be done about public taste these days, least of all by school-masters.'

'You don't seem to like Americans very much.'

He shrugged. 'They're efficient as farmers, they have always invested in water and fertilizer and they even muster their cattle with helicopters, I believe. But I was told the other day by a teacher of juniors that she had a child in her class who could recite which ten "discs" sold most copies in any week, but could not multiply five by five and produce a correct answer. John, I find individual Americans almost uniformly pleasant, but the world they're creating is men-tally off-balance.'

'Horn & Hoof then?'

'A large corporation, with all that means.' He leaned back, smiling. 'You think I'm turning sour, John Close; that I am yesterday's milk left out in today's sun. But my generation had a glimpse—just a glimpse, never a real sighting—of a better world. Imagine this. Imagine you wish to recruit a dozen men who are ruthless, intelligent, aggressive, and morally plastic, men who would do almost anything, to be just a little richer: men like Bad Billy Nixon, who'd turn widows and children out of their homes for the sake of a small debt, and do so without either hesitation or com-passion. Now where would you find your dozen? In a prison? No, no, the average convict isn't very clever. You might perhaps find just one. Would you look among soldiers or school teachers? No. You'd look—you'd have to—among the executives of corporations, because that's where such people go. Many of my boys have. Think about it as you drive away.'

'It's a taxi I need. May I phone?'

We chatted as I waited. When had the better world been glimpsed? He looked at me in some surprise. 'Just after the Second World War, of course. For a while it looked like coming along, but then greed became sanctified, especially among lawyers.' On impulse, I asked if he knew of Mary Ellen Emmett who'd become Stringer—then Green. 'She rings a distant gong,' said Tom Kendrick. 'A woman who won a cattle station; she was that one?'

'Her husband won it. Stringer. He died and then she married a man named Green. Lived sixty-odd years on the fringe of the Kimberleys.'

He frowned. 'Green?'

'John Joseph, known to her as Jacka.'

He thought for a moment, then shook his head.

He's fun. Always was. Prods you with his thoughts, and makes you examine your own. He occupied mine in the taxi and while I drove south again in the Range Rover.

An hour or more later, when I got back to Dawesville, Jane was sitting in a rattan chair on the porch looking out across Peel Inlet. Bob Collis's rifle stood propped against the table beside her. I was deliberately quiet as I walked towards her and was more than ten yards away when she became aware of me. The rifle rattled neatly into her grip and her right hand flicked at the bolt, audibly chambering a round.

'Can you shoot?'

'Try me. I've been practising.'

'Shooting?'

'Handling it. Shots would attract too much attention, wouldn't they?'

'Maybe.' I told her about Tom Kendrick's assessments.

She said, 'Sounds to me like Bad Billy Nixon's our man. Or his son, Bad Billy Two. Or the Northrop man he wasn't sure about. What do we do next, Mr Legal Adviser?'

'Think a bit.'

Jane sighed. 'Would it surprise you if I say I want to *do* something. Actually get off my bottom and make a positive move. It's all right for you. This is your damned country and you know how everything works. I don't, so I have to ask all the damned time!'

'What would you like to do, Cap'n?'

'Catch the pigs who drove us into the desert and dumped us.'

'Me too. Any ideas?'

'I could be a tethered goat. Look—these people are organized to the point where they can play clever games in London. They wouldn't turn down the chance to get at me again.'

'Go on.'

'What's that park in Perth, the one with the restaurant?'

'King's Park.'

She snorted. 'There's been a queen for thirty-odd years! But okay, we put an ad in the Personal column, saying Jane Strutt invites prospective purchasers to meet her at the— what's that tree?'

'Which one?'

'The giant, the one cut into bits.'

'A jarrah.'

'They can meet me at the giant jarrah and make their bids. How's that?'

'You'd get some rum company.'

'I'm hoping for company.'

'Not like them, you're not. Every tart and woofter in WA advertises daily in the Personals.'

'I'll risk that,' Jane said, grinning, 'just so long as you're there to protect me.'

10

STRINGER: J Strutt ready to discuss future with interested parties, Friday, 1.30 p.m., great jarrah tree, King's Park.

It was bald as we could make it. We didn't even say Stringer was a cattle station; to the casual degenerate thumbing through the Personals in search of Heaven knows what, the words would be meaningless. No mention of who Jane was or what the ad was all about. No box number or phone number. Just Friday at 1.30 p.m. Any Friday, at lunch time, there are many, many people in King's Park.

The ad appeared in Wednesday's *West Australian*. No guarantee that anyone who mattered would see it, of course, but then that's true of any ad and they usually seem to be spotted, especially where property is concerned. Jungle drums.

Meantime we'd a couple of days and nothing to do except stay out of the way. So we went south on a little tourist trip and I showed her the Gloucester tree at Pemberton, which is a 60-metre karri you can climb, if you're mad enough, via a continuous stairway of wooden staves driven into the trunk. As we stood at the foot, a pair of lunatic youths were actually climbing, watched by a matching pair of young ladies unsure how impressed to be by this macho display.

'You going up there?' said Jane.

'More your kind of thing than mine,' I said, and pointed to the spot where I chickened out the only time I tried it. I was about eighteen at the time, and the young lady then with me was not impressed.

But looking at those two girls, giggling one moment and open-mouthed with apprehension the next, I had a thought.

'Imagine you're giving a description of yourself,' I said to Jane.

'Why?'

'Just do it.'

She shrugged. 'I'm five feet seven and a half, eight stone six, brown hair, eyes hazel, so the army says. There's a mole an inch to the right of my mouth and a vertical scar on my left knee, a product of a game of mixed hockey.'

'They know most of that,' I said. 'They've seen you. It's time for a new look. You're going to be vulnerable in King's Park.'

'You said there'd be crowds.'

'There will. Now look at those two girls.'

They wore white shorts and bright T-shirts, big sunglasses with coloured frames, and beach thongs on their feet. Both were blonde, natural or otherwise.

'There'll be loads like that in the park.'

'I'm not a teenager.'

'No, you're not. But there'll be plenty twice your age in shorts.'

It was hard going but she gave in at last, and we drove sixty miles to Bunbury to get her hair dyed—'tinted', they said in the shop—and to buy the necessary shorts and T-shirt. She declined to wear thongs because they slipped off her feet, but at the Optical Shop at Big W she bought a splendid pair of pink-plastic, heart-shaped sunglasses. Top that lot off with a Boxing Kangaroo peaked baseball cap, and she'd be a long way changed from the Cap'n Strutt who wore well-pressed, tailored tropical suits. She frowned doubtfully at everything, naturally, and was a bit shy about the outfit when it was all on. But to the casual eye she looked twenty instead of thirty and dinkum Aussie instead of obvious Pom.

It was less easy for me. I rummaged in Bob Collis's wardrobe and found an akubra hat with a brim a mile wide, then a pair of stringy, cut-down denim shorts that must have belonged to a grandson, and a Boxing Kangaroo sweatshirt with a tear in it. Even with sunglasses I still looked like me. So Jane dyed my hair dark brown.

On Friday, we parked in Mandurah and took the bus to Perth, wondering on the way how many would attend? The fine neighbours or their representatives? The kidnappers and/or theirs? A good number of people in the state, to whom the word Stringer was no mystery, wouldn't think it worthwhile to be there. Especially if attending involved flying two thousand kilometres and spending a hundred or two, or three or four, depending where they'd come from. Make it thousands if Bad Billy and his boy had flown in from Sydney.

So far as we could, we'd worked things out. One-thirty on Friday at King's Park is a good time. For Perth long-lunchers, picnickers, sunbathers, tourists, early weekenders, are all making their way along the Avenue of Remembrance, swirling and eddying round the restaurant, the quick food place, the car park. The big tree nearby would be quieter. In general, though, we could merge with the crowds. On the other hand, so could anybody else. If anything went wrong, we reasoned there were plenty of people about. But when it did . . .

Jane and I cruised along the Avenue in a taxi, five minutes early, looking slantwise at the tree. Kids were reading the notice and touching the massive logs, but no one was just standing. We drove along to the roundabout without stopping, round it, cruised back. Inconspicuous. Perth taxis, like taxis in most cities are mainly GM or Ford. Ours was GM, metallic blue like lots of others and with tinted windows. Still no one standing, staring or obviously waiting. There's another roundabout at the city end. We went round that, too, and back again. The taxi-driver, tipped in advance, neither commented nor complained. By the third pass nothing had been achieved and the time was almost 1.42 p.m.

'Stop,' I said.

I paid him off and we walked back towards the restaurant, doubled round the back, then through the car park to the tree. Then we stopped. I'd read about the tree before: height, weight, dates and place of origin, so Jane read it while I looked around. Somebody in a pale suit stood in deep shadow under a nearby Norfolk Island pine, watching us quietly; it was no wonder we hadn't seen him from the taxi. I met his eye and he began to move towards us. Approaching, he said, 'Stringer?'

'Who are you?'

'Neighbour. Anyway I represent a neighbour, George Severy. He'd be here if he didn't have to be in Canberra. Why the mystery?'

I introduced myself. 'There have been problems. I'm interested in bids.'

He pointed out that bids could be attracted by advertising, no meetings necessary except between lawyers.

'But not *only* interested in bids.'

He shrugged. 'You've company.'

Turning my head I saw another man coming towards us from the road. The second man was American, plainly. When he spoke, he had that pitched-down voice so many of them seem to cultivate nowadays, and the short-stepping, buttock-rolling walk that usually goes with it.

'This the lady?'

'She's my clerk,' I said.

He was Brad Dolan from Hoof & Horn, manager of their big spread in the Kimberleys, he said, and what was it I cared to discuss?

'Bids,' I said.

'No need dragging busy folks here for that,' he said. 'You take the number of hectares and you multiply by—'

'John!' said a woman's voice brightly, just behind me, a voice I knew at once: Marye N. Bright, bright as a button, smart as paint, and two above me on the totem pole at MacDonald Slaughter.

I turned. 'Marye!' I cried, still unsure after several years how she wanted it pronounced. I always said plain Mary, like the song says, but all sorts of people said it all sorts of ways, and she never corrected anyone. Saw it as part of her eternal mystery, I shouldn't wonder. 'Whom do *you* represent?'

She gave me her dazzling smile. 'The firm. The partners. You're such a *stranger* these days!'

'You want bids to your office, you better give me your card,' Dolan said. 'And tell me when we can inspect.'

I had a card with me for this purpose and gave one to him and one to Neighbour, who still had not identified himself by name. He didn't do so now; just took it, uttered, 'G'day', and turned away. I watched them walk off, and looked round hopefully for any other respondents to the ad. Hopes dashed. There was nobody.

Marye Bright, meanwhile, was charming Jane. She was dressed, as always, in the crispest and cleanest: you know, shoes-match-bag-and-pick-up-understated-colour-from-hat. A hat-wearer: not too many of those about, not her age, not in Perth. Not many Maryes either. She saw early in life that the law was the way up, and she started climbing. Now had political plans.

Meanwhile Marye is the close companion of a real estate and construction man, Mr Dixie Mackeras, with more millions than I have socks, and she's domiciled with him, as the saying has it, in a modern palace in Millionaires' Row, Dalkeith, just down-river. Precious little stands in *his* way. It must be like living in a lion's cage. This orphan daughter of an alcoholic freelance reporter wears seven-league social boots. Size two. And there's no accounting for tastes.

'I'm one of dear John's partners,' she was saying in that half-gush of hers. 'We worry about him in case he gets lost in the forest.' Marye speaks in sentences, but they're larded with emotion. 'And you must be the heiress, since you're certainly not his clerk!'

Jane nodded and said how-d'you-do, and put out her hand, which Marye shook daintily with her lacy white glove, as though being careful no fingers were broken by accident. It's an act. In an arm-wrestling contest I'd back Marye. Against men, too. *Especially* against men.

'—And we never seem to see him these days,' said Marye, 'what with one thing and another.'

Jane said: 'Probably my fault. He's been looking after me.'

'So he should,' Marye said, and then turned her blinding light on me. 'John, you're to ring the office.'

'All right.'

She smiled. 'Well go on. Do it now. We'll just talk.'

I went to the phone in the restaurant and rang Sharleene who told me she had a letter addressed to me, sent from England. I've been calling you at your apartment. What do you want me to—'

'I'll collect it,' I said.

'Oh, and Mr Close?' When West Australian women speak, they tend to end every phrase on a rising inflection. It's a trick of speech that makes 'The sun's shining' sound like a question. But Sharleene actually *had* a question. She often has, and they usually concern unmarried blokes. 'Do you know Richie Franklin?'

'I know his brother.'

'Is Richie nice?'

I said, 'Do you really want to be a golf widow, Sharleene?'

'He's one of those?'

'Four brothers,' I said, 'and all of them four-handicap or less. Fifty-four holes Saturday and Sundays. Weekdays it's nine before breakfast and eighteen after work. I'm surprised you got to meet him at all.'

'Shame, he's a hunk.'

Mindless chat, lasting no more than a minute, then I hung up and went back to where Jane and Marye stood. But now Marye stood alone. 'Where is she?' I asked.

Marye said, 'She went rushing off.'

I said, 'Which way?' looking round quickly, not seeing Jane anywhere.

'In a taxi,' Marye said. 'She spotted it down there and said, "You'll have to excuse me," and trotted down and climbed in. Went towards the city. In fact—' She shaded her eyes with her lacy little paw and said, 'That's probably the one —just turning at the clock tower, heading into the city.'

'Did she say where she's going?'

Marye's another of your modern women. 'Why on earth should she?' she replied.

124

I didn't explain. The years had given me considerable respect for Marye's abilities, but no great ambition to share my little troubles with her. Marye looks after Marye first except in very minor matters. 'I can give you a lift quite quickly. My car's in the car park.'

I shook my head. 'Probably quicker by taxi.' She gave a little shrug and didn't insist.

I found a taxi—faster than one usually does in the park —but it did me no good. I couldn't leap in and say 'Step on the gas' like those people in the thirties movies, because there's a tight speed limit in King's Park, and if you break it you're in very deep. The driver cruised at strict regulation thirty-k and I knew every second took Jane farther away. The question that hammered at my brain was: who in hell could have lured her into a cab? Because she'd gone voluntarily—that was the extraordinary thing! She knew no one in Australia, except the pilot, Stainsby, and the toughs who'd driven us into the desert. So who—especially when she knew the dangers very well, could have persuaded her? Answer: no one. Marye hadn't mentioned that there was anybody else in the taxi, anyway. She hadn't said the taxi stopped and somebody opened the door and . . . Nothing like that. I pushed my mind back in time to what Marye *had* said, and it was, 'She spotted the taxi down there (i.e. on the road just below) and said, "You'll have to excuse me," and trotted down and climbed in.'

That's what she'd said.

So no one else was involved.

And that was baloney—had to be because Jane had already had one unforgettable demonstration in Australia of how badly somebody wanted to get rid of her.

Which made me wonder, had she *seen* somebody, or something that had scared her, and just got out of the way, quick? Possible. But as a theory it foundered on the same rock: Jane knew nobody except Stainsby. Oh, plus Billy One-Hat. But Billy certainly wasn't going to be in King's Park on a Friday afternoon!

For want of anything better to do, I went to the office to pick up the letter—and kept the taxi waiting while I did so. I couldn't, at a glance, decipher the smudgy post-mark, so I just put the letter in my pocket and took the taxi a bit further along The Terrace, then paid and dodged out and nipped up to Hay Street to pick up another cab. Getting back to Dawesville meant a bus to Mandurah and I fretted and fumed as we crawled southward. Then drove like a maniac from Mandurah to Dawesville.

No Jane when I got there.

I made myself a drink and drummed my nails and looked at the telephone a few hundred times. After a while, I had another drink.

The phone remained silent. The house was quiet, too, apart from my hisses and grunts. Nothing happened.

But too much had happened already—Jane had gone!

Jane had watched me walk off to the phone in King's Park Restaurant, and had then, almost immediately, got into a cruising cab and vanished. She had left no message, no hint, nothing.

It didn't make any sense at all. Yet Jane *was* sensible: head screwed on, as the saying goes. Practical. But what was practical about doing a bunk into the great unknown when she knew her life was at risk? Furthermore, Jane was courteous by nature—yet she'd left without a word to me: and I was her only friend in Australia. Also her lawyer! It made no sense, and two substantial Scotches probably weren't helping me make sense of it. I'd been at Dawesville at least a couple of hours before I remembered the letter, and swore at myself and made a mess of the envelope by ripping it with my thumb.

It was from the Yorkshire Bank, a branch in Bradford. 'The account originally opened by Mrs Mary Ellen Green for the use of her sister, Mrs Strutt, which had reverted to Mrs Green upon her sister's death, and is part of Mrs Green's estate and therefore the property of Miss Jane Strutt,' contained: 'the sum of seventy-eight thousand pounds'! The manager gave details of some investments the bank had made at various times—Mrs Green had asked them to manage the money if it was not required—and he expressed restrained but justifiable pride in the performance. They'd turned ten thousand into seventy-eight, in fifteen years or so. Not bad.

So Jane was even richer. The fact made her seem even more absent.

As the light began to go, I phoned Marye Bright and spoke to a Filipino maid and then a Filipino butler before Marye herself came on.

I told her Jane hadn't turned up, and asked again: had Jane said nothing at all before she left? 'No message for me, is what I mean.'

'John, if there'd been a message, I'd have given it to you. It's not a thing I'd forget. Now would I?'

'Nope.'

'You're worrying too much. She probably saw a friend or something.'

'She *has* no friends, not here.'

'Well, whatever.'

'You didn't hear her give an address to the driver?'

'At that range? Does she shout? I must have been twenty-five or thirty metres away. No, I didn't hear a thing. Don't *worry*!'

'But I am worried. She—'

'John, are you in love with her?'

'No, I—'

'Silly me. But of *course* you are. *That's* why you're so concerned. It's in case she's found a hunk of Australian male to go off with, isn't it?'

'No, it's not! I've reason to wor—'

Marye said, 'No *men*, I promise. The taxi was empty.'

'You're sure?'

'Quite sure.'

'And nobody followed her?'

'There's always traffic, John, you know that. I didn't notice anything.'

'What about the two I'd been talking to?'

'They'd gone. Saw them myself. John, what *is* this? I've heard of jealousy, but you *must* have got it bad. Just be patient. She'll be back, if and when she wants to come back.'

I grunted, that's all. I could see why Marye Bright must have thought of me as love-lorn-loon class one.

Then Marye said, 'Have you considered this—she's English and she's homesick. She's gone back where the Poms come from. Hardly impossible, is it?'

'Unlikely, though.'

'John, it's clear I have to talk to you like a Dutch uncle— aunt—anyway . . .' I remember that because jokes, even feeble ones, formed no part of Marye's normal act.

'Then talk.'

'Is it possible—look, I realize this is a provocative thing to say to a distraught lover—'

'I'm *not* her lover!'

'A technicality,' Marye said. 'You love her—that's why you're distraught. Perhaps there's someone else who loves her too. Someone back in England. Has she a return ticket?'

'Yes.'

'Well, there you are.'

'She also has luggage, and that's still here.'

'Then she'll be back,' Marye said crisply. 'No girl walks away from her favourite clothes. Believe me.'

I grunted again and she said, 'Be patient, cave-man.'

I phoned the King's Ambassador Hotel. She wasn't registered there and I tried a couple more—the Commodore and the more up-market Merlin. Jane, after all, was up-market, too—worth close to a quarter of a million pounds, cash, *half* a million depressed Aussie dollars. She'd make a nice target for a lot of species of wrongdoer.

I thought for a long time about the two men who'd turned up in the park. Brad Dolan from Hoof & Horn, and the one who hadn't even given me his name, but said he represented the Severy family. Logically they were prime suspects. Both wanted Stringer Station, for a start; both were strangers to me; neither possessed what you'd call an engaging personality. But somehow I didn't believe in them as kidnappers, if only for that reason. If a man *had* gone there to grab Jane, he'd have been more cunning: stayed out of sight, not approached us, awaited his moment. We'd advertised our presence, after all. But I still couldn't imagine how the trick had been worked!

I made calls to the Severy family up in the Kimberleys, and then to Hoof & Horn Inc. The Severy I spoke to said, yes, their bloke *was* a bit laconic, but he was really a very good man, etc. etc. In WA a reference from the Severys is as good as one from God, possibly better. I thanked him and rang off and soon after that was being told by Hoof & Horn that their Mr Dolan would shortly complete twenty-three years of unblemished service with the company.

Where *now*?

Bob Collis. He wasn't amused. Called me names. Names like idiot and clown, adjectives like incompetent and stupid, in various combinations. 'Did you marry her?'

'No.'

'Make a will?'

'No.'

'Then I don't fancy your chance.'

'Of what?'

'"Of what?" he says. Jesus! Of getting her back at all, alive *or* dead. You got any idea how big this state is!' He wound down after a bit. Then we got on to the advice. 'The police will be no use. Maybe you'll be happier reporting her missing, John, and maybe because you're a lawyer handling a sizeable estate they'll take really serious notice, but—'

'But be damned! What about the first trip—by Land-Cruiser to the Red Centre!'

'Evidence,' said Bob Collis, 'is there none. *None!* What there is—there's a missing girl. There are people who've got her. There are two and a half million square kilos of land in WA alone, and twelve and a half thousand kilometres of coast. Where do you start looking? Where do the police start?'

'Tell me.'

'With the evidence, John. With what you've already got. Plus what you suspect and/or what you can reason out. There's an old police saying: what you have is *all* you have.'

'It's not much.'

'Another old saw, John. It's always more than you think, *if you really think*! Want me to come on over?'

'Tomorrow?' I said. 'Early. I'll think till then.'

I cursed the Scotch I'd drunk. I sat up, all ready for brisk intellectual action, Inspector Close on the Trail, a blank pad on my knee and a blank brain in my head. My mind wouldn't focus. I sat miserably staring at that empty paper, willing my brain towards action it didn't want to take. About eleven I took a hot shower and then a deep breath and turned the jet to cold. Coffee followed, and while I drank it, I began to go over in my mind the assorted events of our brief stay at Stringer Station. My maltreated mind, by now, instead of being surly and disobliging, had swung a hundred and eighty degrees about and was willing to parade before me small details from obscure mental recesses.

I began on a list of the inexplicables. There were a few things to go on the list. But the one that came tripping on-stage second (after the car in England that knocked Jane down) was a bit of embroidery, the one on the wall of the station house at Stringer. Like a bit of film, the scene ran before my eyes. Jane picking up the broken frame and straightening it, and saying, 'That's funny!' What was funny? What *else* had she said? 'I recognize it. It's a pub at home. I thought it was called the Green Man, but maybe it wasn't, then.' Meaning, when Mary Ellen was young, or something to that effect. I concentrated, trying to remember the framed scrap of embroidery I'd barely glanced at. There had been a name . . . if I could only remember it.

But I couldn't. I could remember everything about the scene. In my mind's eye, I could even see the pub—a grey, sandstone building with white window frames and a green sign swinging outside; the picture was remarkably clear. But the *name*?

I moved on, unwillingly, working my way slowly and steadily through every detail of the events since Jane arrived. And the more I looked at what I'd got, the more despairing I became. There seemed not to be a clue or a signpost in the whole bloody lot.

And Jane, meanwhile, was God-alone-knew-where!

I fell asleep in the chair and woke cold, stiff and frowning at 3.00 a.m., with a half-finished Western fantasy movie cantering away out of a broken dream. I even knew its title: *Sons of the Sons of the Range Men*, and a mass of gibberish it was. I fell onto the bed and slept immediately and when next I woke I was warm and snug but feeling dreadfully guilty that I had been sleeping while Jane . . .

While she died! Because what Bob Collis had said *is* absolutely true—WA is a place where bodies don't get found. There was a case a few years back: three girls whose old jallopy broke down on a lonely bush road that sees a vehicle about once a week. The girls left a note on the car and set out to walk, all together, to safety. Thirty miles, something like that. Never seen again, any of them. No trace ever found: no shallow graves, no clothing, no bones, nothing.

I was utterly certain Jane had been kidnapped. Whoever the enemy was, he'd known where we'd be yesterday, and made plans accordingly. Now he'd got Jane, and it was all too likely he intended to kill her. He'd tried before, after all. But I was convinced, somehow, in spite of the evidence, that she remained alive. The existence of the puzzle, of the pub with the wrong name, gave me the feeling Jane was something more than the heiress to Stringer Station: that she was the key to a riddle.

Bob, when he arrived, said briskly, 'Come up with anything?'

I described the incident of the embroidery. He flared his nostrils in exasperation. 'Embroidery, for God's sake?'

'There's *something* in it,' I said.

'Maybe, but you, you bloody wimp, can't say what it is, can you?'

Suddenly I yawned in his face. I thought for a moment he would hit me. But he controlled himself. I expect he's controlled that particular impulse a lot of times. But not always.

'Did you sleep?'

'A bit. Lot of damn silly dreams.'

'Remember them?'

'Only one. Like a Western movie.'

'Tell me.'

I said, 'There was a title. Lot of horses. Some shooting. All mixed together. Western nonsense.'

'The title?'

'*Sons of the Sons of the Range Men.*'

'Mean anything?'

'Nothing. Why?'

He said, 'Just a chance, that's all. I've talked to plenty of people first thing in the morning. Sometimes they can remember just then—remember things they'd forgotten. Tricks of the mind. Forget it. What else?'

'A few items from the Station, things her great aunt owned.'

'Where are they?'

'King's Ambassador, in Hay Street. Checked with the porter.'

Bob nodded. 'Anything else?'

'Bit of old machinery she couldn't figure out. It's in the loft at Pete Akeroyd's house in South Perth.'

'C'mon.'

Bob does that police driving bit: fast, hard and concentrated, in a Holden Commodore with a 4.2 engine that eats roads. I had with me the power-of-attorney Jane had agreed to, so there was no problem with either suitcase or machinery.

We took the lot to Bob's place, also in South Perth. As we dumped it all on his workshop/study floor, he said, 'Two things. Anybody know you were at Dawesville?'

'No.'

'Expecting any mail or messages?'

'No. Well, maybe at the office, but I can phone. No, hang on, there *is* . . .' I was thinking of Tom Kendrick, and said so.

'Relevant?'

'Maybe.'

'Call him.'

Bob pointed at the phone. I dialled the number, but no reply. Kendrick would, I imagined, be on the beach.

'What was the second thing?'

'That pub,' Bob said. 'What was its name?'

'I'm sure she said The Green Man.'

'You still can't remember the name on the embroidery?'

'No. Why?'

He said, 'You dreamed about Sons of the Sons of the Range Men. Well, Range Men is an anagram of Green Man.'

'You're kidding!'

He chucked a ball pen at me. 'Try it. Question is why. *Why* did the old lady—what's her name again?'

'Mary Ellen Green.'

'Okay—why'd she change it—she did *do* the sewing?'

'I assume so. No proof, but—who else could have done it? There was nobody there for sixty years except the husbands.'

'Okay. She did it. Why in embroidery?'

'God knows!'

'God doesn't give evidence,' Bob said grimly. 'But there's a reason. Was it recent, this embroidery?'

'I hardly looked at it.'

'Not old and faded?'

'No. The room was big and shaded. Sunlight wouldn't get at it.'

'Okay—we don't even know when it was done, except it was somewhere between the twenties and the eighties? Right?'

I nodded.

'And it's a pub in the place she came from—Bradford?'

'Not the city,' I said. 'Some suburb.'

Bob Collis said, 'Remember *anything* Jane said, any bloody detail!'

Brontë, I thought. 'Where the Brontës were born,' I said.

He snapped his fingers. 'Howarth. They were from Howarth, but that's not Bradford! You sure?'

Bob Collis walked over to the bookshelves and fingered out the third in a row of volumes of an encyclopaedia. 'Brontë, Brontë, Brontë . . .' He looked up. 'They were born at Thornton, near Bradford. Your brain's waking up, John. Tell me what we know *now* that we didn't know before!'

I said, 'Maybe it was done recently. The old girl may have been senescent and simply mis-spelled.'

'She *may*,' Bob said. 'But I don't think so. What do we know?'

'Her second husband's name was Green.'

'I haven't forgotten. She changed the name of a pub she hadn't seen since she was a child. And she did it in a fairly permanent form.'

'Permanent?' I said.

'Ever go to auctions? But no—you're a lawyer, aren't you? All your faith in bits of paper. You go to an auction, young John Close, and you'll find bits of embroidery like as not. They're in cushions and samplers and mottoes.'

'This bit was framed.'

'Tell me some more.'

'Wooden frame,' I said. 'Smashed by the intruders, and tossed on the floor.'

'Glass?'

'Broken.'

'But there *was* glass?'

'Yes.'

'Neither moth nor rust can corrupt,' he muttered.

'It wasn't a religious tract,' I said. 'It was a pub.'

Bob said steadily, 'It was protected, that's what it was. Frame would be hardwood.'

'Black ebony,' I said.

'Or ebonized. Right. Plus glass. Plus a wood back-plate.'

'Why does it matter so much?'

He thought for a moment. 'Tell me this. Did Mary Ellen Green know who'd inherit? Oh yair, she must have done.'

I said, 'I have wondered a bit sometimes.'

Bob looked hard at me. 'Everything is important, my lad. Think now! Why?'

'Okay.' I held up a hand, warding him off. Bob looms over you. 'It goes like this: Old Mary Ellen was a million miles from nowhere. Her only sister died in the early seventies, the house in England was sold up, and she'd only written a very few letters to the sister over a full half-century. She was hardly a great letter-writer. The only relative she had left was Jane Strutt, whom she'd never met, and was never in touch with. For all the old lady knew, Jane could have been dead, or vanished—'

'Like now,' Bob said grimly.

I swallowed, and said, 'So Mary Ellen would *expect* that her great niece would inherit, but I doubt if she could *know*.'

He said, 'Hold on a minute. She'd know this, would she? That the only person of her own blood who could inherit was a girl. No men?'

I nodded, puzzled. 'Yes. That *must* be right. But what's the point?'

'How many men do *you* know,' Bob Collis said thoughtfully, 'who'd look twice at a piece of embroidery? Women do. They know what it's about. They look at the stitches and they understand how much work's been put in.'

'Go on.'

He grinned, and it wasn't a grin of amusement: more a baring of the teeth. 'How about this?' Bob said. 'She's a tough old bird, this one: solitary and self-contained. She's got something she wants to say, something important. She's the sole owner of a big tract of land, and it's valuable and she knows other graziers'll want it, and one or two maybe aren't too scrupulous. Now—she knows it's a *woman* who will inherit—'

I said, 'Not necessarily. Suppose Jane had married young,

had children, crashed a car. It could all have happened without Mary Ellen knowing.'

'Could but didn't. There's a bank manager and an account, isn't there? Maybe she heard from him. Point is, it's woman-to-woman direct, and it's in stitches because no man would look twice at a bit of embroidery. But the great niece *will*, and she knows it.'

'Not all women are embroiderers,' I said. 'In fact—'

He cut me off. 'There isn't a woman alive who can keep her hands and eyes off fabrics. She doesn't have to be interested in the actual stitches. If she sees the thing, she'll look at it. And notice.'

'Which Jane did.'

'Yes. And she'll say, "That's funny."'

'Yes,' I said. 'That's what Jane did.'

'So there's a message?'

I nodded.

'What is it?'

'Green Man and Range Men?'

'That's it. What's she saying? She knows her heir will know her husband's name was Green, doesn't she? What if she's saying they're the same thing?'

I said, 'What's a Range Man?'

'Search me. We don't have cattle ranges in Australia, not as far as I know, we don't. America has the range riders— the cowboy culture.'

We kicked it about a little while longer, getting nowhere, and Bob Collis led forward another of his sunny little sayings: If you're doing no good, move on.

'Let's have a look at the other stuff,' he said.

I was on my way across the room to get Jane's case, when I said almost without thought, 'It could be simpler.'

'Like?'

'Well, in order to know there *is* a message, you have to know something else first.'

Bob snapped his fingers. 'That it's an anagram!'

136

12

'Was there more lettering?' Bob demanded instantly.

'In the bag. A couple of strips of letters. Not much—'

He whipped up the suitcase lid and dug like a dog. He surfaced with the embroidered strips of lettering in his hand. 'What do you suppose *this* says?'

Two little strips: the first proved to have three letters on it, and the second, four. They weren't words or even arranged as words. They looked like needlework practice, handsome Roman letters done for pleasure.

'Look,' said Bob, placing them on his desk.

G AD   and   MA RS

'Mars,' I offered, too quickly, 'is the God of War, an orbiting planet, or a bar of toffee and chocolate.'

'I can play silly sods too,' Bob said. 'Gad is the bloke who isn't going to help us. Not unless we bloody well concentrate. Why those missing letters, and what are they?'

To save time I cut a strip of paper and wrote the letters of the alphabet vertically down it and we ran the strip through those empty spaces. GOAD, GLAD, GRAD, we saw, all of which were words, the real thing, the genuine article, even if one was an abbreviation. But the second gave us only MAIRS or MAURS, which looked like items from a glossary of Burns' verse, but neither of which appeared in Bob's dictionaries.

We tried them all ways. Mixed all the letters by writing them in circles and staring at them. We got DAGMARS, and wondered who Dagmar was, and whether there were

Norwegians living in the Kimberleys. We got RAGMADS and DRAMGAS and SADGRAM and RAGSDAM and SAM GRAD (whoever he might be) and assorted combinations which could only be meaningless, like AMSDARG and ARSMDAG and SMARAGD.

It all took too much time, and time was pressing, and we both felt guilty at playing games at such a time.

I suppose we'd both thought, having cracked the puzzle of the Green Man/Range Men, and been shown that Mary Ellen used anagrams, that the puzzle would now be easy to solve.

But there now seemed to be no puzzle here. The letters appeared simply meaningless. After an hour and a half, we followed the police precept and moved on.

To the passport.

The basic facts about it I knew already. One major journey back to the Old Country or Home as Mary Ellen doubtless called it. Then on to Europe. Bob looked carefully at all the details.

He said, 'Holland.'

'And Belgium. France, too.'

'Do we know where and why?'

'She had a brother, killed in the First War at the Battle of the Somme.'

'Half a million people had. Brother, son, uncle. Me—I lost an uncle there. But you wouldn't go to the Somme via Holland.'

'How would you go?'

'Via Calais or Boulogne, probably; Zeebrugge perhaps. Here—' he was going through the little bunch of innoculation certificates. 'This says Antwerp.'

'What does? I didn't see that.'

'It's a restaurant receipt. Café Antoine, Antwerpen. Find me a map, John. There's an atlas in the index volume.'

I've been to Europe several times—about once a year since I've been able to afford it—but never to that area. Bob's big, square-ended, neat-nailed finger traced the old route.

Amsterdam, Antwerp, the Somme, Paris, Caen. Country I don't know.

'Why do you look so puzzled?' I asked.

'Just seems a funny journey, in those days. I can understand the Flanders graves, why she'd want to go there. And Paris—not much damage, and it *is* Paris. But the armies had flattened Caen, and Antwerp had been badly bombed, and Amsterdam . . .' Bob's voice trailed off, which was uncharacteristic.

'Go on.'

He said, then, 'Bits and pieces of paper. Smallpox certificate, yellow fever, all the rest. Even a restaurant bill. Know what's missing?'

'No.'

'This page is blank.'

It was headed 'Foreign Exchange for Travelling Expenses', and somebody had written 'Basic Allowance' in red ink at the top. The page was otherwise blank.

'You could take exactly fifty pounds sterling out of Britain in those days. Exchange controls were very tight.'

'For Australians too?'

He shrugged. 'She was English, remember.'

'Green wasn't. What are you getting at?'

Bob said, 'It's a notion, really. I soldiered over these places in 1945, so maybe I'm too close to it. Answer me a question. What have they in common, these places?'

I thought about it. 'Caen and the Somme,' I said, 'both had great battles, but in different wars.'

'And?'

'Amsterdam, Antwerp and Paris are capital cities.'

'Wrong. Paris is. Capital city of Holland is The Hague. Capital of Belgium is Brussels.'

'So?'

'I'm getting old,' said Bob Collis. 'And it's ridiculous!'

'Tell me.'

He shook his head. 'I have an aversion to looking a fool.'

'There's a life at stake. Never mind your vanity!'

He stared at me, blinking. I could almost see the lights

flashing and the bells sounding as thoughts tumbled about in his head.

'Bob?'

He ignored me and, excluded, I went to find out. Volume one of his encyclopaedia held Amsterdam and Antwerp. I read the entries one after the other. Both were ports, both were great mercantile cities with long histories, and fine art galleries and museums. Et cetera, et cetera. Several words were common to both entries, like 'chief commercial centre', and 'largest ocean-going ships', but it was not on any of those that my attention instantly fastened. There was another word. I whispered incredulously, 'Diamonds?'

Bob looked across the room at me. He was blinking, and his mind must have been like mine, trying to cope with all the new possibilities. He said slowly: 'Stringer's not a million miles from the Argyle field.'

I nodded. The Argyle field is Western Australia's new contribution to the world's diamond supplies. It's a large contribution too. More than large—enormous. For a long time it was thought Australia had no diamonds. But it has. More than South Africa. It's a recent discovery up there, in the north of the state.

Maybe a minute went by, then Bob exhaled noisily and came abruptly out of his trance. He said, with his familiar hard practicality, 'Can't be—it's just bloody coincidence!'

'Explains all the money,' I said.

'Too true!'

'It also explains why somebody's desperate to—'

'*And* why the old girl's been so crafty with her information.' He paused then. '*But*,' he said.

'But what?'

'There's two kinds: alluvials—that's diamonds in river beds or dried-out watercourses; or in diamond pipes, where the matrix of kimberlite has penetrated the earth's crust. Now—there's no alluvial formations anywhere near Stringer Station, so it would have to be mining. The old girl and her husband weren't wandering about the seashore picking up pebbles that turned out valuable. It would *have* to be a mining job. Like the Argyle.'

'You're well informed.'

'I'm a policeman. Or was. Diamonds are valuable. You inform yourself if you've any sense.'

'You think it's impossible, do you? Because it really would explain an awful lot.'

'Move on,' he said.

'Just a minute. What if—?'

'What ifs waste time. Move on. I wish I knew a bit more about John Joseph Green. How much is known?'

'Not a lot. Born Picton, NSW. Arrived at Stringer on camel-back in nineteen-thirty-something, I think. Married the old girl. Stayed there till he died.'

'A life full of variety,' Bob Collis said with heavy irony. 'That's all? Still, I reckon the camel could be significant. Means he probably travelled in the deserts.'

'Doesn't tell us where. There *is* one thing though,' I said. 'Billy One-Hat, the resident Abo foreman at Stringer said Green used to go walkabout.'

'Did he explain?'

I shook my head. 'Used to go once a year, after the Wet, stay away about a month. Till he got older.'

'On what?'

'How d'you mean?'

'Mode of travel. Always by camel, was it?'

'So Billy One-Hat said. Took mules, too.'

'Anything else.'

'His wife used the name Jacka of him in a letter.'

'Jacka.' Bob Collis spoke the word several times, getting flavour, like a wine-taster. 'Short for Jackaroo, would it be?'

'Possibly. It's not a short form I've ever heard.'

He grinned. 'Too young. There was a Jack*er* who captained England at cricket. Stanley Jackson. *Sir* Stanley Jackson.'

'Well, it's not him,' I said, and went to the phone.

This time Tom Kendrick was in, and mildly reproving. 'I tried to telephone your firm, young John Close, and not only were you not there, but they were quite unable to tell me either when you were expected or where you were to be found.'

'I know,' I said. 'The whole thing's too complex to explain at the moment, but—'

'I did as you requested, in the matter of John Joseph Green. Made an inquiry or two.' He paused.

'It's desperately important, sir.'

'It is? Very well. Does the name Lassiter mean anything to you?'

I knew of two Lassiters—one a film character. Not him, then. 'Lassiter of the lost reef—that one?'

'The same.'

'He—Green—was connected with *Lassiter*?' I heard my voice get squeaky and controlled it. 'Surely that'd be too long ago?'

'Not truly connected, no.' I'm fond of Tom Kendrick, and usually I enjoy his mild pedantry. At that moment, though, I could have strangled him.

'Please,' I said. 'It is very urgent I should know.'

'This urgency of yours. It's something more than simple impatience?'

'Much more.'

He said, 'What I have is a cutting from a newspaper. I have made a copy. Would you like me to post it?'

'I'll come for it, sir, at once.'

He said, 'Quickly, please. I was about to leave for my walk.'

Bob said he'd better go, because somebody just could be watching, and if they were, it wouldn't be good management to lead them to Tom. Furthermore, anybody foolish enough to try following Bob Collis through the streets of Perth would quickly be spotted, and then lost. He was almost out of the door when abruptly he turned and said, 'What *haven't* you told me?'

'A thousand things, we've been too busy.'

'The important ones. I have this sudden feeling you know something important.'

I went over it all very quickly, with Bob nodding and

saying 'm-hm', concentrating hard. When I got to the tank and the machine gun he seemed oddly unsurprised. I asked why.

'Because I know all about wartime tanks turned into bulldozers, and unmarked fighter planes, too. Police know these things. May not know where, exactly, but they know. John, have we got everything here that you brought away with you from Stringer?'

'Yes,' I said. 'No.'

'What?'

'Tank manual. Jane brought it for light reading.'

'It's?'

'Dawesville.'

'Hold on.' He opened a door and looked into the garage. 'Al left his Mazda. I'll use that. You take the Commodore to Dawesville. Come straight back with the manual.'

'Planning to drive a tank?' I said, a bit piqued at his superintendent-in-charge manner.

Bob grinned. 'Wouldn't be the first time. This manual, it's big?'

'About like two volumes of your encyclopaedia.'

'Hell of a good place to hide the odd sheet of paper.'

I drove southward fast, eyes flickering all the time to the rearview mirror, wondering how the hell a man can tell if he's being followed. Three times other vehicles stuck fairly close behind me for longish periods, and I suspected them of trailing me. But each time they turned off, and in any case that's the way we drive. West Australians aren't great tail-gaters, or overtakers so long as the bloke in front keeps moving.

But there's another way, I realized. My eye had just caught one of the yellow signs warning of police planes operating speed traps from the air, and then a small aircraft went over, port to starboard, in front of me. The enemy had a plane— they'd arrived at Stringer in it! Simple to follow a car, from above and a little behind, where you can't be seen or heard. Twice on the way, I stopped the car suddenly and hopped out to scan the sky.

Nothing. I was simply jumpy. It was strain. Jane missing and the awful feeling that really I was doing nothing to find her; plus days of stress. I *was* a wimp. Bob had said it and Bob was absolutely right.

I approached the cottage, therefore, in a cautious kind of way. Far from impossible that the opposition knew about it —from Jane herself perhaps. They might have made her tell them. I winced at the thought, and instead of turning into the drive, parked a hundred yards up the road and went on foot along the shore of Peel Inlet as far as the property next door to Bob's cottage. From there I looked through the hedge and trees, checking. No boat bobbed at anchor. No car was parked in the driveway. All was clear—as far as I could tell.

Moving forward, I saw that doors and windows on the water-facing side were undisturbed. I began to circle it. The southern end was okay. I came to the wall that faced the road. It, too, seemed secure.

Fine. I stepped forward, put keys to locks, opened the door and entered.

And stopped, in the little hallway, sniffing. Something in the air. Faint, but . . . farmyardy. I slipped quietly into the bedroom, got the revolver from its cupboard, cocked it, and opened the sitting room door.

There was a sudden grunt to my left, from behind the door and I stepped back fast, under no illusions about the protection wood gives against bullets, in spite of a million Western films. You hide behind a wooden wall, the man with the rifle fires at the wall and the bullet goes through it, you and the half a dozen people behind you.

The grunt came again. Weakness in it. A strained sound, made with effort. And no need to sniff—the stench was unmistakable. I knew now, of course, but it still took nerve to step into that room and look at what lay beyond the doors.

One of Bob's nets had got him, effectively and not very recently. The man must have been searching the room all unaware, when the few ounces of fine nylon filament fell on him. He'd struggled: that was easy to see, and for his pains he was tied tight, head to foot. His weight was on his left shoulder, on the floor, and his legs were twisted up on to the seat of an easy chair. He must have fallen like that; he'd stayed like that. He was trying to move as I looked at him. And he couldn't. Not a muscle, not a finger. He'd fouled himself more than once. The air around him stank. He grunted again as I stood looking down at him, a bisyllabic grunt, unmistakably a plea for water. I ignored it, and examined him slowly.

His face, by now, was barely a face at all; the flesh was divided into swollen, one-inch squares that bulged through the strong, tight, ungiving nylon. It had cut into his nose as he struggled, and blood had run down his face to the floor. Removing that netting might well be hospital work.

I could see one arm, the wrist twisted back, and the fingers tangled in nylon. The hand empty. The other arm was twisted beneath him, and I wanted to be sure it was empty, too. And not free. To do it I'd have to turn him by shifting feet and legs from the chair and rolling him over, and I didn't want any sudden kicks at my face. I looked round until I found an old walking stick and hooked it round his ankles and pulled. He yelled, but by now his feet were on the floor and hand and arm were exposed. There was an automatic pistol in his hand. Thanks to the net, the thing was bent round so that it pointed at him rather than me; but I wasn't sure if *he* knew that. I fetched kitchen shears, then put my foot on both hand and gun, and pressed hard while I cut enough strands to get the automatic out.

After that I got a small jug of water and poured it in a thin stream into his open mouth. He really was in a hell of a state—dehydrated, wracked with cramps.

I cut his feet loose and said, 'Stand.' He couldn't. 'Crawl then.'

He couldn't do that either. I looked at my watch, and calculated that by now Bob Collis might have got back to South Perth from Scarborough Beach.

I phoned and he had. I said, 'You caught a fish,' and heard

the pleasure in his voice as he said, 'Alive but unable to move, eh?'

'Certainly can't move. Not dead, either, but you couldn't call it living. Can't stand or crawl. Had a gun, but I've got it.'

'On my way,' Bob said.

He'd be an hour. I spent it rolling our prisoner on to a loose rug and hauling him on it out of the sitting room, down the hall and out of the door. Once he was on grass I cut more of the net, then turned the hosepipe on him. He began to move, gradually. After a while, when he could stand, I made another couple of strategic cuts with the kitchen shears, sufficient to let him get the net off. Then I clipped the hose to Bob's lawn sprinkler, and set the bloke to cleaning up both himself and his clothes. His face began bleeding again when he pulled the last strands of the netting out of it. It must have been painful, but he did it with visible relief. His nose looked one-third severed, but by now he was recovering quickly, just as I had recovered in the desert; so I kept ten yards or so between us, and held Bob's pistol in my hand, having hurled my prisoner's automatic into the bush.

I didn't recognize him, but it's difficult to recognize any-body whose face consists of one-inch squares divided by deeply marked red lines. He was about thirty, I'd guess; no fat on him, lank black hair, around six feet tall, brown eyes, strong. And naked. His clothes were shoes, socks, shorts, jeans and shirt. Before he washed the jeans, he turned away, removed something from the pocket, and tried to slip it in a sock. 'Chuck it to me,' I said.

'Chuck what?'

I looked at him. He was beginning to shiver and he was considerably goose-pimpled.

'Your wallet,' I said, and flicked the rope at him. Caught him in a tender spot, too. 'Now chuck it over.'

Bob must have driven south like Nigel Mansell on a fast day. His son's Mazda 828, Bob behind the wheel, snaked efficiently into the drive-way before I'd got the wallet open.

'This is the bloke, is it? Okay, let's see who he is. Thoughtful of him. Here's his driver's licence. Three convictions. Jack Gunton. Itinerant worker. Switch off the water, John.'

Gunton, naked, ugly and hurt, now faced fifteen stones of Bob Collis. Thirty years between them, but it was strictly no-contest. Bob said, 'Who's your boss?'

Shake of head.

'Where you from?'

Shake of head.

'Where's the woman you kidnapped?'

Shake of head. Plus what looked like incomprehension.

'Right,' Bob said. 'This is my cottage. I've got family. I like my sons and daughters and my grandchildren to come down here and feel safe. I don't like buggers like you breaking in. So I'll tell you what's going to happen. You are going to tell us everything you know. In return I'll hand you over to the police, instead of doing what I'd like to do. Know what that is?'

Shake of head.

'Full of big blue-manna crabs, this inlet is, just here. I'm going to wrap you in some more netting—I have plenty— and gag you, and pop you in the shallows. You have sixty seconds. Count, will you, John.' Bob walked to the garage and emerged with a big roll of netting, as I was saying 'thirty-seven'.

'What I'll do,' Bob said, 'is knock you down and just drape it over you, and kind of roll you in it.'

I was saying 'forty-two, forty-three', when the bloke shouted. 'For God's sake, *don't*!'

'I won't,' Bob said soothingly, 'if you tell me what I need to know.'

'I will, oh yes.' All eagerness.

Trouble was, he didn't know much. He was a boozer, a drifter, a petty criminal, who'd done time in Fremantle prison, among other establishments; he'd just returned from a brief bout of genuine hard work, labouring in Papua New Guinea, and he'd met this bloke in a pub. The bloke was

147

looking for two or three men who weren't particular about
what they did if the pay was good and there was no chance
of getting caught.

'Who is this bloke—what's his name?'

'Dunno. Just Blackie.'

'Where's he live?'

'Dunno, mate. Meet him in the pub.'

'Which?'

'Dunno the name. Hay Street.'

'Hay Street's miles long. Where?'

'Going east from the Mall on the left.'

'Criterion?' I suggested.

Bob said, 'Topless barmaids are your style, eh?'

'I've seen 'em.'

'That's where you meet him, this Blackie? Not the
Sheraton, for instance? Or the Merlin?'

'No.'

'What's he look like?'

'Black hair. Moustache.'

'That fits every third man in WA. I want _more_,' Bob said
flatly. 'Have you seen the crabs they get round here in Peel
Inlet? Big buggers they are. Claws like wire-shears. Sharks
avoid 'em, they say, even the big 'uns, the White Pointers.'

'Wears fawn boots,' Gunton said. 'High ones.'

'And—hat or no hat? What kind of trousers? Does he
smoke, and if so—what? What time d'you meet him?'

Blackie didn't wear a hat. Blackie was balding and when-
ever Gunton had seen him, had been wearing washed-out
jeans and a denim bomber jacket. Blackie smoked roll-yer-
owns. They met at six, when they met.

'Age is he?'

'Round forty.'

'Go on, there's more.'

There wasn't though. Not much. Blackie had sent Gunton
to Dawesville to break-and-enter and see what he could find.
Gunton had got in through a window that had been left
open, and almost immediately, he said, been netted.

I went to lock up ('Securely, this time, John. _All_ the bloody windows!') while Bob Collis bullied Gunton into dressing quickly. He then handcuffed him and made him climb into the boot of the Mazda. 'See you at home,' he said to me. 'Here's the paper from your old mate Kendrick.'

It was a brown envelope. I put it in the Commodore, waved and set off. Bob shot past me soon afterwards, bound for the police station in Mandurah to hand over Gunton and make a statement.

An hour or so later I was in Bob's workshop-cum-study, opening Tom Kendrick's envelope . . .

13

On the two pieces of photocopy machine paper I pulled out of the envelope, there appeared reproduced cuttings of a feature story which had appeared in 1942 in a newspaper called the *Sunday Mail* in Adelaide, South Australia. Wartime. It was headed, startlingly—

LASSITER TRAGEDY REPEATED?

———

GOLDFINDER VANISHES ON
SOLO DESERT JOURNEY

———

YEAR SINCE LAST WORD
OF MISSING PROSPECTOR

The text followed. For the moment though, I had quite enough to digest, starting with the one word:

GOLD

If there was gold up at Stringer, what had happened already was the merest beginning. Gold would bring men west in rivers, as they'd flooded into Kalgoorlie and Coolgardie a century ago. They'd clamour for the licences called Miners' Rights, stake out other people's land, fight and drink—yes, and die in big numbers. The days of gold rushes may seem over, but that's only because nobody's made a big new strike for a while. But that doesn't mean there isn't one to be made. Especially not in Western Australia, where anything in the minerals line can be found at any time. All it takes is one man to walk in, one day, and ask for a big nugget to be weighed and valued. There are plenty of people who've found fair nuggets, even recently; and everybody remembers the Hand of Faith being dug up in Victoria in 1980, and knows about Golden Eagle being found at Larkinville in WA, a bit more than fifty years ago. One lump. Twelve hundred and thirty-five ounces. Worth at least a million dollars today. And plenty more like it under the surface; *everybody* believes that. The problem is *where*? Could gold possibly be on Jane's land? Could Stringer be a new Kalgoorlie?

Certainly it could—any place can if the stuff's there!

The second striking thing in that headline was the name Lassiter.

Lassiter of Lassiter's Reef.

Who's he? I will tell you.

Briefly, Lassiter was a gold prospector, and somewhere round 1910 he came roaring out of Australia's hot, hard centre. He was covered in red dust, and what he roared was that he'd found a great reef of gold. As you'll appreciate, people have made claims like that before, and not been believed. Lassiter was believed. He was believed because, although he was covered in red dust, he was carrying some of the gold he'd found. Just a little. He talked about tons.

But there was a problem, which he freely admitted. When he found the great reef of gold, he was already lost. Then he became ill. When he recovered, alone in the desert, Lassiter wondered at first if the discovery had been just a dream: one of dozens of fantasies produced by his fevers. But it wasn't. And he had the gold to prove it!

He searched again, but he was weak and couldn't find the reef, couldn't remember where he'd been, and had no map and no position to work out on one, even if a detailed map of central Australia had existed.

Lassiter struggled back to the coast and the cities of the East. For years clever people tried hard to unearth the facts which must be in some locked-up corner of his mind. He was examined in a hundred ways, including hypnosis.

Meanwhile hopeful prospectors took up the hunt, tramping in what they fondly imagined to be Lassiter's footsteps. They searched and searched and then searched some more.

Lassiter's Reef was not found.

At last, Lassiter had another go. This time, it wasn't a one-man or a two-man expedition. His new expedition had horses, camels, an aeroplane. None of it helped. The plane crashed, disaster followed disaster. In the end the rest gave up and Lassiter went on alone. He disappeared, never seen again.

Years later bits of paper hidden under stones and in old tobacco tins were found. Lassiter had been captured by one of the Aboriginal tribes then wandering the great deserts of the centre of the continent. They hadn't killed him, but they wouldn't release him either. He was compelled to wander with them, to make their vast hundred-mile-a-day marches from water-hole to water-hole. He lived on their diet. When he could, he wrote on a bit of paper and hid it.

Eventually he died. He was the only man who ever found the reef. People have been trying ever since. They've used all the aids science can offer, even aircraft carrying sophisticated metal-detecting and ore-analysis equipment. All have failed.

So what had 'Jacka' Green found? Was it Lassiter's Reef —or another?

I began to read . . .

Adelaide, Saturday
A year has now gone by since the last human being set eyes on 'Jacka' Green, the gold prospector who claimed five years ago to have found a reef of gold—'small but rich'—deep in the red interior of Australia.

A year has gone since the bold Green, with his pack-train of two camels and two horses, rode westward out of Alice Springs, and headed into the heat and dust and hardship of the fearful Gibson Desert, in pursuit of the gold he glimpsed once and then lost.

He looked back briefly, and waved. Harry Graham,

resident of the Alice, a postal telegraph employee, waved back.

Since then—nothing. Not a word, not a footprint, not a sighting by another traveller. Green has disappeared.

So now the questions rise.

Is he alive? Or has 'Jacka' Green died—of illness, heat, starvation or thirst—out there in the enormous, unforgiving wilderness that lies at Australia's heart?

Is he searching still? 'Jacka' Green once had a dream that came true: he always claimed that he had actually dreamed of the day he made a gold strike. Then he made one—and lost it. He was a man who spent much of his life alone in the wilderness. He knew how to survive—none better. Can it be he survives still, and searches still, for the 'little pocket of gold' which, he used to say, 'would keep a hundred men in comfort for life'?

Is he a prisoner? Years ago, a wandering tribe of Aborigines captured the far more celebrated prospector Lassiter, and held him prisoner till he died. Could the same fate have overtaken 'Jacka' Green?

For there are many parallels between Lassiter and Green. Both were from the east, from Sydney. Both prospected only for gold. Both found it. Both lost it because illness struck them down at the moment of triumph!

And now that Green has been missing for a full, long year, it may perhaps be said that the final, sad parallel exists—that at the last both men gave their lives to the lure of gold.

A year ago, just before he left Adelaide, bound for 'The Alice', Jacka Green was interviewed by the Sunday Mail.

He was very optimistic. 'I remember most of my last outward trip very clearly,' he said, 'and I plan to follow my old route exactly. If I do that, I'm going to find the vital clue somewhere. Maybe the old embers of a fire, maybe an empty tobacco tin I left behind.

'But this time I'm going to find that gold. I've said there's enough to keep a hundred men in comfort for life. When I find it, I'll be the first of that hundred. The other *ninety-nine will be wounded Australian soldiers, who deserve it more than me.'*

Finally, readers may ask themselves what kind of man he was, this 'Jacka' Green, who took on, alone, the dangerous challenge of central Australia—where the climate has killed so many bold adventurers—in the belief he would rediscover the glint of gold he had once glimpsed before?

Physically he was a shortish man: five feet seven, or so. But he was broadly built and very strong.

He was also a man of great strength of will and character. Many people would have been delighted to invest in his final expedition, but all were turned away. Green was determined he would be in nobody's debt, and to that end he gave up beer and tobacco and for two years banked every spare penny he earned as a skilled mechanic in Adelaide's factories. When he felt he had enough, he bought his horses and his camels and his provisions, and he left.

Just a year ago . . .

Don Gay

I was reading it a second time when the phone rang.

'Bob?' asked a voice.

'He's not here.'

'That his son?'

'I'm just a friend. Bob'll be here before long. Any message?'

'Rick Muir. Tell him I've something for him, if he'll call me.'

'Right.'

I hung up and went back to the article, wondering what Mr Gay, its author, would think if he knew Green *had* survived, had lived for another thirty years, in fact—in complete anonymity up in the north of Western Australia. He'd been so certain Green was dead already. Yet, even as he wrote, Green was hopping about, a bridegroom with a new bride and a cattle station to run. A prospector who'd given up prospecting.

If he had.

It was a nice question. Those month-long absences from Stringer Station might have been camping trips undertaken for old times' sake, or perhaps the weight of domesticity pressed uncomfortably upon so free a spirit and must be escaped for a while each year. Might, but I didn't believe it. What I *was* inclined to think was that 'Jacko' had found his gold—and decided to tell no one. Not would-be investors, not wounded soldiers, nor anyone else except his new wife. If his quoted words to the reporter were anything to go by, Jacka Green had valued very highly the notion of living in comfort all his life. He had found a way to do it.

I gave the article to Bob when he returned, and when he'd finished reading it I told him all this. He pursed his lips and tilted his head dismissively.

'What's wrong?'

'Depends on your idea of comfort, doesn't it, mate? Did Stringer Station look like comfort for life?'

'Not to me.'

He yawned. 'People aren't that different. There's one thing strikes me, though. Suppose he found gold somewhere in the desert between the Alice and the Kimberleys—?'

'It has to be near home. He used to go off for a month. Just a month.'

Bob nodded. 'A few days out and a few days there— wherever 'there' was—then a few days back. He went to fetch something, I'll bet. But it was *not* gold, that's for sure.'

'Why not?'

'One camel and maybe a pack mule. Don't make me laugh!'

'Bloke phoned,' I said. 'Number's on your pad.'

He got up and dialled. 'Rick? Bob.' He listened, then said, 'Thanks for trying.' He hung up, came across to me and said, 'Police plane dropped in at Stringer Station. It's deserted. Not even the Abos. So where is she?'

'We've only one lead,' I said.

'The pub where Gunton met Blackie?' I nodded, and he said, 'Gunton's safe till tomorrow. Then he comes up in court.'

'Breaking and entering?'

'They'll ask for a remand. He's well out of the way, down in Mandurah, but'—he grinned ruefully—'bloody lawyers can always get in and out.'

After that I thought a lot; applied my mind, considered the known facts. The machinery we'd brought from Stringer hadn't been examined yet. Bob, by now, was slowly and patiently turning the pages of the Sherman tank's handbook. There was also that damned lettering! Between them they must hold at least an indication of the secret that made Stringer so valuable somebody would kill and/or kidnap for it. In them might lie the clue to Jane's whereabouts. But I could *assume* nothing at all. Green, setting off in search of gold, might have found something else, anything almost, from diamonds to the famous lost dollars in a Dakota aircraft which crashed years ago while carrying soldiers' pay to an American army camp in (I think) Melbourne. Either would have given him the comfort he wanted. Both were light, and portable for a man with only animals to carry his finds.

But gold wasn't! Gold, unless he'd found it in a great chunk like the Golden Eagle nugget, was barely portable at all. Because not only is it heavy, it's usually found as small specks in heavy rock, unless it's alluvial—heavy machinery and chemical processes are needed to get at it.

Machinery. So I tugged the thing we'd brought from Stringer out into the centre of the floor, into the light, so that I could look it over properly. I suppose with its stand it was about three feet high, and the top was some kind of table: a casting, machined flat, and with two or three assorted holes in it, the purpose of which was far from obvious. The table was supported by a rigid steel frame—so firm that the structure could not be rocked at all.

I walked round it, and called Bob over and had him look. Nothing about it suggested a purpose; there was no trade mark to help: no 'J & C Smith, Ironfounders, Sydney NSW' to push us in the right direction.

'Grommet-grinder?' Bob suggested. 'With automatic grimble-tuckling.'

I didn't smile. Jane Strutt had been gone more than twenty-four hours by now. She was tough and unusually resourceful, but she'd be helpless and we *must* get to her!

I turned the thing on its side. A small electric motor, slightly rusty now, was mounted beneath the table. Red and black push switches protruded through the side of the casing. I turned it over, exposing another side. Nothing there. Then the third, and still nothing. Finally the fourth, which would probably have been the back. I took one look there and thought bitterly that the machine would now tell us nothing. Once there must have been a manufacturer's name plate, with four rivets fastening it to the side of the table. The holes for the rivets were there, but the rivets had been drilled out and the maker's plate was gone.

I swore and Bob tutted sympathetically. I turned the machine right over and leaned forward to inspect the base and bumped heads with Bob. We both staggered clutching our skulls, but were all right a minute or so later. Carefully now, still seeing a star or two, I leaned forward again, and said, 'Something just there.'

'Don't see it.'

'It's been filed,' I said. There was some workshop dirt caked on the base, but a faint glint of bare metal showed through it. 'Give me a cloth.'

I wiped it clean—a patch of metal a couple of inches long, and silvery where it had been filed, showing clearly against the applied finish of the rest of the metal.

'Maker's name, for a dollar,' Bob said.

'Yes. But missing.'

'Not necessarily. There's ways and means, starting with the simplest.' He got a sheet of paper and a pencil, laid the paper over the silver area and rubbed with the pencil, like a child tracing a coin. What came up was faint, but it *was* something, and vaguely identifiable.

DIIDIN

The rest had vanished under the file.

'More mysterious bloody letters!' I said savagely.

Bob said, 'Looks like "DUBBIN" to me.'

'No,' I said, looking more closely, 'there are two b's in dubbin. Can't be that.'

'I'll believe you. So it says DUDIN, does it?'

'Yes,' I said. 'No it doesn't! The first and third letters are "B" or "R".'

'Or "P",' Bob said.

'So it's BUBIN, or RURIN, or BURIN, or PURIN or PUBIN or RUBIN . . . Bloody games,' I said. 'What the *hell*!'

Bob said, 'It's six words and one of them's a name.'

'Yes.'

'Let's try the phone book.'

'You think this was made in Perth?'

He said, 'No. But the phone book's a hell of a long list of names.'

'Hang on.'

'What?'

'There's something else on this paper. Look. It's faint. Top right-hand corner!'

The pencil came out again. The paper was rubbed. What had looked like dots turned into the remnant of other smaller marks. The file had torn most of them away, but because the letters were raised from the surface rather than stamped into it, tiny rough edges remained, invisible on the bare metal.

On the paper, exposed to graphite rubbing, they were legible, if not clear. But the second word was BELGE.

The phone book gave us two of the letter combinations: Purin and Rubin. None of the others appeared.

I said, 'It's not final. It could be either because the others aren't names, or there's nobody of that name here.'

'Two hundred thousand names in the book,' Bob said.

'Show me a Brezhnev or a Gorbachev.'

'You win.'

'So there's a manufacturer of precision machinery, named PURIN or RUBIN somewhere in Belgium,' I said. 'Right?'

He nodded.

'Now get the Yellow Pages,' I said, 'and find me the number of the Belgian Consul. He'll have a trade directory.'

'Would Belgium have a consul here?' He was making his fingers march through the yellow paper. 'Yes, there is a consul—honorary, he's got an Australian name—and there's a trade commissioner. Sixteen, The Terrace.'

'Let's have the number?'

The Belgian trade commissioner welcomed my inquiry. He would call me back, his secretary said, at MacDonald, Slaughter. I said I wasn't there and gave Bob's number.

'Fine,' she said, 'and what's the name of this firm you want to know about?' She had a splendid French accent.

'RUBIN or PURIN,' I said. 'It's one or the other. They seem to make precision machinery.'

'I can tell you that,' she said, and laughed, pleased with herself. 'It's RUBIN. They're very old-established. A famous company in their field.'

'What *is* their field?'

'For the polishing and cutting. Rubin have always manufactured the instruments.'

I felt my stomach tighten. Amsterdam and Antwerp, I thought, with so much in common, including plenty of cutting and polishing. I said, 'But what is the material on which the Rubin machines work?'

'Precious stones,' she said.

Now bit by bit, the secrets were coming out. Planted with care by Mary Ellen Emmett/Stringer/Green, who must have been a woman of considerable subtlety because the task she'd set herself had required deviousness, but in delicate balance and not too much of it. She had had to find a way to inform her niece while leaving behind a puzzle no interloper could unravel. Why did she not simply send Jane a letter? Perhaps she'd done that, and by that time, Jane's great-aunt had died, and young Jane was far gone from the home in which she'd grown up. Hard to set about finding one young woman among the sixty million people in Britain—especially when you're old and a full day's hard drive from a letter box and your lawyer's as far from you as London is from Vienna or Madrid. But Mary Ellen would have known that in the future, when there was a substantial estate involved, lawyers would busy themselves and eventually Jane *would* be found. So Jane must be told, and entry to the puzzle thus gained—and in such a way that only Jane would comprehend.

We knew now about Green, the 'Range Man', who'd vanished in the MacDonnel Ranges, and turned up quietly a year later at Stringer Station. Green who was a prospector, and who had found something that required imported Belgian machinery to cut and polish it. Precious stones, yes.

But what kind?

And we had the anagram. The second one: the random letters on embroidered strips: the one, perhaps which would reveal what stone it was that could be found at—or more probably *near*—Stringer Station.

G AD and MA RS

The goad and the Mars bar. I wrote the letters down again: wrote them in a circle, in a U-shape, in an oval, in an odd-shaped rectangle—all in the hope that accidental juxtaposition of some of the letters would trigger a response in my mind.

Nothing did.

I stared at it for a while, growing ever more frustrated, with an increasing certainty that Mary Jane Emmett had been too smart for me.

Just seven letters! One times two, times three, times four, times five, times six, times seven. That's all. Not hard to do that sum in your head. I did it. There are five thousand and forty possible combinations of seven letters. Hours of weary work just writing them out. Pity I hadn't a suitably-programmed computer. Computer, I thought. Then—Don Freeson, I thought. Don had the University's computer to play with, big fat main-frame thing capable, he'd once told me, of doing twenty times the work they could give it.

I was dialling by now. Don was an old mate. A dinghy sailor.

Woman's voice answering. English voice. Don was away in the East, back tomorrow afternoon. I explained my need and hope of help, at which she instantly turned coldly formal and informed me crisply that the computer was not available for outside use or activity except where such activity had been expressly approved . . . etc. etc. In such circumstances I am not usually patient. John Close in normal form would have blistered and blustered and turned the incident into lifelong enmity. This time I was patient. There are dictionaries on computer nowadays, and games may be played, like taking seven letters, regenerating them in every possible combination of themselves, and then comparing those words with the words in the dictionary, and then junking the combinations which didn't properly exist, and listing the ones that did. I knew this because Don Freeson had explained it to me in a pub one night when I'd rather not have had it explained. Computer-crazy people are like that. So are TV people. They simply don't believe it's possible you are not as interested in their work as they are. I once pinned Don Freeson in a corner and glazed his eyes with thirty minutes on the law of tort just to demonstrate that these things ought to cut both ways, but people like that are deaf.

I said, 'When he arrives tomorrow, will you please give him a message?'

'Naturally.'

'Tell him I have an important anagram to unravel. Please make a note of these letters—g-a-d-m-a-r-s. I want to know what seven-letter words can be made from them.'

She said, 'The machine's not there to solve crossword puzzles, Mr Close!'

'Tell Mr Freeson that I am perfectly happy to pay whatever charges are involved.'

'How do we know you—?'

'Because he and I are lifelong friends,' I said, 'and have a high degree of mutual trust. And if (a) he doesn't get the message, and (b) isn't told how important it is to me, you can expect me at your door with bunched fists and an immigration officer. Right?'

'Very well.'

'What's all that about?' Bob asked.

'One of those women!'

'What women?'

I raised my hands, warding him off. 'Just—'

'You mean English women?' he asked, grinning. 'You've just been given a quick squirt of old-fashioned English snoot, have you? Mate, that's why I emigrated all those years back. Did you win?'

'Remains to be seen.'

'Good idea, though, using a computer.'

I picked up the phone and dialled the office and asked for Marye. Two female voices later, I got her.

'Marye. Hope a call just now isn't inopportune?'

'No,' she said. 'I was just going to call you, as a matter of fact. I just *had* to be sure you've found that English lady you lost so carelessly. I must say she's very attractive and I can quite see why you've been distracted . . .'

'I haven't found her,' I said. 'She's—'

'Haven't found her? Not at *all*?'

'No, Marye, not at all.'

She said, 'But that's just silly.'

'It's worse than that!'

'She can't have just vanished!'

'Seems she has.'

'Anything I can do?'

'You can try to remember what she said before she went off to the taxi.'

'But I *told* you. I mean—there was nothing the least strange.'

'Please, Marye. Go over it again.'

'Well—all right. Let me see. When she saw the taxi, she just said, "You'll have to excuse me." And then she trotted down the grass bank and got in the taxi. That's all there was. It seems unbelievable that . . . John, have you no idea where she could be?'

'None.'

'You've called in some help, have you—detectives, the police?'

How could I say 'no'?—that what I had was a retired copper who was some kind of relative-in-law.

'Yes, but it's no help. This is a big state. She could be anywhere.'

'Poor John. And poor girl! Jane, isn't it?'

'Yes.'

She said, 'Good luck. And if there's anything I can do . . . Oh, John, where can I reach you? I tried your flat earlier, but no reply.'

'I'm with a friend at the moment.' I gave her Bob's number, and rang off.

By now we were well into evening. The light outside had disappeared. Like Jane, I thought, who'd disappeared somewhere over the rim into Western Australia's giant emptiness: into spaces so vast that to attempt a hunt without knowing where to start would be the purest foolishness —like searching the haystack for the needle without the faintest idea on which side of the stack the needle was lost.

Yet it *was* here, that information! It had to be. The one-third of a continent that is Western Australia has a single city at its heart: Perth. The city has the courts, the registries, the government, the men, the corporations, the tycoons, and five out of every six of the population. If Stringer Station were to change hands, it was here the formalities would take place. If somebody were to apply for a Miner's Right and stake out a claim for gold, diamonds, uranium, bauxite or anything else, then *here* is where it would be registered.

Perth held the secret—I was in no doubt whatever of that. Going to the window, I stared out across the water to the tall fingers of the city towers rising in lights into the night sky. Perhaps it lay in one of those thousands of offices. Possibly, I suddenly thought, even my own office contained something important, some fact I hadn't considered sufficiently; some kind of forgotten record of Stringer Station . . .

'I'm going to the office,' I told Bob.

Perth at night, especially in the business district, along The Terrace, can be strangely peaceful. And easy: the air's balmy, the streets quiet, you can park a car and get out and smell that combination of water and flowers that is Perth's special contribution to this world's pleasures. I walked away from the blue Commodore, used my three keys in turn: on the main door, the reception/fire door and my office door, and switched on the light. The usual chaos greeted me: bundles of papers lay all over the place: my in-tray and out-tray, the one filled to overflowing, the other empty. Where to *start*?

With Stringer Station, where else? But the file wasn't there! Brief panic until I thought about the Registry. I had a key for that, too, and found the file without difficulty. All the papers were there. There was nothing I hadn't noticed earlier.

But still, there *could* be, I reasoned, because earlier I had really only glanced at them: I'd read the important bits, then shoved the papers back into the file. This time I would read everything. *Everything*. And carefully. I settled in my chair, rested my feet on the opened bottom drawer and began to concentrate.

Concentrate! I read a few words and saw Jane's face, as though the sheets of paper were so many photographs. Look up at the window and I'd see her reflected in the glass. I read every word in the file, but took in about ten per cent. I told myself her life could well depend on what I was doing. Despairing thoughts came, that she might already be dead. But she wasn't—deep inside me, I knew it. She was alive not for what she knew, but for what she *might* know. Her captors, whoever they were, couldn't know about the pub in faraway Thornton. Only two people could discern that difference, and one was dead. Jane *must* be alive! But where . . .?

I forced my attention back to the Stringer Station file, and read through it again, start to finish, and found . . . well, nothing that helped, until, at the end, routinely, I checked the dates of the documents on the little registry tag at the front of the file. First entry, 1922 etc., etc.—the year that Mary Ellen had gone to live at the station. I blinked. Stringer had won it in a game of two-up, so his title was legal and absolute.

But—somebody must have owned it before! The man who'd lost it to Stringer—*he'd* owned it. Sixty-odd years is more than twice as long as I have been alive, but it's not long in the history of a place like that. So what was his name—this man who'd owned Stringer Station and been damn fool enough to lose the whole thing betting on the fall of a couple of pennies? I looked at margins for pencilled notes, turned the sheets of paper over and examined the back of each. It had to be here—this was the Stringer Station file! And then the penny dropped. I looked again at the Registry tag, turned it over, and saw: 'See also: Emmett M. E. and Dickson, David.'

I didn't bother with Emmett, M.E.—Mary Ellen's file was incorporated with the Stringer papers already. But Dickson, David, was the previous owner. And the son of the owner before that. Dickson, David, was the poor devil with the two cold coins who'd lost the inheritance one night. And no doubt was cursed forever afterwards.

What did that tell me? Not a hell of a lot.

By now I was close to going bananas. I was picking at this bloody great Gordian knot, and unravelling a bit here and a bit there, without ever giving it the ultimate hack bold Alexander gave the original.

Dickson, David, aged 29 of Dickson Station. His signature.

Dickson Station, it had been in those days. For fifty years, until the coins fell badly, and thereafter Stringer Station. Not changed to Green in honour of the new husband. Nor had Dickson, David, spirited Jane away. He'd have been a hundred years old, and anyway a note in the file said he'd died in 1925.

I went back to Bob Collis's place in South Perth, with the beautiful city looking empty and lovely as my car drifted over the Narrows bridge. I felt the prickle of tears in my eyes at the thought of Jane held prisoner, and clipped the radio on to break the mood because I wanted to be able to see to drive. One of these foul Mid-Pacific voices was riding the discs, Australian-American, and announcing in a dreadful, patronizing treacly tone that here was one for those whose memories went way, way, way, way, way, way back: for you, grandpa, and you grandma, the late Count John McCormack would sing, 'When Irish Eyes are Smiling'.

I never actually heard the song—it would have made moisture run through my tear ducts like the falls at Niagara; so I punched the button and found some cheerfully irritating advertising. In my head, though, McCormack warbled on, so I arrived at Bob's place with Jane's face there in the windscreen before me, and a terrible, helpless sadness going for the heart of me. Above was the infinity of Heaven, horizon to horizon, and somewhere beneath it was Jane.

Where? How *could* I find out?

Where?

14

The phone began ringing early next morning: not the way it was to ring later, but its noise certainly started off the day. I heard Bob answer, and natter, and grunt, and then say, 'Thanks.' Thirty seconds later he'd come into my room, booted and spurred, to say, 'Gunton is the last man on the charge sheet. Any luck, that'll be late afternoon.' He was half smiling, looking satisfied.

'Why's it important?'

He looked at me. 'Gunton meets his boss, this fellow Blackie, at six, yes?'

'Yair.'

'Well, maybe Blackie won't be there. But I don't think so.'

'He'll have been told. Gunton must have been on the phone to somebody.'

'Again, I don't think so. I have friends at Mandurah and they say no to that.'

'He'll have a lawyer. Court will appoint one.'

'Not till he appears—late afternoon. Then a remand in custody. But I don't want a story in the afternoon paper for Blackie to see, or a TV news story, or a radio story. I want Blackie there at six, black, hairy and pig-bloody-ignorant!'

'Yair,' I said. I felt dreadful. My mind was full of bits of this and bits of that and they refused to make a pattern of themselves. Jane had now been gone nearly forty-eight hours and I'd done *nothing* to help her—not one single damn thing! Nor did I now know where to look—even for a hint of the direction to take. I spent a miserable hour not eating any breakfast, failing to finish a cup of coffee . . . that kind of thing.

Phone rang for the second time at 8.30 a.m. The dim-but-beautiful Sharleene wanted to know if Bob knew where I was.

'He's here.' Bob's big paw covered the mouthpiece. 'Young lady for you.'

'How the hell did *you* know this number?' I demanded. Not much point in taking shelter at Bob's for safety's sake. If Sharleene knew, all Perth knew.

'Oh now, Mr Close, y'know I used to go about with Jim Collis, so I know all about you and Mr Collis being friends.'

'Right,' I said.

'It was just a shot in the dark.'

'Yair. Okay. What is it?'

'Well, I have a bloke here. He's—' her voice dropped to a whisper—'an Abo?'

'Go on.'

'Says his name is Billy One-Hat and you know him. Do you know Billy One-Hat, Mr Close?'

'Yes, Sharleene, and before you do anything else at all, I want you to take Mr One-Hat and put him in a taxi to this address.' I gave it to her.

'I'll do it right now.'

'Good girl.'

She said, 'Always.'

'Always what?'

'Good,' said Sharleene. 'And don't you dare listen to anybody says otherwise.'

He was with us twenty minutes later, a big, very black, dusty man, who'd looked absolutely at home when he was on Stringer Station, and here looked awkward and unhappy, standing in Bob's porch with his one-hat in his hand.

I brought him in and introduced the pair of them, and wondered, because there are many Australians, and Bob could well be one, who despise the Abos. There's nothing particularly rational about it. The Australian black man used to have a culture that might have been simple, but was so old it made babies of the cultures of China, Ancient Egypt or the Greeks. The forty thousand years of it was wiped out in two centuries. Their land was stolen, their holy places destroyed without thought, let alone compunction, and many Abos have done what the Indians did in North America—taken to the city, and to the bottle. There they live on welfare; they get their money and drink. Not the full-bloods like Billy, who still have tribal loyalties, but the full-bloods stay in the north, out of the cities and away from the bottle. So it's the drunks that Perth's policemen see, and tend to treat with weary contempt, because they see too much.

Bob Collis showed none of that. He put out his hand and drew Billy into the room. 'You look like a man who could do with refreshment,' he said. 'Too early for a beer?'

Billy shook his head. 'Water.'

'Not tea or coffee?'

'Water, please.'

That was no problem.

I asked, 'What brings you?'

'Men come back,' Billy said.

'Which ones?'

He shrugged. 'Same men. Four.'

'What did they do?'

'Tell me go.'

'Why—did they say?'

Billy shook his head. 'Say I get off Stringer quick. Same day, now! Or they beat me, beat my *lubra*, my kids.'

'They didn't give a reason?'

He made a shooing gesture with both hands. 'Say Toyota mine. Take and go.'

'What did you say?'

'I have job, am foreman. Missis Strutt tell me.'

'That's right.'

'They hit me, boss. Tell me go. They have guns. I go. Take family to Kununurra. Come here see Missis.'

'Where's your family?'

'We got friends,' Billy said, simply. 'Be okay.'

'How did you get here—in the Land-Cruiser?'

He shook his head. 'Hitch.'

'How long did that take?'

'Three day.'

Billy and his family would only just have gone when the police plane dropped in and found Stringer Station deserted.

'Billy, did you recognize anybody?'

'No, boss.'

'Pity.'

'But see things.'

'What things?'

'Boots. One man wear tight boots. Make cigarette. Him boss.'

'Black hair?'

He nodded.

'Jeans?'

Another nod.

Back to Blackie, I thought. And Blackie certainly got about.

I said, 'You haven't seen Miss Strutt?'

'No, boss.'

Bob said, 'Are you thinking they've taken Jane up there?'

'Not impossible, is it, if they've driven Billy off the Station?'

'Maybe I could fix for the police plane to drop in again,' he said.

'They'll have thought of that,' I said, and turned to Billy. 'What else did they say to you? I mean, when you said Miss Strutt had made you foreman, what did they say to you?'

'Me not foreman, him say. An' soon Missis her not have Stringer.'

'Soon? You're sure he said soon?'

Billy nodded. 'Soon her not have Station.'

'Did he say why not?'

Billy's head shook.

I said, 'They've got her, Billy. They've got Miss Strutt. They grabbed her and took her away. We're trying to find out where she's been taken. But I think she'd want me to promise you your job is safe. Okay?'

He said, 'Missis Strutt okay, boss. Billy help find. Billy good tracker.'

Pity, I thought, that city streets didn't show individual tracks. If they did, Billy could probably walk straight to her. 'I'll remember that,' I said. 'But one other thing—did they come to Stringer by plane?'

'Yes, boss.'

'Any markings on it?'

He shook his head. No markings.

No way of knowing, of course, how long the day's list would take to hear. Drunks pleading guilty use up a minute or two of the magistrate's life.

But drunks don't always plead guilty; sometimes they have a lot to lose and so produce elaborate defences and impressive professional witnesses and the case takes half an hour. I once watched as a judge faced with a long list of guilty pleas handed out nearly five hundred years' imprisonment before he rose for lunch. Court hearings are unpredictable. We wanted Gunton on remand and in custody, and the advantage of a Gunton listed last on the court sheet was that the reporters might have gone home. The present charge was illegal entry, not burglary. Everything could be nice and quiet. What we didn't want was Bob Collis on his feet as a witness, explaining the knots and tricks of his patent protection-by-net system, because that would have the media blokes salivating, and Blackie would swiftly learn there was no prospect of a rendezvous with Gunton.

But I couldn't face the prospect of a day in court, waiting, endlessly and pointlessly, while Jane, whom I could neither find nor help, suffered yet another day in captivity.

So Bob went alone, and I woke the snoring Billy One-Hat, grilled his breakfast steak, and then sat down to grill him. Billy had been at Stringer most of his life. He must know just about everything that had happened there over the years, so surely he must be able to help pinpoint the predator.

It didn't work like that. Prolonged questioning elicited

only the fact that Billy did as he was told—by The Boss (Jacka Green until Jacka died), and after that by Mary Ellen. He needed orders. When the Station was running properly, a decade and a half ago, Billy One-Hat hired the itinerant jackaroos every season and attended to mustering, branding, fencing and other work, but always under orders. Not that those orders had ever been particularly burdensome; the reverse, in fact, as the years passed.

After Jacka died, things got looser. Mary Ellen was old by then, and didn't care much; so inevitably the place ran down. According to Billy, she stayed indoors most of the time, and spent her days with books and memories or her needlework.

That was how I'd imagined things: Mary Ellen, by now as inured to solitude as anybody could ever be, content with her lot, self-sufficient and self-contained—until she realized that her great niece must somehow be told. Which led to the embroidery instead of letters, and a message kept cunningly inside the station house, instead of a message despatched to England.

'Billy, did she ever write letters?'

'She did, boss.'

'Who posted them?'

'Billy take 'em.'

'Who did she write to?'

He thought about that for a while, then he said, 'No look.'

'You could read her writing, though?'

Billy said with a hint of pride that Mary Ellen made long lists of things: food, fuel, etc. for him to fetch. He could read good.

'Did you bring letters back from Kununurra?'

'Yes, boss. One, two in a year.'

'That's all?'

He said it was. I found the fact hard to imagine: most of us get junk mail alone at a hundred times that rate. But maybe she'd been alone too long to figure on the lists; had no credit cards, store accounts. No—*but* she had bank accounts, and there's nobody faster at selling *your* name for *their* profit than the bloody banks!

'Do you know who wrote to her?'

He hadn't noticed. Except . . . Billy frowned and looked round the room, sought my permission with a glance, and when I nodded, took a biro and then a white envelope from Bob's waste-paper basket and drew markings round the edges.

'Airmail?' He shrugged, unfamiliar with the words, but it was. So she'd received an airmail letter, more or less annually. Yorkshire Bank, no doubt.

Impatient and anxious, I started on Jacka Green and *his* trips, which were also more or less annual. The trips, Billy told me, as he'd told me before, would last about a month, moon-to-moon, which was a statement of accuracy rather than approximation: over the long-term, the moon's a better time-keeper than your wristwatch or mine.

'When he came back, Billy, what did he carry?'

Billy One-Hat shook his head. Jacka Green came back on his camel, leading the pack-horse which bore his supplies. Nothing heavy, no.

'What was he like when he came?' I asked. 'Was he tired, was he happy—what?'

'Happy come home.'

'Did he bring anything—gifts for his wife?'

'Give her something.'

'Always?'

'Small bag of leather.'

'What was in it?'

He shrugged.

'Do you know where he'd been?'

'No, boss.'

'Could you find out, now?'

He frowned. 'How, boss?'

'Find an old trail. Could you still find the track?'

Billy One-Hat looked at me, his broad, black face set in a speculative sort of look. After a moment, the head wagged and there was sudden humour in his eyes.

'Could you, Billy?'

'Mister Green, him like curry beans. Maybe a track there still.'

I didn't ask further. Trackers are entitled to their secrets. I expect tin cans last longer in the desert than dung. But I could be wrong.

There were interruptions. Bob Collis phoned from Mandurah to say he doubted whether Gunton would come up before mid-afternoon at the earliest; Marye called to ask if there was any news. Sharleene called to say Bunbury would be back from his travels sometime next week and had recorded his interest in the outcome of the Stringer Station affair— by which he meant not Jane's disappearance, which happened long after Bunbury left, but the proposed sale of good Aussie land, and the export of the unwanted Pom.

And *still* I was helpless. Impatient as hell, desperate to go after Jane, ready to take on anybody in her defence, I could do nothing at all! There was one slender hope, no more, and for that I must be—of all things—patient. Tonight, if I was lucky, the man known as Blackie would be in the pub at six. If he was, and if he was skilfully followed, he might give a lead. On the other hand, he might not be there—and wouldn't be, of course, if he'd learned of Gunton's arrest.

The day dragged by. Billy lay stretched out on Bob Collis's rug, his one-hat over his eyes, and slept. I paced up and down, made cups of coffee I forgot to drink, and went endlessly over the known facts. The hours crept past, the minutes were lead weights, the seconds eternity. Mid-afternoon I called Freeson at the University, only to learn he hadn't come in on the early flight because he'd been detained in Sydney. He was now expected to be on the six o'clock ex-Sydney, in Perth at 9.00 p.m. That bloody Pommie woman, as she told me the gory details, obviously sensed they hurt. She said every word with a sadistic slowness, made me ask every question twice or more, and didn't attempt to keep the pleasure out of her voice. I swore, as I hung up, that if I ever succeeded in releasing Jane, I'd celebrate by getting her fellow-Brit sacked and deported.

If!

The if moved a shade nearer at four-forty, when Bob Collis phoned with a grin in his voice, to say Gunton had that moment been remanded in custody, and furthermore in a court empty of reporters. Bob was now on his way, would find himself a parking space in Hay Street upon arrival in Perth, and would rendezvous with me inside the Criterion Hotel. There he would give me a very small nod, and I would return the signal. Right?

Right, mate!

15

He must have driven like Stewart used to. At six o'clock Bob appeared behind the pub bar with a big, white apron wound round his belly. I sat as deep in the recesses as I could get. The place was busy already: people pouring out of shops and offices and pausing for a pair of schooners or a chop at the old chilled Chablis on the way home. I sat sipping Bondie's brew and reading the afternoon *News*, watching for Blackie. Black hair, but balding, moustache, high fawn boots. Washed out jeans and denim bomber jacket. Rolled his own cigarettes. Here, at six, with luck. You hear a description like that, and you think it's all very general, fits one man in every two. In some places it would: there are lots like that in the unchanging country towns, or in real workmen's bars. But not here. In this place at this hour people were dressed for offices and stores, turned out smartly. The men wore shirts and ties and the women well-pressed cotton. A few denim-clad kids were there, yes; but a balding man of forty in calf-length boots wouldn't be exactly inconspicuous.

I didn't feel inconspicuous either. The wearing of sunglasses indoors always looks stupidly affected to me, but I was wearing 'em, in case Blackie was one of the blokes who'd driven us into the desert. If he was, he'd recognize me, which wasn't the plan at all. Outside, parked in Hay Street, was Bob's blue Commodore. That *was* inconspicuous, so was its 4.2 litre engine. Even the radio phone was out of sight.

I was reading my paper according to orders. 'What you do,' (Bob's instructions) 'is you actually *read* it. Don't pretend. Read. But get your head and body positioned so that when you look up—and you look up moving only your eyes —you can sweep the room with a single glance. You do that every twenty seconds.' I glanced at my watch, looked up for perhaps the twentieth time, and found Bob looking back at me, and giving an almost imperceptible sideways nod of the head. A moment later I glanced along the room.

Blackie stood with his back to the wall. He looked as advertised, complete with denims, moustache, thinning black hair: I couldn't see his feet. As I watched, he fished in his pocket, took out a packet of RYO tobacco and started making. When the cigarette was lit, he glanced towards the door, levered himself off the wall, went to the bar, and bought a little one, the egg-cup of beer that Brits are always amazed to see in Australia. He swallowed it in one, bought another, and took it back to his position by the wall. From there he could see most of the room and keep watch on the door. So could I. For ten minutes, then, he stood quite still. I watched him watching the door. Then Blackie went for another beer and Bob signalled to me that he'd be in the car, and nipped out the staff way.

Blackie hung on. He had one more beer and two more cigarettes; he looked at his watch every couple of minutes; he was expressionless, but impatient. At 6.40 p.m., he shoved himself away from the wall, glanced once more at his watch, and made for the door marked 'Men'. I went out and waited in the street, and in a couple of minutes out he came, waving for a taxi. While he was still inside, I had slipped into the passenger seat of Bob's car. The four and a bit litres were silently busy under the bonnet.

Plenty of taxis at that time: after the rush-hour and before the theatre/restaurant/pub crowds; our man didn't have long to wait. Nor did he show signs of nerves. Blackie stood boldly on the side of maybe the busiest street in Perth, waving vigorously until a cruising cab pulled over.

'He's not afraid of being recognized,' I said.

'So he's not "wanted",' said Bob. 'Means he's clean, at least recently. Rough-looking bugger, isn't he?'

He was. Big, black and undoubtedly rough-looking. Heavy dark stubble with nothing of the designer look about it; powerful shoulders and arms. 'Looks like that villain in the Popeye cartoons,' Bob said. 'And I haven't even eaten my spinach.'

The white car in front pulled away, and at first did nothing very remarkable, simply going with the one-way traffic right down Barrack Street; left along Wellington, left again into William, following through to Riverside then under the freeway along Mounts Bay Road.

'Fremantle,' Bob murmured beside me. 'Looks it, doesn't he, eh? Aussie docker Ocker—good specimen, suitable for bottling and preserving . . . straight down the Stirling he'll go . . . Hell's delight!'

The exclamation came because the docker's taxi, far from continuing towards Fremantle's Victorian charms and busy docks, had swung left into Hackett Drive and was running decorously into Nedlands and Dalkeith. Millionaire country. There are houses thereabouts at five or six million, a price range which wouldn't, one imagined, be Blackie's. The streets were empty now as dusk deepened.

'I'll take a risk,' Bob said, 'or he'll see my lights.' He swung right for one block, then left for another, gunning the four litres; he was waiting at the crossroads as the taxi went over on its right of way.

We followed, then for no more than a kilometre before the taxi stopped. Bob drove on by, turned in a darkened drive, watched till the cab pulled away.

He'd had the driver's mirror; I'd been trying to watch with the little mirror they put on the visor so women can see their lipstick; it doesn't really work for anything else.

I hopped out. 'I'll have a look. Come when I signal,' I said and began to work my way back along the road. This was an area of sizeable homes—not the millionaire mansions a couple of rows forward, on the Avenue or the Parade, but the houses had land around them, with screens of well-grown trees and shrubs. The cab had turned, I discovered into the drive of Number 26. A wide, dark gateway gaped and what light there was showed a drive of fine pink shale curving off through high shrubs to the pale bulk of the house forty yards or so away.

I looked at it doubtfully. Blackie was in there, and my chances of dealing with Blackie, if I had to, weren't great. Worse, Blackie probably wasn't alone. But if he wasn't, he'd be with others and they'd talk, and I might hear—something about Jane, maybe. I knotted my desperation round me and put my foot on the gravel, which gave a rattle loud enough to carry across the water! I dodged at once into the shrubbery and began to thread my way through it towards the house, wondering whose it might be, because it was worth quarter of a million at least, and maybe twice that, of somebody's money. Good view over the river, and the price would be higher.

No way of knowing, of course; not now. But I was at 26 Something Street, and everything could be investigated later. Meanwhile I moved closer. In front of me the drive forked as it neared the house, the left prong leading to a turning circle, the right to a very big garage. Light from an open door on the side I faced, showed a dark panel van, its rear doors opened, backed into position across the pink shale, and I heard voices, faintly at first, from inside the house, then coming closer. Seconds later footsteps came out, and people began climbing into the panel van. Three, I thought, plus a couple of bags and something on wheels that was lifted aboard.

A variety of sounds followed. A door was locked with a key. The rear doors of the van were slammed, the starter whirred. Meanwhile the vanished light from the house was replaced by the glow of the van's light. The engine was running and the van pulled forward.

I memorized the number plate as it went by; then it halted at the gateway. There the driver got out, and opened the rear doors. And to my horror, Bob came walking into the drive, with his hands in the air and the man Blackie behind him. He climbed into the van. Once more the doors were closed and locked. And now the van moved into the roadway.

I raced to the gate. Bob's Commodore stood just outside. He must have been surprised while he waited for me, and compelled to drive the car to number 26. As the van turned out of sight I jumped in. The keys still hung in the ignition. I started up and gunned the engine . . .

Some things you know instinctively. The van could have been making for anywhere, and when I pulled Bob's trick, I could have lost it. I've shuddered ever since at that thought. But it was bound for Stirling Highway and I knew it and I was right. Dark vans are anonymous as to colour, but not as to height, and trailing it on the highway wasn't hard, even though I hung well back as the van ran past the towering blackness of the park, then swung north. He was going on to the freeway approach, I guessed, and he did and went southwards then, along the Mitchell.

Traffic was thicker here, and I moved closer as the road crossed Canning River. Three or four miles later there's a T-junction at South Street. Turn right if you're making for the coast road south; left if you live in Leeming or . . . My God! I thought—left *also* if you're bound for Jandakot Airport.

They turned left.

So did I. Pulled in until their tail-lights vanished down the next right turn. And followed.

The road bends, but red lights stay in view a long time at night in flat country. Two more turns and that van was running down the approach road.

When I got there I parked and ran close.

There's a fence of course. In Western Australia you fence in your airports to keep kangaroos out, otherwise you're liable to come face to face with a big bull on your take-off with fatal results all round. But it's a mesh fence—you can see through it, and I had no trouble seeing the van standing a few hundred yards off in the shadow of a hangar, in one of the parking areas, beside a twin-engined plane.

There wasn't much going on at Jandakot at that hour. It's not a place where big jets drop in every minute or two; that's all at Perth Airport proper, way inland between the Swan River and the hills. Jandakot's for private and company flying. Lots of little Cessnas and Pipers and the occasional ancient DC-3, one of which, in company livery stood almost between me and the two-motor plane. But I could see, and what I saw in the next couple of minutes was four men climbing in. One of them was Bob, hands behind his back. Another pushed a cargo trolley of some kind. As I watched, one motor started, and after a moment the other, and one of the men lifted something from the trolley and climbed the three steps to the fuselage door, holding it across . . .

Christ!—it *wasn't* a trolley—the man had moved into the light and it was a wheelchair with a shade-hood up, and he was *carrying* somebody aboard!

I tore back to the car, started the engine, and hunted for Bob's hand gun. It wasn't there. What I'd intended was to halt the Commodore where it would prevent the plane taxiing and then . . .

But no gun.

Also too late. The plane was moving. I took note of what came after the V in its registration letters and watched it go roaring off into the evening sky with Bob aboard, and very likely Jane—for who else would be in a wheelchair and shoved into the same plane as Bob? Only Jane. Jane drugged? Or Jane hurt!

But now there were things I *could* do: also things to find out first. The Air Registration Board didn't have a duty officer, but I got a name from the bloke in the tower at Jandakot, and he knew all the planes that had ever flown into and out of the place, and to him EQQ was no kind of challenge.

'Twin Beech,' said the telephone earpiece. 'On charter to Tiptop Mining. Based in the East—Wollongong, NSW, I *think*. Okay?'

'More than okay, and thanks!' Next—but I hadn't the coins, and anyway there was business more important than phoning Don Freeson. I jumped into the Commodore and made for the city. Certainly I should have phoned the police,

I know that; but the rule still applied: you can hide any given number of Beech Twins in Western Australia's deserts. You're helpless and the police are helpless *unless* you know, or they know, where it's going. And I didn't.

Number 26 was still in darkness. Already, though, I knew something else: the street sign said Toller Road. Now . . .

Now I was back in the shrubbery, edging quietly towards the front of the house. The night was cool and still, the trees motionless above my head; windows on the white stucco front of the house were steel-like in the moonlight. Somewhere, on an adjacent block of land, a car door slammed; on another, a dog barked back. I felt alone and ineffectual.

Nervously, yard by yard, I circled the house. There was no sign of anybody inside, no movement, light, sound— nothing. I steeled myself and, suddenly driven, crossed the path to a french window and stared inside. Mess. Old newspapers chucked on the floor; dirty cups and plates, full ashtrays. Furniture, ancient and decaying.

I kept moving. No pilot lights in the kitchen. Show me a modern kitchen without them. But this wasn't modern—it was old, out-of-date.

The whole house was like that. As I moved round it I had an impression similar to the one Stringer Station gave me: this place had been lived in a long time by old people. Doors and windows all had locks and latches, old but strong, and all fastened.

Not until I finally stole into the garage did I find an unlocked door. It opened on to the top of a flight of stairs that led downwards. There was an old bakelite light switch. I took several deep breaths before I could force myself through that door, close it behind me, put on the light and set off down the stairs . . .

The cellar was dry, and soundproof because it had been excavated when the house was built, and the walls were mainly rock. One side had been walled off with heavy jarrah hardwood planks, and a great jarrah door with bolts in it, like something from a medieval castle. Inside: racks for wine bottle storage, floor to ceiling, space for thousands. Plus an inflatable mattress, blanket, chemical closet. She'd been kept here, I was sure of it. Outside were a table with a few magazines on it, a couple of chairs, and an empty bottle or two.

I went through the whole house after that because there was access upstairs from the cellar. It was all the same: unlovely rooms, full of the litter of a bunch of careless men. I searched every room, and found nothing to help me. Not, that is, until I looked out of an upstairs side window and saw the narrow little path that snaked off towards a high brick wall at the southern boundary of the garden. Once outdoors, I followed that path. It ended in a wrought-iron gate set into a brick arch. The gate was locked, the shrubbery on the other side too thick and close to show much.

Yet I had an odd feeling of familiarity with it. Some smell, perhaps. But I realized then I no longer felt afraid. A place as deserted as that seemed to offer no threat.

Advantage lies, as a rule, with the law. And soon I was in my office, with the name of MacDonald, Slaughter to use, and its resources available: in many ways the premises of a successful law firm provides a data base IBM could only envy. I was there roughly an hour. Solicitors who work the courts always know a few cops, and Peter Knowles was among mine. He accessed his computer and told me a few seconds later that the van was, like the Piper Twin, registered in the name of Tip-Top Mining, of Wollongong, NSW. Thanks, Pete.

Do lawyers know stockbrokers? They do. They know good ones if they've any sense. My mate's name is Jim Lindsay. He works a million floors up in the AMP building, and doesn't leave his desk while there's a stock market open anywhere on earth. He's very rich and very weary, and when I called, there he was.

'What,' I asked, 'do you know about Tip-Top Mining?'

'Tip-Top,' he repeated tiredly. 'Lemme see—Tip-Top.

Yah, eastern outfit. Sydney base. Capitalized at two-fifty dollars.' Two-fifty? 'Founded two years ago.'

'Directors?'

'J. Smith, it says here and A. Jones. Secretary, T. Brown. They're not exactly Rio Tinto or Poseidon. You have a tip, eh?'

I said I owed him a drink, then went to the map bay in Registry, and got out the survey sheets. Stringer's not the only property that has changed hands under the benign gaze of McD & S: the firm has conveyed half of Perth, in its time; so attempts are made to keep the maps up-to-date.

Twenty-six Toller Road occupied a block of two point seven acres (the changeover to decimals is still incomplete) and to the names of Mr & Mrs Alfred Grey, the owners, had been added the short-form, 'd'csd'. They were dead. Date three months earlier. The property had, however, been leased. To?

To Tip-Top Mining.

Interesting, mysterious, and probably impenetrable.

I sat holding my head, thinking about Jane Strutt, about Bob, about bloody helplessness, and wimps like me who put people into extreme danger and could do nothing to help them, *ever*, because wherever the wimp turned he ran full-tilt into bloody brick walls and fell on his arse.

In my mind I saw them—the brick walls. One had an arch, with a gate in it. Why were two blocks of land, two houses connected like that?

More maps. Whose property was it that the path led to?

Maps tell all. I had a name. More than one: in fact, names went rattling round in my skull like so many coloured balls in a bingo game.

I had it now: the whole thing. All of it.

Except . . .

One last phone call.

Mr Freeson was at home. Mr Freeson had pumped the letters into a computer somewhere in the innards of America, where Webster's Dictionary was part of the available programming. And out had come a word which seemed remarkably unlikely.

SMARAGD.

'Smaragd?' I said.

'Don't know what it means, eh?' said Freeson scornfully.

'No.'

'So look it up.'

I did. We have The Shorter Oxford English Dictionary, at MacDonald, Slaughter, and 'smaragd' appeared in Vol II.

So now I knew. Smaragd was what all this was about.

I knew. And I knew how I knew. But how did the *other* side know?

SMARAGD . . .

16

Three days now. I prayed she was safe. I felt sick. And felt in my bones she was. Jane had no idea *what* she knew, and that fact should keep her safe—so I told myself as I drove north towards Gnangara, where Billy One-Hat had gone to ground among the families of Abos round the Abo Cultural Complex. Jane, I reasoned, was like everybody else: head full of facts. One or two of those facts were of great importance to somebody else. Her knowledge that the name of the pub was not Range Men but Green Man, was the example. She knew the name had been changed: she'd taken one look and said, 'That's funny!'

There'd be other things, too. Jane Strutt's great-aunt, lonely in old age, suspicious of others, had hidden the secret behind a barrier of what golfers call 'local knowledge', though in this instance it was more than simply that. Everything was there, somewhere, for whoever could find it. But without the knowledge of, say, smaragd, you were lost.

So now there was one other vital thing remaining: the location of smaragd. I didn't know it. The enemy didn't. But Jane *must* know—or be able to interpret something—or the whole of Mary Ellen Green's scheme was without point. Which it wasn't, because sooner or later, in the old house at Stringer Station, Jane Strutt would come across something and say to herself, 'That's funny', and she would then be possessor of a fact that Mary Ellen had been determined nobody else should have.

Complicated, but true.

They had to keep her alive—because if they didn't the secret would be gone forever. Oh, they might wring the word Thornton out of Jane, and could even bring to Australia a native of the place, somebody old and encyclopaedic in the range of his/her knowledge. It wouldn't help them at all —I'd bet on that. Because the final clue would lie somewhere in the relationship between the sisters, and Jane, and the place; in a bit of family history, or gossip, which only Jane, of the six billion people on the face of this planet, would recognize.

A clever old woman had built a wall with knowledge, in case the worst happened. Now the worst *had* happened, and the wall still held.

I believed so. I hoped so!

Billy One-Hat had a half-consumed stubbie in his hand and the patience of the ages in his face. I said, 'Grab your things, Billy. We're going back to Stringer.'

He gave me a long look, nodded once, disappeared, reappeared thirty seconds later with a plastic carrier bag, and climbed into the Commodore. 'Okay, boss.'

I spun the car round and turned south. 'It could be dangerous,' I said.

He turned his big head to look at me. 'But good we do this?'

'Yes. If we can.'

After that it was silence. Billy One-Hat stared ahead, watching the road come at him. I kept my foot down, straight down the Wanneroo Road, on to the Freeway, off at South Street, on to Jandakot.

As I sped in through the gate, the sleek winged needle of a Learjet was inching towards a taxiing position at the end of the runway. Nothing else waiting, it seemed. I parked the car, and, with Billy beside me, ran towards the waiting Lear. Two hours earlier, when I'd telephoned to ask for quick transport to Kununurra, the guy on the phone had suggested the Lear. But how will I pay? I'd demanded. 'Diner's Card,' he said. 'Amex, Visa, Mastercharge.' Not quite what I meant. I'd pay somehow, though. Time mattered so much, and this beast was a dart.

We were in the sky in minutes. Four minutes less than

three hours estimated to Kununurra, and would we like drinks—help yourselves if you like, sir—or a sandwich? Silver salver, smoked Scotch salmon, linen napery. Modern execs do themselves well.

Billy One-Hat slept. It wasn't exactly my first jet, but in this whistling little white dart, which was covering fourteen hundred miles in three hours, *as I ordered*, the experience was certainly novel. But Billy, moving at eight miles a minute, flying for the first time, was unmoved. He slept immediately and stayed asleep as we tore north.

I was tired but wakeful—that foul combination. I sat in my soft, hide seat, sipping Bondie's brew, and trying to apply my mind to timing, which was scarcely in my favour. Simple fact was, there was nothing in my favour. With one possible exception: viz, I'd been in Perth in the evening, so I could hardly be at Stringer in the morning, could I?

I could. Just. Be one hell of a drive in the Land-Cruiser.

Still, Billy knew the way.

I won't weary you with the travel. There was nobody and nothing at Kununurra in the post-midnight span, just a dim blue light from Control, and an all-night cab with a glowing cigarette in the front seat, summoned by Control at the request of the Lear captain, for us. Into it Billy and I loaded all the goodies we'd stripped from the Lear: hard booze and mixings, peanuts and almonds, Bondie's beer and four or five bottles of South Australian champagne plus the smoked salmon sandwiches. I'd be paying for the lot, dead or alive, and they'd be handy at the back of Bourke. The silver salver I left.

Fifteen minutes got us to the Land-Cruiser. Billy'd left it with his friends while he was away, and I will admit to walking round it, and counting the wheels. I lifted the bonnet, too, and tapped the spare jerrycans for fuel. In a shamefaced sort of way, I was surprised to find all was well. Billy's wife and kids were well, too, and still up and about. Oh, well. I shook hands and after that there was only one thing left: fuel. Taxi driver told me where, and a few minutes brought us to a petrol station where a fat, bored man played patience to pop music. People who'd been in town for a thrilling bloody evening, he said, came in to fill up before leaving for home. Since many towed fuel-tank trailers, and bought five hundred, a thousand, two thousand litres, he stayed open. Not too many of them, he said, but then you don't need many.

Billy was swinging the Land-Cruiser round towards the exit when I saw the sign. Gardening Stores, it said. 'Hang on,' I told him, and went to inspect. Plant pots, baby palm trees, bananas, a few tomatoes, lots of paving, the usual stuff. I interrupted the lonely man again as he was putting ten on jack, and said, 'Got some shade netting?'

He reckoned he had somewhere if I didn't mind waiting a minute or two. He went away and came back with a whole roll and said how much did I want? I took the roll. It's useful stuff. Creates shade out of nothing. Strong, too.

Then—off. Blacktop to the edge of the town and a little beyond. After that bumps. In the wet, potholes develop and fill up with mud. Other times they sit there, the mud like concrete, and wait for you to bounce on them. You go along like a kangaroo, bounce, bounce, bloody bounce. Strong, reliable springs required. Strong, reliable springs aboard, sir. It wasn't comfortable, as rides go; but it wasn't slow either. And with Billy One-Hat for a companion, it wasn't a chatty trip.

When I wasn't bouncing, I was thinking. I was sure it had been Jane in the invalid chair at Jandakot—Jane drugged, or hurt, anyway helpless. But Jane alive; Jane being taken somewhere.

Reason worked it out this way: Jane had been held prisoner in Perth, probably at the house in Dalkeith. Someone had hoped she would simply *know*: that the essential bits of knowledge were in her head. And so they were, but not in the way her captors expected. Therefore questions, however many and however carefully calculated, were bound to be unproductive. Because before the contents of Jane's mind could begin to be useful, Jane would probably have to be inside Mary Ellen's house, surrounded by Mary Ellen's possessions.

So they'd have to take her to Stringer Station. Right? Right!

Would they take her direct?

Doubtful. Anybody could be at Stringer Station, including me or other representatives of law or court—and who knows what the nasty little lawyer's been up to, running round Perth! My money was on a scenario something like: Get her out of Perth to somewhere a bit quieter. Then have somebody drop in at Stringer to look things over. And only then, when it was certain all was well, bring Jane into Stringer and spread before her the bits and pieces that ought to jog something out of her memory.

Between bumps and bounces, while the Land-Cruiser drove resolutely on, I went over it again and again. The people who had Jane would be there, but not yet. Jane also would be there, but not now. Soon, certainly. Tomorrow, possibly. But we'd be first.

When we reached Stringer, our job, Billy's and mine, was —rescue. Nothing else; priority one. Jane's life was what mattered; not her knowledge, not her considerable wealth. At Stringer Station, we had to get hold of her, and after that, keep her safe. I spent a good part of that journey trying to work out how.

We were there before dawn, handbrake on, parked half a mile from the station house. By moonlight it was dark and very still.

And I looked at it warily, knowing I could be wrong and that the quiet, sleeping station house could in reality be a-bristle with toughs armed to the bloody teeth. And by now, maybe they'd been alerted by the distant sound of the Land-Cruiser and there'd be rifles at every window. If so, I reflected, it would look exactly as it now looked. Who was laying the traps for whom?

So we sat a minute or two with the engine chuntering

steadily away, and we watched nothing. We didn't see anything move at all. No rabbit, no 'roo, no bird. No lights, no movement. Why would there be in the hour before dawn?

Beside me, Billy sat patiently; behind him on the rear seat, his shotgun lay.

I said, 'What do you think—anybody there?'

'Think no, boss.'

I thought no, also, but being sure was something else. There were no visible vehicles, no parked aircraft. But a truck could easily be hidden in the barn, and there's nothing easier, if you have a plane, than dropping people off somewhere and flying away.

I never in my life wanted to do nothing as much as I wanted to do nothing then. Yet a move had to be made. By me—and soon!

You watch and nothing happens. You have an open mind —to begin with, anyway. But it doesn't stay open; gradually it takes a view. Nothing happening, so your brain argues, means Nobody's There. It keeps saying so, inside your skull, until you begin to believe. The still, small voice arguing the other case is gradually ignored. That's the way it works, and that is what led me, eventually, a few minutes before the sun came clambering up over the rim, to eject Billy One-Hat from the Land-Cruiser and send him off to inspect his caravan home and collect the LMG if it was still where he'd tucked it away.

I went to the station house. Direct. No diversions to the other buildings. The precaution I took was to look in through windows: kitchen, living room, two bedrooms. Bathroom window had the starred glass you can't see through.

The place looked empty. I walked in. And out of the smaller bedroom a bloke came walking with a rifle held purposefully in both hands and a mask on his face. He said, 'G'day, mate. Siddown in that chair over there, and start tying your ankles to the legs. There's cut lengths of rope on the chair.' I couldn't see his triumphant grin for the mask, but I could hear it in his voice.

I sat obediently, and began tying. Not very tightly and not

very quickly either, but trying, as I fumbled around, to find something to use to my advantage. After a minute, I knew there wasn't anything.

'Just you, is it?' I said, by way of reconnaissance.

'More than enough,' he said. And cackled.

'When's the Boss coming?'

'Soon.'

I tied the knots and then looked round the room, casually at first, but then inquiringly, wondering what had happened there since Jane and I had left. The place had changed. But then my eye fell on the framed embroidery of the Green Man/Range Men, hanging from a cup-hook on the wall, and I understood very well.

'You don't look much like a housewife,' I said to my captor.

'No more I am, mate.'

'But you're handy with a tube of superglue, aren't you?'

'Talk too much and I'll glue your lips together,' he said.

'Not mine you won't. Can't talk like that.'

'Makes you think you're so important?'

'Big strong bloke like you,' I said, 'going round with a duster and a wet sponge like a charlady—there's a thought!' I said. 'Bet I know what happened. Boss said, we need to get the place cleaned up. Stitching here, dusting there, making the old homestead look the way it looked when the old lady was living here. So he looked round, and his eye fell on you and he said, "You're a woofter, aren't you? Anyone can see that. Off you go and get scrubbing."'

I couldn't see his expression, obviously, but his knuckles looked whitish on the rifle. Your Australian ocker doesn't like having his gender debated.

'Done a nice job, too,' I said. 'Must have been just like this when the old dear was alive. Takes talent, to do that. You have to think like an old woman, and I expect you do.'

He said evenly, 'Case you wonder, I can shoot you if I want to.'

'The Boss says so, eh?'

'Right. Now,' he said, 'take two more of those bits of rope, and make a running knot on your right wrist and another on your left, and set about tying the other ends to the chair legs. Okay?'

I began to obey. The man was in effortless command of this situation so there was no alternative to obedience. But I wondered if he knew Billy One-Hat was at Stringer Station. Probably he did, but it wasn't certain, and in case he didn't, I wanted to keep the talk going so that Billy, when he came to the station house, would at least hear voices and be warned.

So I asked how he was with needlework and how often he had his hair tinted and whether he preferred Surf to Daz for washing his frilly underwear, and every so often I provoked a reply. I also became fairly sure he didn't know Billy was around. He sat stolidly, facing me. Never rose to go to the window; never cocked his head to listen; never gave the smallest sign of being anything but confident of his position.

My own position, sitting bent over in the chair, was both disadvantageous and uncomfortable, and getting more so. It became progressively more difficult to raise my head to look at him, and the increasing pain in the base of my bent back soon had me thinking of nothing else. After a while I no longer cared what Billy might be doing. The only thing in my head was the agony of my back.

He watched me patiently, and I could sense his amusement at my discomfort.

I said, 'You've tied people up before.'

The hooded head shook. 'Tied yourself up, mate.'

'Clever,' I said. 'Make a bloke tie the knots, he ties 'em loose. Then his back starts hurting 'cause he's bent over. So he straightens and the knots tighten.'

He said, 'Brilliant,' and stretched his legs. He was a big fellow and the straight-backed wooden chair he sat on creaked a bit.

I said, 'Superglue's not strong enough.'

'It'll hold.'

He'd put together all the things that had been damaged in

the initial search—the one before Jane and I first appeared at Stringer. Now everything was restored—near enough. A few rough edges to the woodwork, no doubt, and a picture frame or two not perfectly rectangular; but this was now the room Mary Ellen had lived in, her things in place; even some stuff recovered from the dump outside.

He was patting his pockets, typical smoker, and finding nothing, the chair creaking each time he moved. A weakness? Well, he'd weigh all of one-eighty pounds, and the chair was supporting him, so it couldn't be that weak.

The chairs had all been broken when we arrived at Stringer that first time. All of them. Therefore the chair he sat on had been fastened together again. Glue, screws—however it had been done there must be *some* weakness.

I eyed it cautiously. No obvious discrepancies in the angles—no leg that seemed about to buckle. But perhaps, hit just right . . .

He finished searching his pockets, thought for a bit about his tobacco craving, and resisted. Two or three minutes passed. Then the chair creaked again as he rose. He said, 'Keep still, mate,' and walked towards the second bedroom, boots loud on the wooden floor, leaving me staring at the chair, and thinking that, since Billy One-Hat clearly wasn't coming, for whatever reason, that chair was my only chance.

He was coming back, cigarettes and matches in one hand, rifle in the other. He paused a few feet away, looked at me. 'Chicken tied for the oven.'

Two steps, then, and he was back to his chair, turning to sit, his eyes off me for an instant. I ducked my head yet further, and pushed off with my feet into a forward somersault aimed at smashing the legs of my chair into him.

I felt a hard and painful bang as my head struck the floor, heard a grunt as my chair pivoted over and into him. It tilted then, violently to the side in a tangle of legs—his, mine and the chair's, and I distinctly heard a chair snap.

Stillness. That, I thought, fearfully, was that. Failure. I tried to turn my head, some impulse to look into the gun barrel as the death-shot is fired, I suppose. But I couldn't.

There was a silence in the big warm room, apart from hissing breath, and grunts. I broke it by saying defensively, 'It was cramp. I fell.'

There came a grunt, behind me and another a moment later. And then a groan of pure pain.

About the only thing I could move was my eyelids, and I remember blinking and blinking as I wondered: could it actually have *worked*? I wriggled painfully, trying to achieve sufficient movement to see what had happened.

The response to my wriggle was a screech of agony, and a gasping plea, 'Keep bloody still!'

I blinked more. From the sound of things, I was in control. Tied to a chair, lying on my side on the floor, unable to move. But the boss.

I said experimentally, 'Untie any knot you can reach,' and, a few seconds later, felt fingers plucking at the cord that tied my right hand to my right foot. To judge by the grunts and gasps it was hard going, but in the end I felt the first knot loosen and pulled my hand free. I put it on the floor to get some purchase and begin to lever myself upright, and found I had put it on warm fluid that was bright red when I looked at it.

His blood? Must be. It was hard to believe, but *I* seemed all right, except for the back pain.

'You're bleeding,' I said.

'Bloody right!' he gasped.

'Where?'

'Leg. Me bloody leg! It's clean through me thigh. I'm bleeding like a bastard. I can see the blood pumping. Careful when you move!'

I moved carefully, and again he gasped.

'Got a knife?' I asked.

'Yair.'

'Cut the other knot. It'll be quicker.'

Immediate obedience, and his voice behind me saying, 'Hurry up, for Christ's sake!'

I rose as quickly as a locked spine allowed; then, still bent, turned to look. What had happened was both simple and obvious: he'd fallen hard on to his chair, splintering it, and a piece of old jarrah, rigid and sharp as a sword, had been driven through his thigh. He was right, too, about the pumping blood—plainly the jarrah stick had hit a sizeable blood vessel!

You do some first-aid in West Australian schools and I knew tourniquet-time when I saw it. Fortunately the pieces of rope and bits of wood were at hand, and I got the blood staunched fairly fast. By then he was barely even conscious. I'd removed his balaclava mask, and his face was deadly pale. Shock and loss of blood.

'Is there a first-aid kit?'

He nodded very weakly.

'Where?'

It sounded like 'Dresser', and it was right. I pulled out the jarrah, plugged lint into the wound hard, sprinkled penicillin powder and bound the lot tightly together, but you couldn't call it effective. The bloke was work for a doctor—soon, if he was to survive.

About an hour after that I heard the plane, and left him sleeping and went to the window and watched as it came in. Same unmarked six-seater: neat landing. It stopped, a door opened, and Jane was first out, still in the shorts and top she'd worn in King's Park; she stepped carefully down the wing and stood still. I'd picked up the rifle from where it had fallen, but a single shot of doubtful accuracy at a range of a couple of hundred yards would be no help to anyone, least of all Jane, because now a man had climbed down to stand behind her, pistol in hand.

I suppose I'm simply no damn good at this commando stuff. In my mind was the vague plan that if I shot the Boss, the rest would simply fold up. And I was ready to shoot him. But by the time I'd worked out that in masks they were unidentifiable, and I didn't know which *was* the Boss, they were all marching towards the house, Jane in front, covered by assorted firearms, and I was helpless again.

I thought, too late, of exiting from the back, and then

bursting in on them later. But when I nipped over to the rear door, I found it locked and the key missing. No way out.

Weak, I know, but there was Jane's safety to think about. So I waited for them, while I looked over towards Billy One-Hat's caravan. No movement there. What in hell had become of Billy? And where the devil was the LMG?

17

No change in status: that was the fact of the matter. I'd been prisoner before and I was prisoner now; Jane likewise. I'd achieved nothing, except to half-kill one of them.

The door crashed open, and a man came in yelling, 'Hello! G'day, Bert!' I could have shot him, of course, easy as pie; but I didn't, because there were three more just like him outside, Jane precariously among 'em.

She gave a little gasp and a grin of relief when she saw me, and then she strode over and gave me a hug and a kiss, but I had to say, 'They've got me, too.'

She nodded. 'You know what it's all about?'

'I can make a guess or two.'

At which point something, probably a gun, jabbed into me. 'What happened to Bert?'

I said, 'Diagnosis: overeating. Sat on a chair and it collapsed under him. Ought to be in hospital.' I pointed at the wide pool of blood on the floor. 'Maybe he'll die anyway.'

A man said, 'I'll bring the Chief down.' He went to the door and fired a Verey pistol. Not too many seconds later an aircraft blasted by low overhead, in a terrific roar of engines, and I heard the sound swing about us as the plane came in to land.

Jane said, 'It's the P38 Lightning. I saw it on a parallel course as we flew here.'

'From where?'

She shrugged. 'North, somewhere. I don't know. A ranch.'

'Station.'

'Yes, Station,' she said. 'Big place.'

*

Outside, the roar of mighty engines came and went and came and went as the pilot played the revs game, and flew in and taxied. Then the engine was cut and soon there were footsteps outside and the door opening.

Enter the Boss. Regulation balaclava, denim work-shirt, jeans. They were designer jeans, though, and the calf-skin knee boots were superb.

'You'd be in charge?' I asked.

He looked at me. 'Total charge.'

'Chief . . .' The men led him away to look at Bert. I heard mutters and murmurings and then the voice of the Chief, being decisive. 'Personally I don't care if the stupid, careless cretin lives or bloody well dies,' he said, 'but you'd better get him to a doc. Whip him over to Ord River, dump him on the runway and get off again quick, right?'

Two of them carried Bert out. One came back. The other would be flying the plane. Still, numbers were down by two for the time being, if I could find some way to act, or if Billy One-Hat hadn't gone walkabout with LMG.

The Chief sat on an upright chair, boots in the blood. He sounded, when he spoke, like the chairman of a meeting. 'Well now, we all know—'

'Not me,' I said. 'I don't know anything.'

'Oh, you know, all right. You wouldn't be here otherwise.'

'What is it I'm supposed to know?'

He inhaled noisily: impatience audible.

'Now listen,' the Chief said. 'I'll say it once. After that—'

'Just say it,' Jane said.

So he started again. 'Somewhere here,' and he gestured round him at the room, 'there's what I'd call a location concealed. The old woman hid it in a bloody cunning way, so only one person in the bloody world would understand it. Well, that person is here, right this minute, and here she'll stay until we know where that location is. Everything clear so far?'

I said, 'Why would she tell *you*?'

'Because,' the Chief said, 'that way she can leave here alive, take the money she inherited, and go back to England.'

'Bypassing the police?'

'That's right. She'll have made a decision to sell this place —Stringer Station—and when she does so, the money it raises will go to her. All of it. Fair, isn't it?'

'Do you think it's fair?' I asked Jane.

'I just don't like being pushed,' Jane said.

'The tails side of this coin,' the Chief went on, 'is that WA is so big and empty—'

'That nobody'd ever find us?'

He said, 'They'd never even stumble across your bones! You'll be dinner for the dingoes, the pair of you. Tonight, tomorrow night. So start looking, and start thinking.'

'What do *I* do?' I asked.

'You bear in mind that you're absolutely disposable— you're as valuable to me as used chewing gum. So you sit, and you stay quiet.'

'Right.' I sat obediently.

I watched Jane search. I'd no doubt that he'd kill me, eventually; he was keeping me alive only because killing me would upset Jane and he didn't want Jane upset. For his purposes, Jane needed to be both clear-headed, and a bit scared, so that her instincts and perceptions were in top working order. He wanted her prowling that room alert as a pussy cat.

He radiated tension. It was clear that he not only expected Jane to accept his terms, he expected action this minute: expected her to leap joyfully upon one or other of the dozens of items in the room yelling, 'Eureka!'

But she didn't. Jane began by taking the pictures and embroideries down one by one and looking at each one carefully. She'd turn each one round, to be sure she was looking at the item right way up; then she'd turn them over and examine the back, in case something was written or hidden there. After that, off with the back plate and a careful look at the picture, or the piece of needlework, or the photograph, or whatever.

And every so often, the rasp of the Boss: 'What is it?'

Jane said, 'My grandmother, when she was young.'

'What is it?'

'A white rose, embroidered in *petit-point* on a blue ground.'

'Why white?'

'She was a Yorkshire woman. It's the county emblem.'

'Show me.' Then, after looking: 'Looks like a bloody daisy to me.'

'It is, nonetheless,' Jane said speaking crisply, 'the white rose design as worn by cricketers playing for Yorkshire. Check it in *Wisden*, if you know what *Wisden* is!'

So it went on. It was plain Jane was giving her attention to the task. And it was plain, too, that she was finding nothing. The problem, of course, was that she hadn't the remotest idea what she was looking for. What everybody believed was that Great-Aunt Mary Ellen had left behind something only Jane would recognize and/or comprehend.

But what it was, none of us could begin to guess. She could only continue and hope. The Boss could only watch and wait. And he didn't like it. The Boss was a man accustomed to command and to results: you could see it in his impatience and in every line of his tall, tensed body. Eventually—maybe an hour and a half had gone—he pushed himself away from the wall he'd been leaning on. 'Better try another way.'

I said, 'She hasn't finished trying this way, yet.'

'All the same. Maybe if we *all* know.'

'About what?' Jane asked, cool and polite.

'This place Thornton.'

She said, 'But you do know about it, don't you? Told me you had somebody go there and send you a report. You even made me read it. About fifty pages, all dull. Population, statistics, acreage, etc.'

He said, 'Tell me what *you* know.'

Jane shrugged. 'I last lived there more than ten years ago. Mary Ellen was there sixty years ago.'

'Describe it.'

So she did. Jane could have been in no doubt as she stood there that her life was in real danger. Watching and listening,

I knew, this tense, impatient man dared not behave as he'd promised; dared not release her; because the moment he did, she'd go to the police and he'd be arrested and charged with kidnapping.

Except, I realized suddenly, that he still believed we didn't know who he was! Which was true of Jane. Bob—wherever Bob might be—also didn't know. There was just me, and the Boss didn't know *I* knew—that was why all the pantomime of balaclavas was maintained!

Okay. There was a mine. Emeralds. Found, appropriately, by Old Man Green. But no claim existed—I'd already checked the files in Perth, and Green hadn't been listed. So somewhere out yonder was a seam of pegmatite—the matrix material in which the crystals are usually found. If the Boss learned the location, he could then hold Jane for long enough to buy his Miner's Right, peg out his claim, submit it, acquire exclusive rights to mine the stones, and that would be the end of that. If Jane were then to turn up, saying, 'That drongo swiped my emerald mine,' the courts would laugh at her. Equally, if she didn't know who was behind the balaclava, it would be pretty hard to prove she'd even been kidnapped.

So he *could* do it! His only problem was that there was a witness. And my problem was that I was the witness. Kill me and he was home and dry.

I'd be damned lucky to get out of this alive! That happy thought brought me back to events as they were happening.

Jane was saying: 'Really, it's still not much more than a village. A suburb, perhaps nowadays. On a steepish hill that starts to rise gradually about half a mile out of Bradford— all roads out of Bradford are uphill—and goes up close to a thousand feet. Thornton's not technically a mountain, but the next village over, a place called Queensbury, certainly is.'

'Tell me where you lived. About your family.'

'Well, we'd lived there a long, long time. I know my grandmother's grandmother lived in Storr Heights in Thornton, and she knew several people who'd been baptized by Patrick Brontë when he was there, and he left in the early eighteen twenties . . .'

It went on for a while: Jane talking like a guide book, and the Boss pretending he was Birkenhead, cross-examiner supreme. Then he got bored and said, 'Just go on looking,' and told his men, 'Watch them both,' and left. A few moments later, one aircraft engine started. Then another, and the Lightning went roaring on its way.

When he'd gone, Jane simply carried on examining things. She kept her eyes on the various objects, and moved in a steady, consistent way, and didn't speak. After a while, two things struck me about her; the first, that she was, for Jane, remarkably submissive; the second, that I wasn't among the things she looked at.

Why not—did she know something already? It seemed unlikely. I suppose I thought that when Jane spotted Mary Ellen Green's hidden secret, great bells would begin to toll; that she'd start back abruptly, eyes wide, like somebody in a comic strip. But, thinking about it, that wasn't Jane at all. She was tough, self-contained and resourceful. And at the moment, convincingly demure and submissive.

The Boss flew back after about an hour and a half, flung the door wide and demanded, 'Well, where is it?'

'I haven't the faintest idea,' Jane said.

'Christ, you've been at it bloody hours!'

She smiled faintly. 'It seems like months.'

'Nothing? No hint—not a clue?'

'But I've been thinking,' Jane said. 'If this supposition is correct—in other words, *if* Mary Ellen wanted to pass this knowledge to me, and to me alone—would she put it in a place where I'd spot it immediately?'

He said, 'Well,' and paused. Then he went on, 'She'd have to. Wouldn't expect you to like it up here would she? No place for a woman, after all. She'd expect you to take one squint down your Pommie nose and head straight back to Perth.'

'*She* stayed sixty years,' Jane said drily.

'Well, yair, but—'

'I think,' Jane went on, 'that we're talking about the final piece of knowledge—the really important bit. She'd—well, either I'd have to work for it, or it would be something I'd only realize gradually.'

'What does that mean, "realize gradually"?'

'I don't know,' Jane said. 'I really don't. But think of this: she was leaving me this place.'

'Plus the mine! Little something extra.'

'But this place first of all. She'd lived here so long—and liked it—that's obvious. She could have sold up and gone any time she felt like it, and she never did. So maybe she wanted *me* to stay here a while—a few weeks, a few months. Get to know Stringer Station. She'd know I'd spot the pub embroidery quickly. And I did. The rest was available for a *gradual* follow-up. But the last bit—'

'For God's sake!' said the Boss. 'You want to spend six months here? You think that's what it will take?'

'She didn't know anything about me, did she? Didn't know what kind of man I might be involved with. I'm not married, but I could have been. Some louse or another. She wouldn't want *him* finding out, grabbing the advantage, and running off, leaving me.'

'Crap!' The Boss waved a dismissive arm.

Jane said, 'This whole thing was very carefully thought out, by an intelligent woman and *for* an intelligent woman. Embroidery, you see. The whole thing exists in the world women live in.'

He said, 'You're in a bloody kitchen now, aren't you? That's a woman's world, isn't it!'

She didn't even spit in his eye. Jane, who'd have beaten my skull flat with a shovel for even thinking such a thought, let alone expressing it, merely lowered her eyes and said, 'If you choose to think so.'

She said it gently, and softly. This was your Victorian miss submitting to authority. *If you say so, sir . . .*

'Christ!' he said. 'Let's have some bloody tucker and get

on with it!' He stamped outside and came back a few minutes later with two Esky-boxes, the first full of sandwiches and Australia's eternal meat pastries and pies, the other full of cold beer. It was well into afternoon now and the house was hot, and he had a window opened and left the door wide to permit the passage of air.

Then he sat to watch Jane work. His two remaining men, obviously bored out of their minds, sat lazy and almost inert, opening an eye only to reach for food or drink. But the Boss was alert. Jane had reached the sink, and was looking carefully at a rust-spotted mirror fastened to the wall above it, when the Boss suddenly said: 'Rugs.'

Jane turned. She had a can of beer in one hand and half a meat pie in the other, but still she contrived a garden-party air, which I felt like applauding.

'Yes, there are,' she said, and this time I did clap.

He said, 'Shut up—and remember what I told you!'

Jane said sweetly, 'If you're thinking they could be maps, I agree with you. But I've looked at two already and they're not. The third is smothered in drying blood and I don't propose to look at it till it's clean.'

'So wash it. You have a sink.' He laughed. 'Women's work, eh?'

'And if the colours run?' Jane asked. She bent and picked up a corner. The rug was the kind people used to make by threading small pieces of cut cloth through holes in canvas: five feet by three, I'd judge, and two-thirds of it blood-soaked.

'So they run. Who cares?'

'You really are several kinds of idiot,' Jane said, and he was on his feet in a second, yelling, 'Don't be bloody cheeky, you Pommie bitch, or I'll—'

'Go without, I imagine,' Jane said coolly. 'The point is this: imagine the pattern is basically blue. Assuming she'd made it, and what's more made it *as a map*, with places indicated in, for instance, red on this rug—you can see bits of red here, and here—and when you wash it the dark blue dye runs and the reds turn into blues, you have destroyed the map. You've done your best as it is, with all this blood.'

'I haven't spilled any. Not yet,' he growled. 'Your smart bloody lawyer did that!'

'Anyway, I doubt if it's anything as crude as a map. Though of course, it could be. And you have two great big men dozing in here. Why not send one of them to rinse the blood off before the stains set.'

His eyes glared at her through the holes in the balaclava, and she said, 'Or Mr Close would do it, I'm sure. In the meantime, I could get on.'

He transferred the glare to me. 'Mr Close probably has a gun tucked away out there—I wouldn't trust the bastard an inch. No—you go.' The instruction was to one of his men who had just stifled a yawn.

'Take the bloody rug and wash it.' He looked at her. 'How would he do it?'

'Soak it in cold water for an hour. Then rinse under running water till it's all gone. And don't just dump it in the water tank!'

'You heard the lady.'

Jane resumed her careful study of miscellaneous objects. An old frying pan was looked over for significant scratches; a silk thread sampler carrying the message, 'Every House is The Lord's House', and bearing the stitched signature Mary Jane Emmett, 1870, was taken from its frame and looked at seriously for the first time in a lot of years.

'Let me see.'

She handed it to him.

'Who's this Mary Jane?'

'Her mother.'

'Whose mother?'

'Mary Ellen's mother. I doubt if she was involved in this particular plot—she'll have been dead sixty years.'

The Boss grunted and waved an impatient hand. 'Get on with it!'

It went on like that. Hour after hour after hour. Events, such as they were, were of the kind I have described. It was hot in the Station house and—tension or no tension—warm air

206

made us soporific. I sat yawning on the floor by the window. The Boss's two men, rifles across their knees, sat yawning at the table. The Boss wasn't yawning; he was watching Jane. Jane pursued her steady path.

By mid-afternoon, tea was drunk. Sugar available, not milk; Jane with an enamel cup and her little finger raised, intending to irritate. Which it did. She was working on him for whatever reason. Probably she'd been doing it for days. At any rate, she could make him rise to any of a dozen baits, and every so often, she did. He'd have enjoyed beating her down, but he couldn't because he needed her mind. She knew it, and played on it. The only defence she had.

Then, about five, with the light outside beginning to lose its fierce dazzle, something happened.

The Boss said, 'What's that you're looking at?'

And Jane replied, 'I rather think it's an old cardboard box with several different polishes inside. Brasso, Silvo, that sort of thing.'

Lord knows what it was that upset him. Suddenly the Boss changed character explosively and completely. A minute earlier he'd been simply a rough character, the tough, impatient business man, anxious for results, but accessible occasionally to reason. Now, suddenly, he was in a fury. You could almost smell the capriciousness, the latent brutality hissing to life on the raw surface of his personality.

'You bloody Pommie bitch,' he snarled. 'You know already!'

Jane shook her head. 'No—'

'Course you bloody do! You know and you're trying to fox me—tell me you don't know and then wriggle away after to get the stuff for yourself and—' he waved a hand towards me—'for this bloody booby here!'

'No!' Jane said. 'It's not true.'

'Bloody well is though. You've got the bloody message, you cow! I can see it, I can bloody smell it. All right—if you know, you'll bloody well tell me.'

'There's nothing,' Jane said. 'Really, honestly, there's nothing!'

'You'll tell me, I promise you that! World of women—bloody sheilas! More trouble than . . .' He strode quickly to the door. 'Bring her out—and don't forget that shyster lawyer!'

The two rifles were pointing, and the message was: quick march. I let Jane precede me through the door, out into the sunlight, and moved after her. The P38, its aluminium skin glinting and unadorned, stood maybe fifty yards away, and the Boss was walking towards it with a purposeful air. When he got to it, he climbed to flip open the perspex canopy over the cockpit, reached in, and pulled out a yellow Esky-box by the handle on its lid, looked at the fastening, then closed up the cockpit and strode towards us.

Now he jerked his head. 'Take 'em over there—to the chapel.'

Beside me, Jane said, 'What makes him think that's where Mary Ellen hid the big secret?'

'Doubt if that's it,' I said. 'He's got a nasty idea.'

And indeed he had. He dragged open the door when we arrived, and stood in the wide entrance looking at us. Then he pointed. 'See those pews?'

I said, 'Difficult to miss 'em.' Apart from the lectern with the Bible on it, and the paintings of Jesus and Mary facing each other from opposite walls, the pews were the only furnishings.

'One each,' he said. 'Stand 'em on end and lean 'em against the wall.'

'Why?' I said.

'Do it.'

So I did it, and he said, 'Check. Make sure it won't fall over.'

So I did that, and asked what the hell this was all about, and he chuckled and said, 'Better be sure the sheila's done it right. You know what they're like.'

'I can do it,' Jane protested angrily, but I checked anyway.

'Okay?' He called.

I nodded.

'Now get up there!'

'Where?'

'On the end. Stand on the end. One of you on the end of each bench.'

Jane turned to face him. 'Stand, sit—or what? And you *are* mad!'

He laughed again. 'Stand, that's best. Go on—get up there.'

'I don't think so,' Jane said.

'Well, now, if you don't, I'll have some holes made in your boyfriend.' He turned and said, 'Use birdshot. When his backside's full of lead pellets . . .'

She turned back to the upended pew. In normal use it was about five feet long, with three rough arms, one at either end and another in the middle. The arms made a ladder of sorts so it wouldn't be hard to climb. The ends of each pew were large, flat pieces of wood, an inch and a half thick, and undecorated, making a platform about two feet by eighteen inches.

'Go on up.' Jane and I looked at each other, and obeyed.

This was some kind of test, we both knew that. Its purpose . . .

'Get two tin mugs and two spoons, understand,' the Boss ordered one of his hooded men, 'and be bloody quick! Run, run, *run*!'

When he returned we were given a mug and spoon apiece and I said, 'What's this for?'

The Boss laughed. 'Alarm bell,' he said, 'because I'm going to leave you two alone to think about things . . .' He stepped into the chapel, lifting his box with him, and stooped to tie a length of line to the lid and unfasten the catch. Then he went back to the doorway, lifted the heavy door into place, and called to us through the metal, 'Keep your eye on the box.'

'What is it, John?' Jane asked, in sudden fear. Truth was, I think she'd guessed.

We watched the line tighten between the doorway and the wooden box. Then the lid began to open on its hinge. He kept pulling until the box fell over backward and something fell out. In the dimming light, it could have been thick, coiled rope; but rope doesn't writhe of its own accord.

'See it?' the Boss yelled. 'Know what he is? King Brown, that is. One of my blokes caught him, week or two ago.'

'Get the damn thing out of here!' I yelled back. 'It's no good threatening her. She's been trying hard.'

'She bloody well knows and won't tell!' he shouted. 'So I'll tell *her*—about King Browns! Know what they say, do you Missus Strutt? They say, if you ever get bitten by a King Brown, what you do is, you look round for a nice shady tree. Then you go and sit under the tree and light a ciggie. Then you enjoy three good puffs, because that's all the time you've got! So you just make a noise with those spoons when you're ready to tell me.'

'And if the bloody snake kills her?' I called. 'What then? I'll tell you—you *never* find the answer. Never!'

But he didn't reply. He gave a bellow of a laugh, and I heard them walk away.

It's not humorous, I'll tell you that. I stood for a long time, rigid with fear, with my gaze locked on the brown snake. Then Jane said, 'What will it do?' She was eight or nine feet away, marooned like me on the little wooden island of the pew end, each of us five feet or less off the ground.

'I'm a townie,' I said. 'I don't know much about 'em.'

'You told me once that Australian snakes are deadly but shy. You said they moved out of the way if you made enough noise. This chapel's built of corrugated sheets. We could make a heck of a noise!'

'Jane,' I said.

'What?'

'None of that applies. The brown snake's the exception. Especially the King Brown. It's aggressive, and it can move very fast.'

'The deadliest, is it?'

'Not quite, but near.'

'So what will happen—what can we do?'

I said, 'They're deaf. No ears or eardrums. Very sensitive

to vibration, though. It'll go looking for warmth as the heat leaves its body.'

After a moment she said, 'That means us. We represent warmth?'

'And food, I expect. There are two of us.'

'Oh, God—I can't even look! What's it doing?'

'Nothing, yet. Lying coiled. Jane, had you really spotted nothing in there? The easy way out is something to tell him. Give him a clue of some kind.'

'No—there's nothing. God, I'd tell him in a second—if I knew anything! I don't. Heavens, I'm *shaking*! I've a horror of snakes.'

There wasn't a lot of light by now—it was just the reflected light from white paint on the tin walls that enabled me to see anything at all. But when I looked away from Jane to the earthen floor, the Brownie had moved: that flat, slender head was no longer part of the coil; instead it jutted away a foot or more, weaving gently, and in our direction. I wondered how long the brute had been in the Esky—which is insulated. If the snake had been warm when he went in, he'd be warm still. Therefore active.

No knowing the answer.

We were in a catch-twenty-two situation. The Boss wouldn't let us out unless Jane gave him the news he wanted. And Jane couldn't do it, because she didn't *have* any news.

I said—it was a whisper because you do whisper when you're faced by that kind of lethal brute—'Could you make something up—some fact—something he'd believe?'

She said, 'He'd only find out, and be madder still. We'd be back in here.'

'We could try, though!'

'Yes, all right. It's worth—oh, John!' Her voice went in a moment from a whisper to something like a screech of pure terror.

Because the King Brown was now moving slowly across the floor below. And towards us.

18

My heart did one of those lurches, as though falling ten feet on the end of a piece of elastic, and then bouncing up again. It was my perch, *my* upended pew, towards which the Brown snake now moved. He was taking his time. Head low, body entending and then extending again. I realized that this was a *big* snake. Oh, I know it doesn't matter how big the snake is if it kills you, and small snakes can often be worse than big ones. Death Adders for instance. I wished it was a Death Adder, because they're short and fat and can't climb. This one was ten feet long and our legs were five feet off the floor, or a shade less. There was nowhere for us to climb.

My body turned cold and shivery with sheer terror: bare hands versus venomous fangs is no contest. The snake can hold that head of his a long way from you, biding his time and choosing his instant to strike, and when he does, his fangs are through clothing and skin with effortless power: through leather, too, unless it's extra tough. You hear these stories of the bloke who grabs snakes by the tail, cracks them like whips, and the heads fly off. Well, I'd no thoughts of anything heroic like that. I knew already that there were no weapons I could use. The only chance was to climb, somehow, and find safety under the roof. But there was nothing to rest on up there. Or was there? The chapel's roof was shallow-pitched, and there seemed, in the dim light, to be some kind of metal rail, running the length of the little building. But even if I *could* climb up, which was unlikely, I'd have to hang by my hands, and that could have only one ending.

'*John!*' A sudden yell from Jane.

I looked across at her. While I'd been staring desperately up at the roof, she must have glanced downwards. The snake, for whatever reason, had changed direction; had abandoned its twisting approach to my pew. Now it had turned its head and was moving towards Jane's.

Frantically I looked round the little chapel and its few contents: the portraits of Jesus and Mary, the lectern, the pews on which we stood. Not a thing to use as a weapon against the big, aggressive snake. It could simply pick us off. Writhe up, until it could bite, and kill. First one, then the other.

First Jane!

Because by now, the flat, narrow head was raised, and rising more, searching first about the base of the pew on which she stood, then questing higher, to the arm in the middle; touching the arm; testing its strength, easing upward.

I'd almost forgotten the tin mug in my left hand. But I'd have to use it; have to summon the only kind of help there was.

But before I could do it, there was a sharp rap on the tin wall behind me, and the voice of the Boss said, 'Fun started yet?'

I yelled back, 'Get us out of here, for God's sake!'

'I'll maybe give that snake a bit of a gee-up if he doesn't move soon,' he yelled. And laughed. Then his boots went walking away, despite my calls, and Jane's.

I'd been watching the snake, as the Boss played his sadistic game. At the first reverberating bang on the tin wall, it had instantly withdrawn its head to ground level, and its body into the shelter formed by the angle of the pew's back and seat, and now it lay coiled there, as far as I could see. Truth is it was damned hard to see anything: the pew was brown, the snake was brown, the floor was sandy grey; and it moved so fast—hidden and coiled in no more than a second or two!

'What can we do?' Jane's voice was tremulous, terrified.

'We can hope,' I muttered, 'that it stays where it is!'

But it didn't. I suppose it was tuned to the vibration of

the boots. As that lessened the snake must have felt safe in emerging. Because emerge it did: the narrow head first, then a long slide of slim body, and the head questing upward once more. I've read since that there's enough poison in a King Brown's venom sacs to knock down and kill a pair of cart horses weighing a ton apiece.

Then Jane dropped her tin mug. It must have brushed the snake as it fell, because in a moment the head was again withdrawn. But only for a second. Soon it was searching the air again, finding the mug, the head hovering, testing the scent, then rising once more. This time, though, there had been a small change in its behaviour: the whole body had not withdrawn into the safe corner of the pew. The tail had swung through a long arc, and now stretched out towards the middle of the floor, as the head inched slowly upwards. Past the arm it paused—I thought it had done so to deposit a coil on the shelf there—but no, the head again began to float menacingly higher. There was less than a couple of feet to go before that deadly head would find Jane, before the savouring, testing tongue touched the warmth of her skin; before . . .

It was too late now—too late to strike spoon against cup, or cup against iron wall and get help in time; the help, if any came, would be unable to fire a shotgun without hitting Jane.

I jumped. It was no carefully calculated action, no deliberate piece of heroics. I realized quite suddenly that if the pew on which I stood fell across the King Brown's body, where it trailed along the floor—if *that* happened . . .

I leaned against the wall to push the pew away from it, feeling the wooden platform rocking unsteadily beneath me . . .

Then I jumped, and as I jumped, I pushed, with my feet —shoving the heavy jarrah pew towards the snake.

It tumbled the way a tree does: the top arcing downwards, the base steady. It also hit the snake.

But without breaking its back.

What happened next was very fast. First I landed on my

feet and jumped again to grab for the only thing to hand—
the lectern. A glance showed the snake flowing swiftly
through a gap by the pew, lancing towards me.

I hurled the Bible off the lectern first, and hit the snake,
and slowed it, but on it came. I picked up the lectern
then and swung it by its base, and this time it halted and
reared, and behind it I could see Jane hopping lightly down
from her perch, wrestling her own pew off the ground and
preparing to hurl it with all her strength . . .

But in that fraction of a second, something else had happened. To my left came a scratch and a long scrape as the
door was lifted. The by-now-angry King Brown snake reared,
making that awful hiss deep in his throat.

And out of the dark arch of the doorway a shadowy thing
flew at him and over him and he began to thrash and writhe
helplessly, in the coils of something more flexible than he.

Then Billy One-Hat stood in the doorway. He was apolo-
gizing quietly. 'Billy went hide,' he said. 'Billy have to wait.'

Billy was sorry. Jane and I, needless to say, were not. And
now Billy proved to be as dexterous as he was knowing.
While the furious snake tried to writhe its way, hissing, out
of the length of netting in which it was entirely enveloped,
Billy was shrouding it in more of the stuff. He had a length
of wood with him, and now he lifted it to kill the snake.

I said, 'Billy, could you get it back in the box?'

He gave me a startled look, then glanced down at the
heaving pile of net and serpent.

'Yair. Could do that.'

'Don't take any risks,' Jane ordered.

Billy smiled. 'Easy,' he said. And easy it seemed. He took
the Brownie behind the head, and lifted, and in the box it
went, net and all, and the lid closed in what seemed like a
twinkling.

Then Billy led us outside, and pointed to one of the Boss's
men spread-eagled on the ground on the side of the chapel
farthest from the house. Soft Abo approach and a thump
with the piece of wood, I expect; I didn't bother asking.

'They won't even know we're free,' I said. 'Not until the Boss man comes for another gloat.'

'What exactly,' Jane demanded, 'have you in mind for the snake?'

'In through the window, box and all, lid unfastened, that's what.'

She nodded. 'And blast them with the shotgun as they come out, I suppose.'

'Something like that.'

'They have guns in there,' Jane said. 'And the snake's wrapped up like a parcel. They'll kill it, and then—'

I said, 'That's what I mean. We strike first.'

Out here in the moonlight I could see the glint in her eye. 'Three men in there, is that right?'

'I reckon.'

'Well I,' she said, 'am not going to murder three men.'

'They're asking for it!'

'Maybe they are.' She grinned suddenly. 'On the other hand, I have no objection at all to their dying of fright. I nearly did, after all. Come on!'

What she meant by that was getting the Land-Cruiser and putting our shoulders to it. Already it stood four hundred yards from the station house: Jane wanted it a hundred yards further off before the engine was switched on.

The Land-Cruiser started the way diesels do—with a noisy *clank-clank-clank*, and a *duh-duh-duh* and a couple of *trsk*s, and when running sounded loud enough to me to awaken every dozing drunk from Stringer to Sydney. I looked back at the house, expecting to see the Boss and his men come hurrying out to investigate. But they didn't.

'Funny,' I said.

'Over-confident.' Jane gave another of those grins. 'They've been passing a bottle round in there, that's what they've been doing.' She'd taken the wheel, the initiative, and command, all in a couple of moments.

She pulled up about three hundred yards from the south-west corner of the house, with the Land-Cruiser tucked back behind a little wave in the terrain. Now she grinned a third time and said to Billy One-Hat, 'May I have your rifle, please?'

'What for?' I was looking at the moonlit scene: Stringer Station all at peace; two aircraft parked fifty yards or so away from the house.

Jane said, 'You know all those Western films where people fire at each other from the shelter of doorways and windows?'

'Yair.'

'Well, it ain't feasible. Not against our old friend here—' she held up the rifle—'the old 303 Lee Enfield would put a bullet not just through the window frame but through the entire house, walls and all. How many rounds have we, Billy?'

'Got 'nother clip, missus. More at home.'

'That,' Jane said, 'will do very nicely.'

She settled herself on the ground, correct firing position, and all that, raised her head to adjust the back sight, then put one into Stringer Station. She kept her head down, waiting. After a moment, the lights went out.

'Ground level,' Jane murmured, and squeezed the trigger again.

Another pause, then a silvery window slid up.

Jane said, 'Perfect,' and fired her third shot.

'Where were you aiming?'

'Bottom right-hand corner. That's where he'd be.'

'You're a good enough shot to put one there?'

'Still air,' she said, 'and I'm not bad.' The bolt clicked and she fired once more.

The bullet must have hit pot or pan because we clearly heard a clanking as it flew about. We also heard the flat crack of an answering shot.

'They don't know where to fire,' Jane said, easily. 'We're just a dark ridge. They'll have to run. No alternative.'

'To the planes, you mean?'

'Yup.'

'What then?'

'They'll fly away. Off *my* land,' she said with emphasis.

'They know we're free, and armed. There's nothing else they can do.'

'They can come after us when it's light.'

'If they live.'

'I thought you didn't want to kill anybody!'

She turned her head and smiled at me. 'I don't. But they're on my property, and they're playing dirty games, and I'm rather cross about it. So—' She moved her eye to the back-sight, and fired again.

One more answering shot, then silence. After a few moments I saw a man appear at the corner of the house, first trying to shelter, then dashing for the light plane. Two more of them followed. Jane did nothing and the engine-roar swept towards us and the plane moved forward, turning into its take-off run, while Jane, head still and concentrating, fired once more and then stood up, smiling pretty broadly.

'What did you hit?' I asked.

'Just speeding them on their way,' she said, 'whoever they are!'

We watched the little plane lift into the night sky.

'You don't know?'

She shook her head. 'They all wore masks the whole time. And I was never allowed to see anything except the room I was kept in. They blind-folded me sometimes.' Then she stared at me. 'Do *you* know?'

So I told her, and she nodded, and gasped a bit, and when I'd finished, she said, 'He's going to get a nasty shock, isn't he, when we roll up in Perth with the boys in blue?'

I shook my head. 'Can't do it that way, Jane. After he'd got you, he grabbed Bob Collis. Still has him—where, I don't know.'

'So that's who it is! Look, I was kept at his "place" and there was someone else there, in a cellar—I heard two of them talk about him. Where's his "place"?'

I looked at the horizon, and at the dark blue of the sky; I looked for the odd star or two I can actually recognize, and then I pointed roughly north-west. 'That way,' I said. 'Forty miles or so.'

Abruptly she said, 'I wonder.'

'What do you wonder?'

'I don't see why not.' She moved off down the shallow slope to the Toyota and slipped into the driving seat. 'Hop aboard, gents!'

'Where are we going, Captain?' I asked.

'To take a little look,' Jane Strutt said, 'at that tank.'

I'd forgotten just how big it was. Fact is, the Sherman's a sizeable beast with solid armour about two inches thick and in that shadowed cave it looked simply colossal, like something from an inter-galactic world.

The first problem was light. The small generator burned petrol, and the fuel in it was very old. I pulled a lot of times on the recoil starter rope, but it didn't even cough. So all we had for light was the hand-lamp from the Toyota.

Jane said, 'Billy, d'you mind driving to the house and finding some fresh petrol?'

'No, missus.'

'There won't be anyone there. Oh, but there's the man you knocked out!'

'Yes, missus.' Billy waited for instructions.

'Tie him to something,' I said. 'A long line, and near to water.'

He nodded, and took the rifle with him, and a second later I was running from the cave to catch him up and tell him not to forget the LMG when he came back.

When I got back inside, Jane had the tank's engine-cover raised and was carrying out an inspection by torchlight.

I said, 'You'll surely never get it started, will you?'

'Little ray of sunshine, you are, John.'

'But it must be fifteen or twenty years since it was running,' I protested. 'It'll have—'

'Have what?'

'Well—everything will be kind of set like glue!'

Jane said, 'If this engine was laid-up correctly, I don't see why it shouldn't start. Have you anything to write with—or on?'

'Nothing.'

She shrugged. 'Doesn't matter. I'll just take it in sequence. If I were laying it up for good—which is what Green must have known he was doing—I'd drain down the radiator first, okay?'

'This the radiator cap?' I asked, taking hold.

'That's it.'

The radiator was empty. Jane nodded.

'Then I'd check the oil, and fill her right up with long-term-storage oil.'

I found the dipstick. 'Oil okay,' I said. 'Full right up.'

'But what kind? It matters.' She shone the torch round the cave, pausing several times to focus the beam on drums and barrels. Then she walked across to a white-labelled drum with the Caltex trademark, and picked it up by the handle.

'Empty,' she said. 'Caltex—long-term store only.' She carried it towards the engine compartment.

'So far so good?'

'So far—perfect,' Jane said. 'Old Man Green knew what he was doing. Now—the fuel tank. It ought to be full.'

I took off the cap. 'Brimming,' I told her. 'You couldn't get three drops more in there.'

'That's because it was filled at night,' Jane said. 'Everything as cool and contracted as it could get. You get no condensation later.'

'Doesn't the diesel fuel get stale when it's years old?'

'Nope. Look—the air filter's blanked-off. If I just unwrap this . . .' This was kitchen foil.

'Now what?'

'Now we get the correct oil—there is some, I saw it. Then we drain the storage oil and put the right oil in.' Jane peered at the engine by torchlight. 'There's the drain tap. I'll just get a spanner.'

By the time Billy returned, twenty minutes or so later, the oil change was complete, and she was waiting for him, holding a strong pair of jump leads, with cables long enough to stretch from Sherman to Toyota—naturally enough, since they'd been made for the purpose.

'Did you bring water?'

Billy looked at me as if I were mad. Your full-blood Abo doesn't forget water. Not for a second. Ever.

So we filled the radiator.

Jane held up crossed fingers when the jump leads were clipped to both the Land-Cruiser's battery and the Sherman's. 'Okay, Billy,' she called to him, 'start up!' We heard the Toyota's starter.

The tank engine didn't fire. There was grunting and grumbling as the big GM6046 dual diesel turned. The Land-Cruiser's own sturdy diesel began to roar more loudly under pressure from Billy One-Hat's boot. Still nothing.

And then.

Suddenly . . .

Ber-roe-argh, broar, brrr. The first deafening catch became a tremendous roaring snarl like a dozen hungry lions at feeding time, and Jane climbed like a monkey up and into the driving position.

The next problem was to get our mountain of metal out through the cave entrance.

And when that was done—not without trouble, but there's no point dwelling on it—I had a question to ask, as Jane came clambering out of the Sherman. 'What are you actually proposing to do with this thing?'

'I thought,' she said coolly, 'that we might huff a bit and puff a bit and blow his house down.'

'There's no main gun on your tank, ma'am.'

'But there *is* a bulldozer blade—look.' She tapped it with her fist. 'So we'll go to his "place"—and we'll damn well level it! And if Bob Collis *is* there, we reclaim him for our side, first. If the Boss is there, we—' She stopped. 'Who *is* he, anyway? I don't mean just his name. *Who* is he?'

'Hop into your golden coach, Cinderella,' I said. 'I'll tell you a story as we go.'

19

I didn't though. The inside of a Sherman tank, under way and with its twin GM diesels blasting within inches of you, is no place to carry on conversations. You see pictures of tanks and everybody's wearing headphones; I'm not surprised. I tried to shout and Jane tried to hear but after a few seconds she smiled and shrugged and I shut up. There'd be time later.

After a while, a moonlit Stringer Station appeared in the observation port and Jane stopped the Sherman in front of it, climbed out, and went to talk to Billy in the Land-Cruiser, chugging behind. When he halted she said, 'Where'd you put him, Billy?'

The man was shut in where we'd been imprisoned with the King Brown snake, in the chapel, wrists efficiently tied behind his back and to his ankles—Billy had tied and branded a lot of calves in his time—and when I removed the balaclava helmet, and Billy shone the lamp on his face, he turned out to be Blackie: he of the roll-your-owns and the Criterion pub.

He was a nasty, unshaven, black-chinned rough, and he didn't take baths very often, but he turned out to be realistic enough.

When I said, 'Your lot have lost and our lot have won, and how do you fancy a ten-stretch in Fremantle Gaol?' he said, 'You can't prove a thing against me.'

'You're on this lady's property.'

'I got lost.' His grin showed a fair number of blackish teeth—probably where he got his nickname.

I said, 'I'm a solicitor—an officer of the court, that is. The lady's an army officer. We're both prepared to swear to several criminal acts you've committed, including two of kidnapping, two of attempted murder, and so on. You have a record already—' I was guessing, but it was something to bet upon with confidence—'do *you* fancy your chances, mate?'

'Whole thing was his idea,' Blackie said.

'Whose?'

'The Boss's. Said it was all a practical joke. What happens if I leave him and join your side?'

'You get a pretty muted welcome,' Jane said. 'You ride in the back of the Land-Cruiser, like we did, and you stay tied up. And if we've any trouble, I'll run you over with the Sherman tank. Accidentally, of course.'

That made his eyes widen. Or maybe it was her tone. Very brisk, Jane was now. 'Come on!' she said. 'Let's toss him in the back and get moving.'

A couple of minutes later we were rolling north-westwards. In those minutes I'd nipped indoors and found paper and biro. If I couldn't shout the tale into Jane's ear, I could write it down and she could read it when ready.

So that's how I occupied myself while Jane drove the old tank to the north-west. A mere two or three miles brought us to the first sound wire fence, and there she halted the tank and stole my paper and wrote, 'My fence or his?' I looked out and saw the neat posts and fresh wire and knew this wasn't Mary Ellen's legacy.

'His.'

'Goody,' Jane said, and set the Sherman trundling at it. 'Maybe his cattle will emigrate to *my* station.' She ripped a mile or two of wire and poles out as we went, and when I raised my eyebrows enquiringly she slowed briefly and scribbled 'Petty vengeance' on my paper.

We were about three hours on the way, coming up on the big station an hour or so after midnight.

Dark it may have been; certainly it was a time when the God-fearing might have been slumbering. However a

Sherman tank, roaring cross-country doesn't leave much scope for surprise. Jane juggled track-levers and throttle for a swift stop as we raced into the wide yard.

Into silence. Nobody there to greet us. No welcoming rifle fire.

We sat there for a moment, engines throttled back to no more than a furious rattle, and looked out of the ports at a scene in which nothing moved. The earth was still, the buildings, silvered by the moon, stood without a gleam of light, a quiver of curtain, or a changing reflection on an open window. No bark from a dog, no hunting cat.

There must have been noise, though; drowned of course by the racket we were making. But then we saw. The big, blue door of an out-building flew wide, and big headlights dazzled and a car hurtled out and past us, smashing down a five-bar gate.

'What the *hell*—!'

'Mercedes,' Jane said. 'Pale blue. Four-fifty SE. We can't catch it. I didn't see who was inside.'

'Three people. Or four.' I'd glimpsed silhouettes.

'Recognize anybody?'

'Er, no.'

'Entire population, would you think?'

'Yair.'

I still left the steel shelter of the Sherman with a certain reluctance: a couple of inches of steel armour are wonderfully reassuring if you suspect the presence of a sniper. I tried to copy the low, infantryman's run as I dodged round the tank to Billy One-Hat's Land-Cruiser to collect a rifle.

Then Billy and I bounced Blackie out of the Toyota and on to the earth and I said, 'Who'll be here?'

'Search me, mate.'

'If it'll help, a pale blue Mercedes just went out the gate, going like the hounds, three or four people in it.'

'Be nobody left, then. Just Boong jackaroos down at the barns.'

'You're sure?'

He nodded. 'Be nobody, mate.'

I said, 'Except the prisoner.'

Blackie looked up at me. 'Prisoner? What prisoner?'

'The one you picked up in Dalkeith. Where will he be?'

He glared at me.

'Remember,' I said, 'whose side you're on now.'

'End of the stable line,' Blackie said reluctantly. 'Barred windows. Made of cement block.'

We went there second. First came a search of the house: it was luxurious and empty and had been left in a hurry, a fact demonstrated by a video machine still turning and a TV set showing an old Presley film. Easy to guess that somebody'd heard the Sherman afar off, turned down the sound to make sure, and then run. The sound was still off and I didn't turn it up.

We went looking for Bob and found him, as advised, and totally unsurprised. He, too, had heard the Sherman and known what it was; the difference was he'd waited, having no option.

He wanted a whisky, and wasn't alone in that. Nor was it hard to find. We stretched ourselves on various expensive couches and chairs and sipped at our choice of single malts, and I said I was relieved to have found Bob alive.

'Even that bunch had doubts about murdering cops, including ex-cops,' Bob said. 'All they wanted was a location on a map, but it was nothing I knew anything about. Where is this bloody place anyway?'

'Nobody told you?'

'No. But we're well up north.'

'You didn't recognize anybody?'

'Nah. They wore woollen helmets. Slits for eyes. I thought it was the IRA for a while.'

'Knock you about?'

'A little. Nothing serious. Do you know what this is all about yet?'

'Tell me while you're at it,' Jane said. 'I'm puzzled, too. Start with the Boss, so-called. Who on earth *is* he?'

It's a happy rôle, that of the bloke who knows all, answering the questions of the uninformed. I settled myself in my chair and took a swig of Glenfiddich and said, 'Well, here we are at Northrop Station. Private company ownership but not by anybody named Northrop, or not recently. And the story doesn't really start with your inheritance, Jane, it goes much farther—' And that's as far as I got.

Jane's yell interrupted me. 'Blimey!' she said suddenly. 'My God, I must be stupid!' She was looking almost wildly round the big sitting room, muttering and pointing. 'North,' she said. And stopped. 'Paper and pencil,' she suddenly demanded.

I found both without going out to the tank, and she sat at the table and said, 'Just let me think for a bit.'

Then she began to draw . . .

She began by sketching a rectangle with corner cut out of it. 'The living room at Stringer Station, okay?'

'It's like that,' I said.

'Right. Now—' Bob and I were peering, one over each shoulder, and trying not to jump up and down, because Jane plainly had the whole puzzle by its treacherous throat and only needed to apply reason.

She made a cross on one wall of her plan. 'The pub embroidery was *here*, right?'

I nodded.

'Which would mean north.'

'Of what?'

'Of anybody standing in the middle of the room.'

'Let's assume so.'

'But *was* it?'

We discussed it—in relation to dawn and sunset, in respect of winds, etc. We tried to remember where the stars were. We concluded, finally, that it must be north.

'Fine,' she said. 'That's The Green Man. Now—on the south wall?'

'That's the funny thing,' I said. 'That embroidered plus-sign with the middle missing. Have you worked out what it means?'

Jane whispered, 'Not sure. Give me time. Now what was on the east wall?'

'Several things. That picture of Christ at the door, for a start.'

She shook her head. 'No, not that.'

'Roses. She'd embroidered roses.'

'You're sure it was on that wall?'

I said, 'Hang on a minute! Remember that some of those things had been taken down, and then broken. We don't know they'd been put back in the right place.'

Jane gave a tight little smile. 'They were right. Most of them, anyway. I checked the frames with the fade marks on the walls. So it *was* those roses!'

'Yes.'

She looked at me, eyes shining, and said, 'Got it!'

'The message?'

'This message anyway.' Playfully, she adopted my own lecturer's tone of a few moments earlier. 'Gentlemen, let me introduce you to the village of Thornton.' She made a little cross in the middle of the living room. 'We are here. And here—' pointing with the stick—'is The Green Man. Here, lies what is known as Four Lane Ends. A crossroads where four roads meet, that's all; no more, no less, but that's its name.' She paused. 'Now, gentlemen, let me draw your eyes and attention to this point here—to the roses. There was once another family of Emmetts in Thornton. Tom Emmett and his wife Mercy. They lived in Rose Villa on Storr Heights. Windy spot, and they'd grown big beech hedges to protect the roses.'

I said, 'The other wall was blank.'

She laughed. 'The *wall*, yes. But not my mind, and not Mary Ellen's! There's another road just here. Come on, John —ask me where it goes?'

'Where does the road go, Jane?'

'Chat Hill. And it wasn't entirely blank, was it?'

'I saw nothing.'

'It's the south wall, John. Chat Hill, to the south of Stringer Station—that's the message!'

I said, 'What were those heights?'

'Storr.' Jane spelled the word.

'You think it's a store in the other sense, too?'

'There was a delf at Storr Heights—'

'A what?'

'Delf. A hole in the side of the hill. It was once a quarry, so I was told. Tom Emmett filled it in for his garden.'

'So we've Chat Hill, and a hole in the side of it which may or may not be a store. And that's where the stones are. Is that it?'

'Yes. And I've been wondering,' Jane said, 'how *you* come to know about emeralds. But that can wait. Where's Chat Hill?'

I thought for a moment. 'Billy's lived here all his life.'

'So he has.' Jane rushed to the door and called 'Billy?'

He came trotting in. 'Yair, Miss Strutt?'

'Does your people have a talking place—a hill somewhere?'

'Corroboree?' I added, and cursed myself as I saw his smile vanish and a stubborn frown replace it.

Jane turned accusingly. 'You've upset him. What on earth did you say?'

'Just the Abo word for a dance, or a party.'

'Why's he cross, then?'

'Because their culture's sacred to them.' I turned to him. 'Sorry, Billy. I didn't want—' But he had already turned away, scowling.

Jane walked after him. 'Billy, Missus Green left me a message about a place where Mr Green used to go when he went walkabout. So it must be about seven to ten days away on horseback. I'd like to find it. Will you help me? Will you —please?'

He wanted nothing to do with it, or her, for that matter. Not at first. But Jane Strutt, officer and lady, undeniably had a persuasive way with her. I stood well back and watched her talk to him, sensing she was making progress. I also felt more than a bit ashamed, because here we were, replete with the old white greed once again, and there Billy was, remaining guardian of the secret places of tribe and belief. For him the land itself was sacred and wondrous, full of the mystical powers of the Dreamtime. Two hundred years had seen so many of the Abo secret places desecrated as their land was stolen, their culture defiled, their Dreamtime and the Rainbow Serpent derided, their tribes dispersed. A meeting ground might well be one of the holiest places of his tribe, reserved for the elders, for the initiations, for sacred dances to make the wallaby more fertile or make fire behave when fire was put to the bush to promote regrowth: these places were held sacred ten times longer than Rome and twenty times longer than Mecca.

So Jane talked, and Billy listened, frowning and occasionally shaking his head, and sometimes, as she talked on, giving a reluctant little nod.

There was just the sibilance of Jane's whispering in the big room. I couldn't hear what she said to Billy and didn't want to and I suppose my mind just quietly went walkabout among the Thorntons and Stringers and—

The aircraft!

Where was that damned Cessna?

The Boss had flown it out of Stringer Station while Jane pumped .303 rounds through the corrugated steel walls. Had he flown it here? Well, he must have done! But here now seemed deserted. The Boss had gone, his transport plane with him, and the apple of his eye, the old P38 Lightning, was still on the ground at Stringer!

Or was it? Think about it! He'd two pilots, himself and another. What would have been easier than to have himself dropped off at Stringer to reclaim the P38?

I went outside, opened the rear door of the Toyota and demanded of Blackie, 'Where's he keep his little plane—the six-seater?'

'There's a red-painted barn doubles as a hangar,' he said, readily enough. I slammed the door on him and went looking. Possibly the Cessna was still here, and the Boss had departed by Mercedes. But the red barn stood empty, when I got there, so it wasn't and he hadn't.

And then, as I stood in the doorway, my eye was caught by a notice at the far end of the building, readable only because the letters were in bold red on a white ground. 'WARNING!' it said. I trotted over to see more. Underneath the warning were the words 'Ammunition Store'. The words were on a door and the door was locked. I got it open with a prise bar from one of the neat tool-racks on the walls. Inside were wooden ammunition boxes in two sizes and I opened one of each.

'Not just machine guns,' I told them. 'Belts of cannon-shell —that P51 has a pair of cannon!'

Bob looked at me levelly. 'The radio-phone has been smashed. In there.'

'So—tank or no tank, we're outgunned.'

'If he intends to attack,' Jane said.

Bob Collis chipped in. 'He's got no bloody option, has he? His identity's known.'

'Not to me,' Jane said.

'Name's on his writing-paper in there. Dixie Mackeras owns this place.'

'But why would a man who owns all this—?'

'Because he's like that. Because he's rich, and wants even more,' I said. 'And here we are, still without any way of talking to the outside. And there *he* is, sitting in the cockpit of his fighter, which may be World War Two, but it flies and it shoots.'

'Bloody good plane, that,' Bob said. 'Saw 'em attack with bombs once, near Caen on the breakout, carrying two thousand pounders.'

Jane gave a slightly forced laugh. 'I don't think he's got one of those with him, not tonight.'

'So now?' I asked. 'We've got a military matter and you two are the soldiers.'

Jane said, 'We get away in the dark.'

'To where?'

'Mister One-Hat,' she said, 'has kindly agreed to show us where.' She must have seen my frown, because she added, 'He and I have a very clear understanding, now.'

On Bob's advice ('You can't really run a Sherman on its tracks more than thirty miles or so without a breakdown crew in attendance to repair the tracks when they break') we left in the Land-Cruiser at around three. Blackie we shoved in to the concrete-block stable which had held Bob. There was bread and cheese and twenty litres of water, and all being well *somebody* would release him one day soon. Who did it depended on who won. Mackeras, if he won; the police if we did.

The Sherman was abandoned, too. If Mackeras flew over his station, he might pause to shoot it up, thereby using ammunition he wouldn't be able to use on us, or replace. Because just before we set out, I made a little fire from wood and paraffin and tossed the lot in among the ammo boxes. The bangs, a little later, were many and loud.

We could have done it the other way, I suppose. Could have concentrated on getting the hell out, getting the police in, getting Mackeras out of the way and only then going after the mine.

But we didn't. At that moment only Billy One-Hat knew where to go, and his knowledge came not from maps, but only from familiarity with the great sweep of his own land. Jane drove. Billy sat beside her, Bob and I rode in the back. All of us had guns but, faced with a fully-armed fighter, we might as well have been carrying nail files . . .

20

'Why?' Jane said, or half shouted at me over the Toyota's roaring engine note. 'A man like him—rich already. Everything he would ever want. *Why?*'

Six o'clock in the morning now, and the light clear, golden and intensifying, and once more we were bounce-bounce-bouncing as the Land-Cruiser's well-exercised suspension proved barely equal to a hellish track. We were making speed, too, to smooth the road, so God knows what it's like going slowly.

I leaned forward, keeping my chin well clear of the seat-back in front which threatened every couple of seconds to rear, break my jaw and loosen all my teeth, and half shouted back. 'Does the name itself—Dixie—ring any bells?'

'No.'

'It's a diminutive—of Dickson, in fact.'

'Still no.'

I said, 'Man name of Dickson owned Stringer once. Those days it was Dickson Station. He's the bloke who lost it in a two-up game.'

'But that was centuries ago!'

'Nineteen-twenties. Not so long. Lost it to Mary Ellen's first husband.'

Jane glanced back. 'What's Mackeras's relationship with him?'

'Grandson,' I said. 'Born poor and nursing a big grievance, that's my guess. Grandad had squandered what Grandson should have had. Somebody else had it instead. First Stringer, then Mary Ellen, then Green came into it, then Mary Ellen again, and then you. By that time he's already rich and— remember he made his money in the Perth building booms

—he's both tough and unscrupulous. Had to claw his way up, when he thought things should have been his by right.'

'He could have offered to buy after Green died!'

I said, 'He could. Probably did, more than once. But she must have been a stubborn old lady. Not only that, but she *liked* living up here. And beyond that, she'd decided to leave it all to you! A fact which Dixie knew.'

'How did he—?' Jane began. Then stopped. 'That woman Marye. It was her!'

'Marye with an "e",' I said. 'Marye N. Bright, shares his home and his life and many of the little secrets that lurk in deed boxes and files in lawyers' offices.'

'She still couldn't have known about the will,' Jane insisted.

'Why not? If Mackeras was in the habit of dropping in on the old lady, making offers for the station—as he must have been—she'd have told him, wouldn't she, that she had other intentions? I have a picture of her in my head, haven't you—?'

Jane said, 'It's mine by right.'

'When they lifted you in King's Park,' I asked, 'what exactly happened?'

She glanced back at me once more. 'We were standing together—you had just gone off to the phone—and she sort of spun round. Said she'd something sharp in her eye; she dropped her bag at the same time and everything in it rolled down the grassy slope. I went after them and a car stopped and I was lifted in. Quick as that. Two men. I was pushed face-down on the floor—never saw a thing until they took me out at a house, and I saw damn little there either because they shoved me straight in a cellar!'

'And Marye N. Bright?'

'I don't know. Busy with her eye, probably.'

'She told me,' I said, 'that you just hopped into a cab. Vision must have been distorted.'

'Values, too.'

'The daughter,' I said, 'of a fellow called Bright. Freelance journalist, semi-perpetual drunk, writer under many names. One such *nom-de-plume* was Don Gay.'

'That rings no bells either.'

'He wrote a piece years back in the Adelaide *Sunday Mail*, about Jacka Green, the gold prospector who vanished. Then Mary Ellen married John Joseph Green, and Marye's just the girl to put two and two together to Marye's advantage.'

'But is it worth all this effort, I mean to people like that? His station's ten times bigger than Stringer.'

'Acquisitive people,' I said, 'like to acquire. But there's another point. A few years ago you could have got good odds against diamonds existing in Australia *at all*. Now the Argyle field's very likely the richest on earth, and here we are with emeralds! We don't know the quantity, though we can make some guesses about quality.'

Jane said, 'Must be easy to get at if a lone prospector can dig them out.'

'Right. Could be valuable beyond belief, and Marye N. would be delighted to be proprietor of one of the great gem mines. My name is Marye—and the "e" is for Emeralds. She'd adore all that.'

Jane laughed. 'Wouldn't mind it myself! But how did they learn about the emeralds?'

'My guess,' I said, 'is that Mary Ellen must have worn something ostentatious. Ring, perhaps, or a brooch. Remember she and Jacka had done the entire thing. Between them they'd found the stones, learned to cut them, made the mounts, all using the skills learned in Holland and Belgium post-war. There'd be strong sentimental value in jewellery like that—especially with Jacka dead. Hey, Billy, did Missus Green wear jewellery?'

He said at once, 'Yair, big green stuff.'

'What kind?'

'Hands,' he said. 'And here.' His big dark hand patted his throat.

'And when Mackeras saw those,' I said, 'he began to feel greedy.'

'Egged on, no doubt.'

'Marye,' I said, 'would egg on with high efficiency.'

*

234

From time to time I pushed my face against the side window, squinting upwards, or leaned awkwardly back over my seat to try to scan the sky. Couldn't see much, though, because all the angles were wrong. I felt in my bones that Mackeras was somewhere not far away, but the chances were all against our spotting him.

Facts: Mackeras must destroy us, to remain free and continue to enjoy his wealth and position. Furthermore, he had the means: two aircraft, one too fast to use for shadowing us, but beautifully effective in attack; the other near enough a spotter plane: low stalling speed, high wing, several hours' duration.

What I feared was that Mackeras in the Cessna was circling slowly above us like the wedge-tail eagle, all sound of his engine masked by the racket of the Land-Cruiser's diesel, and all sight of him cut off by the Land-Cruiser's long, steel roof. Easy for him: he could just hang up there out of sight, watching our dust trail point the way, waiting until the position of Jacka Green's pegmatite deposit was revealed, and only then moving in to the attack.

In the right circumstances, notions like that can rapidly turn into obsessions, and mine did. Soon, in my mind's eye, he was right above. I demanded that Jane stop, then I got out to stare up into that cobalt sky with eyes which, fresh from the shade, couldn't cope.

I listened, then moved off a hundred metres into the scrub and listened again. The fact that all I could hear was the diesel didn't damp my fears.

'Switch off the engine!' I called to them, and Bob Collis bellowed back, 'Don't be bloody stupid!' because when you're in a solo vehicle and miles from anywhere in the outback, you don't switch off engines unnecessarily. Sometimes they won't start again.

'What was all that about?' Jane demanded when I returned.

I explained, and then everybody was looking at the sky, and all ears were cocked. We saw nothing.

We pushed on. Then Jane yelled, 'He wouldn't even

have to stay with us. He could just pay us little visits from time to time. The dust trail wouldn't be hard to spot!'

'No,' I said. 'It wouldn't.'

'We could stop for a bit,' Jane offered. 'If he flew over we'd at least know whether he was after us.'

'Noon in a couple of minutes,' said Bob, succinctly, ruling *that* out. The sun was overhead; none of us needed reminding of its power.

So we bowled on, air-conditioned, running now over characteristic Kimberley green-country-land, rolling between stony outcrops and deep scars worn by rains over the ages; it looks a bit as though a lot of green velvet cushions had been pushed together edge to edge.

Once, when Jane swung the Land-Cruiser abruptly through three quarters of a circle to avoid some kind of obstruction, I thought I saw a plane above, but by now the windows were heavily red-dusted and I couldn't be sure. It could have been a bird, even an insect.

Billy, meanwhile, was immune to such concerns. His attention was upon route and terrain, as he indicated changes of direction with turns of the wrist, often in places where no change of any kind looked necessary. Once, for instance, while we were travelling easily over the top surface of one of the green cushions, he guided Jane insistently 'left, left, left', and half a mile on we glided nicely down a gentle incline to the bottom of a gulley that had sheer, twenty-foot sides—starting a few yards away. It was quite an astonishing feat of memory Billy was performing. He'd walked over this country twice as a boy, he said. Now forty years on, he still seemed to know every gum and gulley, practically every pebble, and blade of grass and, what was more remarkable, to anticipate each of them. Without him, not only would we not have known target or route: crossing this terrain we'd have spent much of our time trying to extricate ourselves from situations varying from foolish to impossible.

*

We'd been *en route* something like seven hours when Billy One-Hat pointed ahead to a hill that rose a couple of hundred feet a mile or so ahead, and said, 'That one.'

Jane said, 'You mean we're actually *there*?' in a voice full of relief, and Billy gave a haunted sort of smile and said this was the Hill of the Talking: not of his tribe, but of another to the south with whom discussion had ever been necessary in order that fighting be avoided.

We reached it four or five minutes later. Jane stopped the Land-Cruiser and I hopped out, stretched and looked. Chat Hill (I'd better call it) was a curious formation; the hill itself was guarded in the approach on three sides by a low ridge that could almost have been *built* for defence, like the man-made earthworks of early history in Europe. It hadn't though: this was good, tough Australian rock; only Nature could have moulded it.

You could see why the Abo warriors had favoured this spot. Anyone arriving had to show himself on the ridge-top before even approaching the hill. Clever stuff.

I reported my findings, climbed back aboard, and we drove to the end of the ridge, round it, and back down the fold which lay between ridge and hill, and where high bush, in the form of twenty- to thirty-foot gums, grew in numbers.

The Land-Cruiser we parked at the foot of the ridge, half screened by trees on one side and protected on the other by rising ground. Then, in the heat, we began climbing Chat Hill. Soon the soldiers, male and female, were looking back doubtfully.

'Camouflage,' Jane suggested.

'Agreed,' Bob Collis said.

So we set about finding brushwood and breaking off dead branches to hide the Toyota from questing airborne eyes.

It was good thinking, but just a shade late. Few people enjoy hard physical work in the heat and we were tugging and sweating, carrying wood towards the 4-WD when there was a sudden startling blast of sound and as our heads jerked up, the six-seater Cessna passed low overhead.

Worse—bullets sprayed at us viciously from the side window . . .

21

Viciously—but, thank God, inaccurately! I glanced quickly round. No one was hit. The Cessna, having now overflown, was turning swiftly, like a crop-sprayer, nearly ready to attack again. We raced up the hill, into the trees and I flung myself at a thick-trunked ecualypt and stood tight against it, putting a good foot of hard timber between me and the gun.

Then he was blasting back, flying low down the valley, firing once again; a spray of bullets thumped into earth and trees, clipping bark and branches. Edging round my tree, sheltering, as he went by, I got one swift glimpse of the plane at a range of less than a hundred yards.

He was alone. He was flying one-handed at nought feet, and firing an automatic weapon out of the side window with the other hand. He was a maniac—and a desperate one: now swinging into a turn again for the next pass.

'Everybody okay?' I yelled.

No reply: the engine made too much noise for voices to be heard.

Then he was back, the automatic weapon poked from the left-hand window and firing at random into the trees. No shots came nearer than a couple of yards.

I yelled, 'Jane!' with lungs of brass and by the grace of God she must have heard or guessed and she glanced out from the shelter of a gum a dozen yards away, and waved at me, while behind us the Cessna stood on its left wing-tip and readied itself for a fourth firing run.

God, but it was frightening! That time one bullet hit my tree, high up, and a small branch fell on me. Makes you jump, that does. First time I ever heard the *zoop* of a bullet and it's a sound I don't ever want to hear again. But if it was frightening, it was also ineffectual, thus far. Nobody hit, no damage: the precious Land-Cruiser parked where he couldn't fire at it directly without risking a crash into the ridge.

He turned again at the end of the fourth run . . . positioned himself . . . and then abruptly changed his mind, because the engine was suddenly louder yet, and he was climbing over the top of the ridge and heading home!

I left my tree and stepped out into the dappled sunlight. So did Billy, so did Jane . . . lastly Bob Collis, holding on to the trunk, hopping. I ran to him and saw the pain in his face, the blood that stained his right trouser leg.

'Shin bone,' he muttered as I reached him. 'Must have hit something else and ricocheted!'

'I'll get the first-aid kit.' Jane was already lopping towards the Land-Cruiser as I helped Bob to sit on the ground and he took a look at the wound, inspecting it with an almost professional interest, in spite of his pain.

'Not much to look at, is it?' he said wryly. 'But the tibia's broken. I won't be walking far.' He gave a taut grin. 'By rights it should have taken my whole bloody foot off at that range.'

Rapid first-aid was carried out by Jane: clean the wound, penicillin powder, bandaging to apply pressure. The bullet had sideswiped him, entry hole and exit hole an inch apart.

'Sit here,' I said. Bob leaned resignedly against his tree, and said, 'Find the damn mine and let's get out of here!'

'Where do we go, Billy?' Jane asked.

He shook his head and shrugged, voluble as ever.

'There's a hole of some kind, perhaps a cave or a quarry, in the side of the hill,' she insisted.

'Dunno, missus.'

'We'd better see what we can find,' I said. 'Let's go in opposite directions and at different heights—thirty feet apart on the hill.'

So we did—and we'd gone about twenty yards when Jane called to me, 'How soon d'you reckon he can get back here?'

I already had the answer worked out. I climbed down to her. 'We drove seven hours at about thirty-five mph average. About. Therefore we've come just short of two hundred and fifty miles. If the Cessna flew at around one-twenty or one-thirty as it probably did, he'd take near enough two hours to return to Stringer.'

'And then come back in the Lightning?'

'So I imagine.'

'How long?'

'You'd know better than I do. What's its speed?'

'It was very fast for its time,' Jane said. 'Four-fifty or so maximum in level flight. So it's a half-hour ride, not much more. Then when he gets here he's a pair of aircraft cannon to blast us with, as well as the machine guns!'

'*If* he comes back,' I said. 'Maybe he won't. He's a rich man. He'll have resources abroad. He may have decided to just walk out.'

'But he wouldn't. He's mad, for one thing. And he can't bear losing.'

'It's an Australian trait.'

'Yes.' She smiled and glanced at her watch. 'We have about two hours, then. Better get busy.'

We were above the tree line, and out in the still-hot sunshine as we tramped across the slopes. Gradually I went up a little higher, to cover more ground as we passed, reasoning that the pegmatite wouldn't be located too high, or else Jacka Green would never have found it.

Up there, walking steadily, with a long view across miles of empty country, I got the feeling that often comes when you're off the track in Australia—that you're probably the first man ever to put a foot down where you just did. Oh, Jacka Green might have been there, or numerous long-vanished Abos, but had they stepped there, or there? With long miles of emptiness here, it was long odds against a human foot on any bit of it.

I was looking out for two things: the shadowed entrance to a cave, or some sign of a path. You may think a path would inevitably have vanished in the decade and a half since Jacka Green died; but you're wrong. This landscape is fragile, the vegetation thin. Scars show for a long time, and Green must have had a preferred route on the hill for his horse and camel or mule. By this time I was walking on the low side of a small ridge that ran across the slope, wondering if I shouldn't be on top of it.

Every so often Jane and I would wave to each other, or shrug at each other, or grin, or whatever, as a change from marching along in silence; and it was while I was doing something like that, round the far end of Chat Hill, that I managed to fall over my own feet and tumble—and roll bruisingly, about twenty feet down the slope towards her, crashing through a low thorn bush as I went. I wasn't hurt much, except in the area of pride, but Jane had come to help and suddenly said, 'Hey, you're bleeding!'

And I was. Clean cut on left forearm, about an inch and a quarter long.

'Sit down for a minute. Get your breath!'

'With Mackeras due back?—No, thanks.' I was winding my handkerchief round the cut. 'Tie this, will you, Jane?'

She tied it, looked up at me, and said, 'Too tight?'

'Tighter still if anything.'

'Right. Look—this could be neater. Let's start again.' She unwrapped the makeshift bandage, and began to tie it, then said, 'What made a cut like that?—it's as though it had been done with a knife, look at it, straight and the edges are clean.'

'Must have been a sharp thorn.'

'Nope.' She tied it quickly and started up the slope, towards the point from which I'd fallen; only a few steps, really. Then halfway she stopped beside the thorn bush and carefully reached her hand and arm in between the thorns, picked something out and lifted it clear.

'Empty tin can,' she said, 'wedged in the branches. Mr Heinz's beanses from the look of it.' A remnant of a blue label remained attached. 'Jacka—*his mark*!' She grinned exuberantly.

'Um,' I said.

'Excelsior,' Jane now urged. 'Higher, higher!'

So we climbed, easily for a few yards; then we encountered the small, steep ridge, almost vertical at this point and perhaps four feet high. I half-jumped, half-climbed it, turned to offer my hand, and found Jane standing beside me, saying, 'It's scraped clean along there. What's pegmatite look like, anyway?'

Her question put me straight back in the classroom with Tom Kendrick pointing the finger at me. I never actually studied geology in any formal sense, as an examination subject, but the school sensibly took the view that in a state as mineral-rich as Western Australia, you might as well know what you've fallen over. 'Pegmatite,' I said, thinking, 'it's . . . er . . . an igneous rock . . . er . . . and the colour is pink or whitish-grey.'

Jane was scooting along the ridge. 'Pinkish-white,' she said, 'does that count?'

I followed her along. 'Any sign of digging?'

'No. Just exposed pegmatite.' She stopped, turned, looked back. 'My guess is that this whole thing, this little ridge, is made of the stuff. Does it do that—occur in veins?'

'Don't remember. Keep going.'

'Heavens, look!'

It was a football-sized rock, split apart, its interior like the inside of Aladdin's cave—a mass of quartz and mica crystals in blues and greens and pinks. You see them sometimes in the windows of jewellery shops.

'Beautiful. Keep going!'

We found Jacka Green's workings sixty paces or so further on. Well above us, on a kind of corner on the end of Chat Hill. Just where the hilltop began to slope downwards, stood a curious formation which looked as though a giant had leaned over and taken a bite out of the hillside—but a delicate bite, direction upward, so that the stone overhung it.

There the pinkish-white pegmatite of the little ridge had

risen with the hill, for all the world like a long squeeze of toothpaste across the side of the slope.

The natural hole—the giant's bite—went perhaps fifteen feet in and six or seven feet down, but all around us were tailings of broken rock, and in the back of the hole lay a tarpaulin tied with rope.

'Your mine, my lady,' I said, 'is ready for inspection.'

She jumped easily down, and then looked up quickly, laughing. 'I haven't the faintest idea what I'm looking for!'

'You're just rubber-necking,' I said. 'The looking is done with a pick-axe, and it's a search for crystals.'

'Right.' She turned this way and that examining the rock, and suddenly pounced upon something. 'Catch, John.' It was a piece about the size of a cricket ball, and a tiny, pyramid-shaped hole sank into it at one point. 'Do you think that could have been an emerald—one that Jacka Green found and took away?'

'Could be anything. But yes, maybe it is. Seen enough?'

'Not yet. I want to see what's in the tarpaulin.'

She picked at the rope then unwound it, and removed the covering: inside were pick, shovel and hammer. 'No use carrying them back and forth,' Jane said. 'Early labour-saving, eh?' She rewrapped the parcel of tools. 'Okay, pull me up.'

I was just doing so when Billy One-Hat arrived, in complete silence as usual, and both of us nearly jumped out of our skins. He was barefoot on the stony slope, boots fastened together and slung over his shoulder.

'Find him, eh, missus?' he said. He looked a bit sombre about it, and once Jane was out of the delf she went to him and said, 'I won't let you down.' What she meant I didn't ask.

After that, we moved ourselves. Mackeras in his appropriately named Lightning could be here in an hour, if he was coming back—and I had little doubt he was. Our task now, was simply to survive.

No point in debate: there were just two obvious facts. First the Toyota must be preserved to take us out, otherwise we'd never *get* out. Secondly, we ourselves must find somewhere safe from Mackeras's heavy armament.

We began by shifting the Toyota about a hundred yards, then toiling in the heat to pile on it more branches torn from the bush. If he'd spotted it before, we reasoned, it was now elsewhere and better hidden, and should not be hit unless by bad luck, protected as it was by the ridge.

That left the four of us. We had rifles—and nothing else. Not a thing, in other words, with which to defend ourselves against a powerfully equipped aircraft which, though forty-plus years old, remained fast, efficient and very dangerous.

And we had little time. Billy One-Hat, walking one-way round the hill while we had gone the other, had discovered no convenient caves, or if he had, wasn't telling us.

That left the mine. Plus the difficulty of getting Bob Collis up there. Hopping four hundred yards uphill on one leg, with the other one broken, is no kind of picnic outing. Could Bob do it?

'My bloody oath, I can!'

One arm round Billy's shoulders, one round mine, and instantly a question; up through the trees first, and then along the bare ridge? Or along the valley bottom first, to climb when Bob was already tired? Method two would mean Bob had shelter in the trees if Mackeras arrived early; two was therefore adopted, and off we staggered, Billy and I, with two hundred pounds or so of beefsteak, beer and barbecues suspended between two rapidly sweating men. It was the first time I'd actually seen Billy sweat; and the cause wasn't the heat but the weight. I remember threatening Bob, 'If we ever do get home you go first on the scale and then on the diet!'

But that was the limit of badinage or even talk. Pretty soon there was neither strength nor breath for it, let alone disposition. Bob hopped and hopped and hopped again, grunting with pain each time, and by the time we'd gone a hundred yards he said, 'Sorry, blokes, but we'll have to splint it.' We found a pair of straightish sticks and I tore off the long sleeves of my shirt to make ties and in a few minutes we were off again, until Bob said, 'Where's Jane?'

'Jane!' I yelled.

'Up here.' Her voice came thinly from above and ahead: she must be going diagonally up across the slope. 'Need help?'

'No.' We struggled on, half-carrying Bob. Jane would be ferrying our firearms, a tough enough job without taking on one-third of Bob Collis. But perhaps I'm overstating Bob's condition; he was anything but helpless and the leg that worked functioned powerfully: fact is that though progress appeared slow, we moved quite quickly and the trek along relatively flat ground already lay behind us, and we were halfway up the hill when—

'Listen!' Billy said, head cocked.

We did. There was no mistaking that sound: the distant hum of aircraft engines was faint but very clear. At the speed a P38 commanded, we had only seconds now, and then we'd be a clear target, the three of us, on the slope above the trees with a hundred feet still to climb. And Jane would be alone at the diggings. Frantically we tried to increase our pace, while in our ears the distant sound became less distant and the Lightning hurtled towards us. The strain of dragging Bob up that thirty degree slope was murderous on all three of us, but worst on him, as the broken leg bashed against the ground with each step. But still he thumped the good leg against the earth like a pile driver, forcing his big body remorselessly upward. By this time he was no longer upright, but on his side on the slip, his arms no longer round our shoulders. We had him by the arms, pulling as he pushed, legs braced on the slope. Forty feet to go . . . thirty five . . . stamp, stamp . . . thirty . . .

And then the blast of sound fell on us, a blanket woven of pure noise and, close as we were to the earth, we all crouched instinctively closer as Mackeras and his silver Lightning flashed across the sky over our heads!

'Leave me,' Bob gasped into the sudden quiet as the noise tore away over the other side of the hill.

'Don't be stupid!'

'I can force myself up, no worry. Bit at a time, eh? Go on, the pair of you.'

I glanced after the Lightning. Mackeras had announced his spectacular arrival to his victims, and was climbing a little now, probably to get a better look . . .

'Just go! I'll pretend to be dead.'

I looked at him doubtfully, hearing the racket in my ears as the Lightning's twin engines roared into position. How could we . . .?

'Don't *give* that bastard two lives,' Bob shouted. 'Make the bastard work for 'em. Go!'

I couldn't have done it. I'd have had to stay, forlorn and helpless. Billy One-Hat wasn't like that. He was over fifty, a big man but no athlete, no mass of bulging muscle—but now Billy, still holding on to the arm, took a step back down the slope and suddenly Bob was draped over his shoulder and back, in the familiar fireman's lift, and Billy's slim black legs were driving like a rugby forward's on the slope, and I was running and scrambling beside them, struggling just to keep up, as the Lightning came flashing down at us.

And now it was firing!

Mackeras must have seen us, small light-coloured figures on the greenish-brown of the slope, but he chose to ignore us. Why? Maybe his line was already determined. As I scrambled higher, I glanced up the hill to the lip of the mine, but could see nothing of Jane. I looked down quickly then and saw the plucking of his bullets in the dust of the valley. Had he seen the Toyota?

Beside me, Billy was grunting and shouting with effort as he lifted Bob ever closer to the dark gape of the mine-opening. Like him, I drove my aching legs and empty lungs towards it. Behind us the chatter of gunfire ended and the Lightning lifted and tore away.

Why? My brain was too busy with the effort my weakening limbs required, to offer any answer . . . and the lip of the hole was now edging slowly towards me. Billy's astounding burst of strength hurtled him forward, and I yelled and chanted again, 'Three, two one—*go!*' as we flung ourselves down and scrambled over the lip into shelter!

Into the hole Jacka Green had dug, where Jane, crouched on a rock below the lip, was coolly working the bolt of the .303.

'Bob okay?' she demanded.

'Been worse,' he replied. 'What're you up to with that thing?'

She smiled tautly. 'I put one into him.'

'Rubbish!'

'It's not even hard! He passed a hundred and fifty yards away and he's thirty-odd feet long. Matter of aiming off, that's all.'

'All!'

'He's coming back!' Jane said warningly. And then, her voice rising. 'At us—he's coming *at* us!'

Heads just over the lip, we saw him come barrelling in from our right, swinging wide, then banking towards the mine, and everybody ducked, Jane boldly last, as the savage blast of the engines was supplemented by the *batter-batter* of his guns and suddenly a burst of fire zipped into the opening and thudded on the back wall.

Bob, lying on the flattish floor said, 'He had to climb damn sharp then—or he'd have been into the hill!'

'Got another one into him!' Jane was triumphant. 'He couldn't hit me. I couldn't *miss* him!'

'He'll be back,' I said. 'And we were lucky last time that nothing flew about inside here. Stay down—next time we might get ricochets.'

'Or him,' Jane added grimly.

We waited.

Now Mackeras came round in another skimming turn, and flung the Lightning's guns into level line with the mine entrance, the ridge was behind him and beneath him, the guns flickering fire as . . . we ducked and the rounds came racketing up the slope and in through the entrance hole, filling the shallow, curving space with flying metal . . . but only for a second, no more, then he roared upwards.

And Jane yelled, 'Got him—third time!'

But the situation was deadly dangerous. It seemed to me his turn was wider each time, giving a longer direct flight —more time to pour more fire into us. We were in a small space. We couldn't be lucky forever. He'd get us all before long, and we'd no way—despite Jane's triumphant rifle-fire —to protect ourselves. No defence at all.

Unless—

I raised my head to look out. Late afternoon had brought the first stirrings of a breeze, as it often did.

'Matches!'

They looked at me blankly.

'Quick,' I said, realizing as I spoke that I had little chance. Neither Jane nor Bob Collis smoked, and Billy—

'Here, boss,' Billy said. It was a gas lighter.

Mackeras was still straightening for his firing run as I climbed to the lip and flung myself down the slope towards the trees a hundred feet below. I kept my head down, trying to stay on my feet long enough to be clear of the fixed guns as he thundered in.

He began firing. I could hear the rounds zipping by and one seemed to fan the bare flesh of my arm . . . and then I was tumbling head over heels, rolling over and over, catching glimpses of earth and glimpses of sky, dropping breakneck down the slope until I fetched up with a hard whack against the base of a small gum that cracked as it broke my fall by uprooting itself.

I was a bit bruised, but little more, and the bone-dry ground yielded bone-dry kindling that caught fire fast and the dry eucalypts did likewise. Dry tinder in Australia catches like galloping horses and flies like the wind.

I could hear Mackeras's fighter plane swinging in its wide circle as, pushing the now burning eucalypt bush before me, I began to make a path of fire through the trees, and behind me smoke began to billow, and under my feet the flame began to spread.

I was running and pushing into the wind, and glancing back as often as I dared, calculating that Mackeras might have time for possibly two more passes before smoke made aiming difficult and increased his danger in flying towards the hilltop. I think I yelled a prayer that he'd miss, or crash or—

His turn was steep and complete now, and above me he was hurtling in again, guns blazing at the mine. My eyes dropped to the swift blaze, spreading behind me like lightning across the ground and up the trees. Mackeras must have sensed this was almost his last chance, seen the smoke begin to billow as the breeze picked it up and it began to draw a fine grey veil across the end-face of Chat Hill.

Exactly what happened next I cannot be sure, because the smoke was obscuring my own view, too—the trees were torches in a matter of seconds—but it seemed to me the Lightning somehow wavered just a trifle in its headlong approach, recovered, then hurtled higher, and missed the hilltop narrowly only because the pilot lifted the nose recklessly into a near-vertical climb.

After that the sounds were hard to interpret. But plainly his flight pattern had changed. Not now the organized turn into a firing run. Though I could see almost nothing for smoke, I could hear an engine whose pitch varied, whose running sounded . . . not ragged, exactly, but strange.

I ran down the slope, out of the belt of trees, crossed the valley bottom and began scrambling up the ridge.

When I reached the top, it was just in time to see Mackeras in the P38 dropping towards the ground maybe half a mile away where the dome of one of the green cushions looked fairly flat.

He was going fast. Too fast, I thought. But he brought her down, wheels retracted, belly flat to the ground, pancaked her, skidded for a while.

Then stopped.

No fire—not yet.

Mackeras didn't get out.

22

What made me run towards that plane? I've wondered, since, if it was not some momentary madness. The danger was always clear: for the Lightning had come to rest, by some fluke, with its nose, and therefore its weapons, pointed directly towards me as I ran; and that nose contained Hispano cannon plus machine guns. So he had only to press the firing button . . .

But if madness had me, I was not the only one. Jane must have bounded from the mine-workings and plunged at once on to the smoke-blown slope, because I'd gone almost no distance when I heard her yell, 'Wait—wait for me!'

I didn't, though. I was running with one hope uppermost in my mind—the hope that the Lightning wouldn't burn; that I could drag Dixie Mackeras out of it. I wanted him alive. I wanted him in *my* hands, to put in the *law's* hands. I wanted him, ultimately, in court.

Half a mile may not look far when you're in front of your TV watching athletes whisk twice round the tartan track while commentators yap of tenths of a second. It's a bloody long way across open country, though, in ordinary clothes, and with a day's high heat lingering, and a drop into a gulley and a climb out before I could even approach the plane itself.

I was terrified the whole way: terrified that the Lightning would burn. Astonished that it wasn't a pyre already: impossible, surely, that petrol dripping from a ruptured pipe or tank had not been ignited by heat from engines or exhausts —two of them, remember.

And if Mackeras was there, as he must be, strapped in the

seat, I was surprised his thumb hadn't touched the firing button. For five full minutes as I ran I must have been dead-centre in his sights.

The questions raced through my head: why didn't it burn, why didn't he fire, why didn't he climb out, had the crash killed him? But it couldn't have, because I glimpsed movement behind the cockpit hood. Was he trapped—by the legs, maybe; waiting to burn?

All the time, from well back behind me I heard Jane calling faintly for me to wait; but I dared not. Seconds counted. Lost seconds could cost Mackeras's life—or mine, as I tried to get him out—and the last thing I wanted was Jane close to the dead plane when its fuel flared and ammunition began to explode.

So I tore on, with growing exhaustion taking the strength from me. My throat was dry and aching, my lungs felt on fire, my heart thumped and thudded in my chest, and my legs were starting to wobble.

And now I could even smell petrol! I knew that it needed only a spark.

Madness.

But I ran on because now I saw him wave to me, frantically, beckoning almost, but visible, just, through the tiny windshield.

I seemed almost to be swimming through petrol vapour as, at last, I swung to the side, swerving away from the pointing guns. It was clear now that the Lightning had ploughed into blown sand, for her engines were half-buried, her propellers grotesquely bent. But still it would be a high step from the ground up on to the wing. I halted—to look, briefly, to gather an ounce of strength—and was struck by the most intense silence I have ever heard. A complete hush, but a waiting one; a silence that *expected* to be broken, and violently.

And into it a scream erupted—from the cockpit!

I jumped up on to the wing, and stepped towards the perspex cowling that shrouded the pilot's seat.

For a fractured moment he seemed still to be waving, as

I looked for the place to grip the canopy, to slide it or tilt the thing on a hinge. And as I did so I saw clearly the dreadful scene in the pilot's seat.

In a second I understood that scream, and knew the awful meaning of what I had believed to be Mackeras waving . . .

For Dixie Mackeras, eyes bulging from his head, mouth wide, hands still desperately fighting a battle he had already lost, sat rigid and upright in his seat.

While at his throat, mouth agape and fangs embedded, was the King Brown snake! The man's hands still held the writhing body of the ghastly, venomous brute, and he seemed to be trying to drag its head away. But it was hopeless in so confined a space, and even as I looked, the snake's venom, pouring into the great blood vessels of the neck, must have reached his heart, for suddenly his body slumped, and one hand fell limp. Dixie Mackeras was dead.

In that moment the wing rocked as Jane jumped up beside me, and gasped, 'Get him out, for God's sake!'

'Too late,' I said.

'Of course it isn't—'

But then she saw—saw the long body of the King Brown writhing in Mackeras's lap, and the serpent's head, spread wide like some obscene bow tie at his throat—and she was jumping down, and running, and then vomiting and gasping into the sand.

I stepped down more slowly and went to her, and gently led her further from the wrecked plane. I was still murmuring the pointless things one says at times like that, when the crunching noise came and, turning, I saw the wing we had stood upon had given way at the point where the engine was mounted. There was a pause of perhaps a second, then, the *whumpp*! as the petrol fired.

Nothing to be done, of course. Not then. Mackeras was dead, and I recall thinking the King Brown was unlikely to co-operate in any rescue. I stood and watched the funeral pyre, and after a moment or two, Jane straightened and did the same. But we didn't watch until the end: the story was over now. There were other things to do; so we turned and left the burning wreckage, and began to walk back to Jacka Green's private emerald mine, where Billy One-Hat waited with the wounded Bob Collis . . .

And that's it really, except for details that had to be cleared up, mainly by me because that's what lawyers are for.

We got back to Perth, pretty soon, all of us, courtesy of Toyota, Bluie Stainsby and Ansett WA, and I had time to ask Mr One-Hat a couple of questions, the answers to which I believed he knew.

The first concerned the arrival in my own hands, that day in the Terrace, of Mary Ellen Emmett's will. Delivered, you'll perhaps remember, by an Abo full-blood capable of disappearing into thin air.

'Aw, yair,' Billy said. 'He do that.' Billy was grinning, a sight rarely even glimpsed.

'Tell me.'

'Missus die. Priest put her in ground, then him go,' Billy said.

'And then?'

He looked at me.

'The envelope sent to me?' I prompted.

'Ah.' He nodded. 'Missus say she die send papers.'

'So you did?'

He nodded.

'Ah.'

He had friend, he said, drove semis, Kununurra to Perth and back. He take papers south. Second friend live at Gnangara. He go into city. He was the one who could vanish. Mr One-Hat grinned again.

I said, 'Billy, *why* did the Missus send the papers like that?'

The grin vanished. 'Men come see Missus,' Billy said. 'Many times they come. She afraid station stolen when she die, so she give to Billy. Missus trust Billy One-Hat.'

'And quite right,' I said.

Jane said, 'What are you two conspiring about?' At the

time we were in the airport building at Kununurra, and not exactly alone.

'Nothing much. Just chatting.'

'Looked fairly earnest to me,' she said.

'Earnest? What you need's a nice cold stubbie!' I said, and bought her one. And one for me, and one for Bob Collis, and one for Billy. At that point somebody somewhere said, 'Look at that bastard buying beer for boongs!' There's still a fair bit of that kind of attitude about in WA. I didn't see who'd said it, but Jane did, and before you could say Jack Robinson she'd taken three strides and swiped a bloke across the chops; and *that* set the place buzzing a bit, as you'll understand, and my chat with Billy ended for the moment.

I got at him again that night. We were all at the hospital, waiting while Bob had his leg looked at and resplinted, and I led Mr One-Hat away down a long shiny corridor and asked him Question Two.

Question Two was herpetological by nature. 'Just tell me,' I said. 'How did that ten feet of King Brown snake climb into the cockpit of a Lightning?'

Billy said he had watched a television set two years ago in Kununurra. On TV was aircraft. In aircraft was snake. He remembered it when he put King Brown in Esky-box. 'So, when boss send me to Stringer house, I give Esky-box to aircraft.' There was a space behind the pilot's seat, apparently, into which it fitted nicely.

'Yes,' Jane said, when I told her, 'I can see now how it got *in*. But how did it get *out*—just at the right moment?'

'How's this?' I said. I'd thought about this, too. 'Box top not fastened. Either that or Billy unfastened it. Then so long as the plane doesn't move, the snake's not disturbed. Possibly there's a brick or something keeping the lid down. And even when the Lightning takes off—well, it's more or less level flight for half an hour or so. It was only when Mackeras began his aerobatics, in attacking us, that the box tilted over and the lid fell open, thanks to gravity, and out comes Mr Snake!'

Jane said, 'My God—I'll never wipe that picture out of my mind!'

Nor I. Even now if I let my eyelids down unthinkingly, I find a picture on the backs of them of Dixie Mackeras with the King Brown at his throat.

Next morning we went in a bunch to my office. Sharleene greeted me with her enormous smile and two bits of news. The first took the form of a solitaire ring which shone like the headlight on the trans-Nullabor railway engine.

'That was pretty quick, Sharleene,' I said.

'Oh, well.' She smiled yet more brightly. 'You know my Simon, I'm positive. He's a brother of Bruce Fernaby.'

'Another golfer,' I said.

'Well anyway,' she said, as though getting her own back, 'Mister Bunbury wants you. Soon as you get in.'

He was in his King Kong stance by the window, ready to thump his chest or swat fighter planes, and he was roaring already. 'Who are all these people?' Miller Bunbury demanded of me angrily. 'I'm not throwing any bloody parties!'

'I'd like,' I said, 'to introduce Captain Jane Strutt, who is a client of the firm.'

Bunbury bared his teeth in a menacing grin.

'She has inherited Stringer Station, up in the Kimberleys,' I went on, 'from her great-aunt, Mrs Mary Ellen Green.'

There was a pause. Then, 'I did hear,' Bunbury grated, 'that you felt obliged to sell Stringer to an Australian.'

'Wouldn't think of it,' Jane said. 'Not for a moment.'

'If I were you, I'd think,' Miller Bunbury growled. 'I'd give it plenty of thought. This is gonna be a republic one of these mornings, and maybe the Poms won't be too popular. If I were you I'd sell—and quick!'

'I shan't sell. Ever,' Jane said sweetly.

'You couldn't even work the place!' he grated. 'It's wrong for you and you're wrong for it. Go back to England—a real Australian's what that station needs!'

'And a real Australian is what it's getting,' says Jane, cool as you like. 'I shall require your firm's assistance in the setting up of Stringer Station as an Aboriginal Co-operative.'

'Jesus bloody Christ!' said Miller Bunbury. Then he glared at me. 'You prepared to do that?'

'Certainly.'

'You can bloody go and do it somewhere else!'

So I did, leaving Bunbury two partners short: the second because Marye N. Bright seemed no longer to be among us. Like, and probably *with* Dixie Mackeras, she'd vanished. There's talk of Brazil, where the nuts are, but it's just talk.

I didn't go to another firm. Decided instead to put up my own plate. First job was to give legal form to the co-operative; now Billy's picking the people to work it. I also registered the claim on Jacka Green's mine, and it's all pegged out and properly documented by this time.

And Jane's gone home.

A blow, that was. She was all set to resign her commission and go into the emerald business, but then she learned the details. You want to employ Aussie labour in outback locations, you have instant trade union problems. The men do two weeks there, then two weeks back home. You pay for them to travel back and forth, provide air-conditioned bungalows, movie theatres and swimming pools, plus three-squares a day, etc. etc. etc.

So just before she got on the plane, I said, 'Why don't we go up there in the winter with a pick and shovel apiece, and see what we can dig up?'

'Just you and me, you mean?'

'That's what I mean.'

And she winked and went, promising to write.